The Fall and Rise
of
Champagne Sánchez

Rudy J. Miera

FLORICANTO PRESS

FLORICANTO is a trademark of Floricanto Press.

Berkeley Press is an imprint of Inter-American Development, Inc.

FLORICANTO^{TM} Press

7177 Walnut Canyon Rd.

Moorpark, California 93021

(415) 793-2662

www.FLORICANTOPRESS.com

ISBN: 978-1539869160

"Por nuestra cultura hablarán nuestros libros. Our books shall speak for our culture."

Roberto Cabello-Argandoña, Editor

Leyla Namazie, co-editor

Dedication

Dedicated, in Love

*To: My father and mother, who protected
and passed on the precious flame of life to me,
To: Rumaldo 'Juju' Miera, who taught me honesty
and loyalty, and the power of family,
To: Agnes Miera-Chávez, who taught me
compassion, charity and the power of music,
languages and culture,
To: MariAnne Brunacini Miera, who has filled my
life with joy, and who, as a loving wife, has made that
flame of life glow brighter,
To: my brothers and sisters, John, Cathy, Bill,
Susi, Joey, Marlene and Margaret, who continue to
spread the light of life into the world.*

I

No, not now. The cruel, navy-blue Malibu gasped its last breath of gasoline as Adelita bitterly muttered, *"Dios mío,"* and coasted to the curb. Running out of gas on the way to the most important assignment of her journalism career could not have something to do with the so-called *Champagne Sánchez Curse.* Or could it?

Adelita decided that sitting in her pitiful Malibu, doing a slow burn and giving into paralysis would not solve anything, so she grabbed her notebook and camera, slammed the door extra hard (to punish that old *carro* with a mind of its own) and started to walk east on Central Avenue.

If she were here right now, her mother would remind her to "Pray to San Rafael" or was it to "Pray to San Cristóbal?" See, that was one of the things that made Adelita and guys like Champagne different from their parents. That World War II generation always knew exactly which Saints' Intercession to ask for whenever troubles showed up.

Ka Plooossshhh! Adelita's skinny arms shot up past her long black hair (now slightly wavy because of the passing rain shower) in the universal gesture of cursing the sky as an uncaring Monte Carlo disappeared around the corner, oblivious to its drive-by damage from the puddle splash.

Great! Now, not only would she be late for the most

critical assignment of her three-month-journalism career, but Adelita Zoila Augusta Chávez, daughter of Delfina Margarita Chávez, would arrive at the press conference, dripping as if she had taken a detour through one of the spring run-off *acequias* that flowed into the Rio Grande this time of the year. Adelita now allowed that maybe there was a *Champagne Sánchez Curse* that made a rare, arbitrary visitation on some poor soul in Albuquerque.

"Hey, *Chula*! What's happening, baby? Would you like a . . . whoa! Never mind." The red-bandannaed cruiser, riding shotgun in his homeboy's Impala, recoiled at the sight of the *mud- woman*. "Yo, homeboy, let's get the hell out of here, *ese!*" he shouted. The driver of the customized *carrucha* floored it without having to be asked twice, overlaying a second, fresh- mixed coat of early-April rain and dirt on Adelita's mid-morning skin of mud.

Adelita Chávez continued, more determined than ever, putting into practice her sharp habits of observation and imagination. Magnificent *Mexicas* marched by the dozens through this desert trail centuries before these asphalt streets were pounded by Chicanitas, like twenty-year old Adelita Zoila Augusta, and rolled on by lowriders, like the air-brushed, chrome-wheeled ride that now faded into the distant clutter of Route 66 motels, pawn shops, and cholesterol- guaranteeing restaurants. Those ancient Aztec wanderers never dreamed that their journeys through this desert they called *Aztlán*, in search of a homeland, were laying the foundation for this pilgrim girl's road. They could never have imagined that their paths would be re-traced by late twentieth-century *mestizo* saints, in their search for love and adventure, for cheap thrills and spiritual elevation. And, just about the time that Adelita Zoila Augusta Chávez' daydreaming kicked into full Technicolor, wide-screen clarity, she was startled by a *Bahoooohhmmmdt!*

A non-muddied, obsidian-black stretch limousine hummed up to the curb. And stopped. And waited. Adelita looked around. A mistake, she thought. They are supposed to meet someone very important at some other corner, not Central and San Pascuale, and they will soon realize it is not me, right?

"Good afternoon, miss." The tall chauffeur behind the aviator-style sunglasses opened the door and gestured for her to get into the back seat.

Who? Me? Adelita's piercing, jade eyes surveyed the man, the car, and the passenger up front who was clouded in a haze of cheap-smelling cigar smoke.

"It's okay, miss. My client says he recognized you, in spite of the mud overcoat, and would like to give you a ride to wherever you're headed."

Adelita was still convinced that there had been some mistake.

"By the way, where, specifically, is it that you are headed, miss?"

"Uh, the . . . uh. I was on my way to the KiMo Theater, but I don't need a ride, really." "Must be quite an important meeting."

"Pardon me?"

"Ah, a coincidence. We're headed to the KiMo, too.

9

You'll find complimentary beverages on either side of the TV in here. If you need anything, here's the button to communicate with me, or my special client, up front, while I drive. You're free to decline the ride if you really want to walk instead. Oh, and don't worry about the mud, I have to clean the limo after every outing.

Adelita's Gypsy-green eyes locked on the driver's innocent face, scanned the gently – purring sailboat of a car and locked on the dark-skin skinny guy in the front seat, whose face was not visible to her. Why not? After all, it's just a matter of about a half-dozen blocks and what could happen right in broad, gray daylight on Burque's most-traveled boulevard. She stepped into the cavern of a car and settled down on the couch-like seat.

The decadent scent of well-worn leather blended with a faint trace of whiskey and stale cigar smoke. The chauffeur and his unique client were having an amiable conversation on the other side of the tinted, indoor window that separated her from them in the moving yacht. She occasionally had spotted a black limo on Central Avenue on her way to classes at the University and always imagined this is what it smelled like inside. Strange how the old familiar main street seemed so much smaller through tinted windows, she thought as she settled into the luxurious burgundy seat. The black beauty glided forward, navigating over the numerous potholes like a boat trolling in Navajo Lake on a still afternoon.

A mosaic of memories stirred in her mind as she relaxed into the first overwhelming feel of pampering, since when? Remembering her mother, Delfina Margarita Chávez, taking her to the *San Felipe Fiestas*, every first week in June. Recalling the long, Sunday forever-afternoon drives up to Chimayo, to dig handfuls of the sacred dirt from *El Pozo* in *El Santuario*. And then there was the time Auntie Linda López, Champagne's mother, presented her with a bright red spiral notebook on her fifth birthday, for her to write her *cuentitos* and other word creations. Adelita melted into the limo's backseat in silence with her most recent journal in her lap, closed those restless green eyes, and recalled her first baby steps into the world of words.

Adelita's Notebook #1

Tía Linda gave me this book. I will write stories. My mom made Chaquegüe (she spelled Chaquegüe for me) this morning. It was dark blue. She made it sweet for me with brown sugar. That's all for now. Ok, goodbye from Adelita

Adelita became suddenly aware that the sleek vehicle had been still for some time and then the chauffeur whipped the door open. "The KiMo Theater. Here we are, and I hope your ride was pleasant, Adelita."

Adelita? How could he possibly know her name? *Kerchunkack*! The driver's side door almost ripped off its hinges as a denim-jacketed and denim-panted joker jumped out. Now she could see her *cousin's face* clearly!

Impossible. No, actually, journalist and faithful,

journal-writing Adelita Zoila Augusta Chávez could have predicted this surrealistic scene. Standing there, next to the front passenger freshly-slammed limo door—like a gunslinger who discovered that the gun he just drew was a water pistol—was the eternally-hopeful, strangely-charming, bad-choice-making, bad-luck- attracting, always-scheming, *entre-movidas,* sad-sack Chicano survivor. The exhaled smoke from his cigar encircled him like a drunken halo. In fact, in spite of, indeed, and in spirit, like a poor- man's Lazarus in the Prodigal Son's Converse sneakers, here stood her *primo*, Santos 'Champagne' Sánchez.

II

Champagne 'Sánchez' was not always called *Champagne*. He did not earn that nickname until he was in his twenties. In fact, his *apellido* was not always *Sánchez*, either.

Back when he was six and in the first grade, Santos looked at the world as a generally friendly, but sometimes unpredictable dog. The world was a constant companion, except when things got strange. For the most part, the world followed young Santos wherever he went, occasionally comforting him, sometimes nipping at his too-large-for-his-age feet, but every once in a while, the world suddenly growled and bit him for no apparent reason at all. Dammit, the hell!

Duranes Elementary School was his world. The spotted green tile hallways were scrubbed clean by Angelina Baca so that her precious children could have new clothes for the first day of school. "*Muy bien hecho*, Santitos. What a good job you did on your capital *M*s." Mrs. Martínez held up the bright red Big Chief notebook that Santos had focused on for the morning. Writing in cursive letters was a tantalizing, time-eating activity for Santos, almost as intriguing as the Friday afternoon sessions spent forming dinosaurs, volcanoes, and dogs out of oily artificial clay.

"Class, let's all try to make the curves on the tops of

your letters as smooth as the ones in this excellent example by Santitos."

Santos liked it when she called him that. He liked it when he was able to follow directions, and when he was the first one to learn something new. What he did not like was when things could be going along, *como un río riendo*, when suddenly, *Gurrehrrah!*

The world bit him deeply, abruptly, and permanently the afternoon his mother, the frail and shy Linda Sánchez López, pulled him out early from school, drove him to the Dairy Queen (on a *weekday* no less!) and told him that his father, Eddie López, had left that morning for California. Santos left the vanilla ice-cream cone untasted and stared ahead. The southbound Fourth Street traffic was a cruel, buzzing soundtrack to the most unending, steel trap bite in his life. He never ate vanilla again. Enchantment, in his corner of the North Valley, had dissolved like the morning dew in the burning desert morning.

After that afternoon, ice cream of any flavor never tasted as sweet, clay never seemed as smooth, and being the first to write, add or multiply did not feel as significant. Every day seemed just like every other day, an echo of days before his father's exit, and tinted with a touch of stale gray.

Two years later, Santos abruptly wandered out of the fog of his personal grief, not by accident, but on purpose.

A couple of painful memories returned to Santos, like hungry crows coming back to the place of a previous feast, finding only stale crumbs. Santos remembered a cold Saturday night in his father's Chevy, parked on the side of Cisco's barber shop on Bridge Boulevard. He recalled a moment of pure terror, looking out at a young man in all-black, pointing a gun straight at Santos and then running off. Santos ducked quickly and then felt anger at the loud laughing voices coming from behind the cloudy windows of Cisco. What kind of father would leave his son outside in a freezing car for hours where guns and desperate men crisscrossed in front of cars parked outside near late-hour games of poker?

§ § §

Another drunken Saturday night. Linda had been gone for hours, visiting with Herminia, one of her *primas*, over in Martineztown. Eddie was about on his sixth beer when he shuffled into the small room where Santos was halfway into his Superman comic book.

"You must think you're so smart, because you read so much, huh?" Santos looked up and then back at the bubble of dialogue over Lex Luthor on the musty page. He had been through this kind of thing before and knew how to ignore the mean words, which were finally, usually silenced by beer number seven or eight.

"You really think you're smarter than me just because you can read, little *mocoso*?" Just stay calm, Santos decided, he'll go away in just a little while and then I can find out where Luthor hid the Kryptonite.

"You answer me when I talk to you, Santos. *¿me entiendes?*"

"Dad, I'm just reading my comic book. Don't you

want to listen to your *Alegres de Terán* on the stereo?"

"No, I'm not in the mood tonight for hearing those *llorones* on the stereo and don't you talk loud to me, you little *cabroncito!*" Sometimes, the best thing was to get physically away; so Santos trembled inside as he passed Eddie López on his way to the bathroom, noticing that his father's eyelids drooped over the eyes he tried to uncross while struggling to stay upright and not wobble.

After several moments that felt like hours, Santos heard the uneven shuffle of footsteps outside the restroom, a couple of thuds against the thin walls and, finally, the slamming of a door. Santos cautiously crept back to his bedroom. From the doorway, he looked on in shock at the sight.

His favorite Superman comic, the one he had cut so many weeds for, months ago, and guarded so carefully, in an old shoe box, lay on the bed . . . in a shredded pile.

§ § §

His third-grade teacher was the infamous Mrs. Jaramillo, the terror of his school. Upon discovering that she would be their teacher the following fall, kids were known to go through an entire Summer of Depression, but caution suddenly took a long vacation for young Santos.

Fear no longer touched him as it did his eight-year-old classmates. Hidden behind his large watery eyes was the knowledge that he was now going to have to grow up without the dad who, at least sometimes, would pass on *dichos* like

"*Es bueno ser importante, pero es más importante ser bueno.*" Those words of wisdom, about trying to be good instead of important, even if they only came once a month, were his verbal connection to a long line of men who walked under a cloud of melancholy in their journeys towards self-sufficiency. But now that voice was gone forever. Santos hoped that he would be able to remember at least a few of those bits of guidance for a future that seemed grayer than the *Nuevo Mexico* November skies.

That Fall, Mrs. Jaramillo had left the freezing classroom for a moment, quite likely in pursuit of a maintenance man, who was probably hiding in the boiler room, warming himself as the rest of the school silently shivered in their Catholic desks.

Santos, led by an April Fool Spirit lost in windy November, walked over and opened one of the windows just for the hell of it. He then sat down in his laminated, wood desk and got back to work on his math assignment. Mrs. Jaramillo stomped in, janitorless, and alternately stewed and refroze at her massive real-oak desk. When her snake-eyes spied the source of the chilling draft, she waddled over, cursing under her bad breath, "Worthless janitors, careless *cabrones*."

Again, for reasons known only to the god of mischief, Santos took advantage of her limited visual capacity and padded past her and the expensive oak desk, quiet as a cat, and arrived at the front-of-the-room blackboard. He took the shortest piece of chalk and placed it, dead center and perpendicular, into the soft layers of her favorite eraser, sticking out like a fat index finger. Quiet as a spider spinning a web, Santos returned to his desk and his boring, dammit, math assignment.

Still muttering, Mrs. Jaramillo waddled her 242-pound frame to the front of the classroom, announcing, in real drill sergeant tones, "Put away your math books now! Get out your grammar." How come women seem to change their minds a lot, Santos pondered. She began to erase the equations on the board. "What the heck?" At the same time that she erased the sample multiplications on the board, she inadvertently, unintentionally drew a wild thunderbolt pattern on the blackboard. Billy Tabet was unable to suppress his laughter and made himself the number one *suspect* and the primary target of Mrs. Jaramillo's escalating wrath.

"So, Mr. Tabet, you think this is real funny, do you?"

"No, Mrs. Jaramillo, I really don't." He covered his mouth. "Ha, haw, hawhwwh." It was the second burst of guffaws that sealed his fate of having to write, two hundred times, "I will not laugh in class and show Mrs. Jaramillo disrespect."

Just like we will never know anything about some of those books burned in the ancient library at Alexandria, we'll probably never know exactly what possessed Santos Sánchez López into taking full advantage of the situation. Santitos walked over to the Jaramillo real-oak desk, while she was over there, taking care of business in Row Five of Room Four, explaining the use of commas to young Frutoso. When Ruth Jaramillo, once again at the front of

18

the classroom, opened her Teachers' Edition of the *Third Grade Grammar*, the students all heard a loud, ripping noise, due to the strategic placement of chewing gum between pages 37 and 38, that day's grammar lesson. Room Four no longer required artificial heating.

The seed of *La Soledad*, solitude, was passed on from father to son for centuries from its origins in the Basque countryside in northern Spain. Eddie López didn't know the entire reason that sadness always seemed so present to him as he pilgrimaged alone, past the quiet Golden Gate Theater and the Record Sun, pounding the midnite streets of LaVerne and Arizona, feeling like the most solitary ghost of after hours East L.A., but he felt shamed by the faces of the young Chicanitos that stared at him from those *barrio* porches along some forgotten streets in dark city Aztlán . They reminded him of the boy he had left behind in old Burque.

§ § §

Walking through the dusty, lonely alleys of Barelas, Santos carried this feeling of being *desafinado*, of being constantly out of tune with most of the players that he encountered in the urban orchestra of chaos and change, murmuring under a *menudo*-scented cloud of *barrio* dust, another restless *peregrino*, wandering in some forgotten dirt roads of urban Aztlán.

At the tender age of nine, Santos gave up hope of ever

seeing his father again, dropped his father's López, adopted his mother's Maiden name, Sánchez, for his last name, and proudly took on the role of official (and, depending on the situation, unofficial) class clown.

Adelita's Notebook #2

O.K. I like to write a lot in my book. My mom gave me a pen. Now I don't use just a pencil all the time. My cousin Santos helped me. He showed me how to do smoother little mms. I like m words. Like much. And mucho, mother, mujer, máquina, menudo, mundo.
Hmmmmmmmmmm, funny . . .

III

What is not generally understood is that class clowns are not always happy. Even some who take on the role of a lifetime. Their smiles are *puras mentiras*, pure lies. *En verdad*, many young jokers are actually quite sad loners for the majority of their haunted waking hours.

Things might have turned out differently if there had been an *hermano* or *hermana* for Santos to talk to, but that is something we will just never know. After he had accepted the fact that his father was never coming back, Santos tried unsuccessfully to find a reason for the significant departure, but nothing made sense. He knew only to blame himself. Why? Maybe because he thought about 1,001 other things, while he suffered through Father O'Malley's 5:30 a.m. Sunday Mass. No. Was it because he muttered cuss words when forced to cut the weeds in the backyard? He knew it wasn't that. Was it because of that time he stole a Butterfinger from old Manuel's *tiendita* on the corner of 12th and Griegos? No, that wasn't why fathers left.

Santos never thought that it was something inside his father that caused him to leave. Santos sometimes believed that he, himself, had done something wrong and was somehow responsible for his father's leaving, in some unnameable, forgotten, indefinable way.

Santos was too young to understand about La

Soledad, the seed of solitude, but not too young to feel its presence inside of himself. One afternoon, as he gazed into his burnt-butter eyes in the bathroom mirror, he remembered seeing the same look in his dad's watery eyes when he had come home after visiting with his own father. Eddie talked to Santos briefly after that visit and told him that it was a terrible thing that some fathers treated the eldest sons worse than the younger ones.

When Santos passed his parents' room that night, on his way inside the house after another friendless walk through the high-desert Duranes barrio, he thought he heard his father sobbing, alone, on the other side of the thin, shabby door.

Adelita's Notebook #3

Mom told me about Uncle Eddie. She said that my cuzin Santos has no Dad, but he duz but he went to Calfornyah. But I dont have my dad. Really. He died when I was three. When I ask my Mom how he died, she says when the time is right I will tell you mee heeta. I always wonder when the time is right.

Panzón. Frankie, *El Feo.* Big Mike. Lupe. Even Frutoso, from Wells Park. And Elfego, who sometimes came to hang out, venturing out from 5 Points, in the South Valley. All the guys kept and liked dogs. Except for Santos. Santos never understood dogs, and they never understood him. Or rather, they always *mis*understood him. He could be walking down Lucero Road, reasonably happy, when some cocker spaniel, Chihuahua, or mutt would suddenly wake the world with its barking; only the worn wooden yard fence prevented them from tearing into Santos' leg. Dogs that had not yelped for years would awaken from their canine slumber and yip, growl, and howl when Santos, unaware, came within eye contact.

One *Día de Los Santos* morning, after the 5:30 a.m Mass at the San José Mission Chapel, Santos, in his backyard, gazed at a dirty-yellow sunflower stalk when he heard a little sound.

Under a small cave of leaves, a delicate black paw scratched at the frozen First of November soil in rhythm with its own mournful cry. Santos picked up the coal-black kitten, looked into its turquoise-green eyes and sealed a pact of companionship with the powerful act of naming. "You little lost jaguar. Had to take off from your *familia*, huh? From now on, you shall be called Maldito. My own, bad little cat." Santos knew Maldito could be his because nobody else in the Duranes neighborhood had a cat. He must have wandered here from far away. Duranes had three, four, or five dogs for every woman, man, or child, but no one ever saw cats and kittens.

And before leaving for school that day, Santos confided in Maldito as he lapped up the stale milk from a potted meat tin, "Maldito, *mi* Maldito. I can talk to you. I know that anytime, I can speak to you."

IV

The tempting appeal of comic books was the tantalizing mysteries in the back pages: the mail-order promise of exotic magic tricks, proven muscle-development secrets, and replicas of Wild West Troop Forts, with a six- to eight-week shipping time in the U.S. mail. Of course, it didn't matter what it was that Santos sent for, *lo que sea*, it always arrived six to eight weeks later, either cracked, crumpled, bent, folded, squashed, dented, or smashed. To say that Santos Sánchez suffered from bad luck would be tantamount to declaring that the color green sometimes made its appearance in nature.

If he had sent in his 95 cents for a pair of Scientific Wonder X-Ray Specs, they would invariably arrive with one lens missing or shattered. After paying $1.35 for a Midget Spy Camera and waiting seven anxiety-filled weeks, he exuberantly tried the new tool of espionage only to discover that the shutter was frozen shut. Out of the 100-piece World War II Toy Soldiers Set that he sent for, only twelve of the fifty riflemen, bazooka carriers, or marksmen were actually un-deformed enough to stay in position on their base for more than a minute without toppling over. The Personalized T-Shirt that he ordered read *SUNTOS* instead of *SANTOS*, and when he returned it for a Satisfaction Guaranteed replacement, he then received one that read *SNOTOS*. A Money Order for a $1.88 produced a Marked

24

Deck of Cards alright, but there was no King of Hearts, Seven of Spades, Queen of Clubs, or Jack of Diamonds. His 85-cent Hypnotic Whirling Coin came with the screen-printed vortex so badly misaligned that instead of his buddy Elfego getting hypnotized, he merely vomited. On Santos. Of course.

Santos was in Old Town one Saturday morning, watching the tall, pale, wealthy tourists from places like Chicago and Houston when he spotted a five-dollar bill fluttering in the February breeze. In a sincere desire to follow his conscience, like Father Julius had instructed him to do, he walked over, picked it up, and handed the precious money to the fat woman with the camera and said, "Excuse me, ma'am, is this yours?"

Without even looking in her purse, she grabbed the five and admonished him. "How dare you young punks treat the tourists so badly? You tried to steal this, didn't you? But then it started bothering you, huh?"

"No, I just saw you standing close by."

"Don't try to talk your way out of getting caught in the act."

"But I'm just trying to find out who the owner might be like Father Julius tells us to do."

"Get away from me this instant, or I'll call the police on you."

So much for trying to do the right thing with the tourists. So much for Santos following his conscience.

Back in his backyard, under the naked gray limbs of the big cottonwood tree in the corner, Santos gave Maldito another sliver of precious, hardened cheddar cheese. "Maldito. You and me. We know how to ignore those kinds of people. Yeah. We just have to ignore them. Just me and you."

Panzón's dog was just as overweight as he was, and Frankie, El Feo, had a mutt whose raggedly looks begged to be put out of his misery. And, coincidentally, Big Mike's German Shepherd was the biggest dog in the neighborhood. Funny how everybody's pet eerily resembled their owner, down to the smallest detail. Even Elfego's Diablo had a scar over his right eye just like Elfego himself. Lupe's pet, Blackie, walked with a limp, just like *cojo* Lupe himself.

"*Escúchame, pero bien*, Maldito. We will always be able to share our secrets. *¿Es una promesa, qué no?*"

At the exact moment that Santos whispered to his scrawny, black companion, José Vásquez happened to glance out of his kitchen window as he sipped his morning *cafecito*.

The pre-dawn blue always brought out the truth and sympathy in people. "What is it, José? *¿Qué estás mirando?*" Esperanza Vásquez became immediately concerned whenever her husband went longer than five consecutive minutes without finding something wrong in this *pinche mundo* to be angry about.

"Oh, *nada. Nada.*"

"*Dime*, José, *que estás . . .*"

"Linda López's kid."

"What about him?"

"From here it looks like he's talking to himself."

"*Pos, pobrecito*. Without his dad . . . you know, José, you should . . . "

"I know, I know. You've only told me about a thousand times I should think about taking him out to a baseball game. Maybe someday. I've just been so tired lately."

"I know. You're so busy with the case that you're working on. Face it, José, someday never comes for you, and there's always the case you're working on now."

"*No me hables así, Esperanza.*" "Never mind. Here's your lunch."

"Thanks. I gotta get going. Wish Mónica a good day for me. Oh, and tell her that I will be dropping her and her friends off at the KiMo Theater for their Sunday afternoon movies. And tell her that for getting a good report card, she gets to go out to the Dog House for a foot-long chile cheese dog, with onions, afterward."

José gave one last glance at the boy down on his knees talking to the ragged black cat in the frost-lined leaves and walked away from the faint patterns that started to attach to the early Winter windowpane. Frozen, silvery teardrops remained.

§ § §

The ancient New Mexican sun gently warmed Adelita's shoulder as the murmuring of the limousine got mixed into the muffled sounds of Central Avenue lowrider Impalas, college student Vespa motor scooters, and the pathetic homeless' pleas for spare change. The trio of

Santos, driver and Adelita stood in the ancient sun, and Adelita flashed back to the very first time she wrote in her journal in a limousine, fifteen minutes ago.

Adelita's Notebook # 3,800

Qué memoria tan linda. Sitting here literally cruisin' Central in a limo with the backseat to myself. Of course, no one that I know can see me due to the ultra-tinted windows. Lástima. I just flashed back to when I was five years old, and the only ones who knew me were my mom, my Auntie Linda, my cousin Santos, pobrecito Santos, and a couple of our neighbors. Mi mundo era muy, muy diferente en esos días, it really was, and yet, it's the old cliché: "The more things change, the more they stay the same."

Central Avenue is still more cruised and patrolled than any other street in town, punctuated by blasts of stinking exhaust from city buses filled with urban Indians, kids from the *barrios*, some homeless immigrants, working-class college students like me . . . but back to *mi memoria*.

While scribbling here in my Reporters' Steno Pad, I remember my first journal, a little bright red notebook that my mom gave me along with a sharpened pencil and the encouraging words, "*M'ijita, ahora puedes escribir tu librito*. Just promise me that I will always be the first one to get to read your books."

I'm content knowing that it's a promise I will keep.

The limo driver cleared his throat, and the breeze cleaned the air of the stinky cigar smoke and the skinny Chicano spoke.

"So, it looks like you're covering the big press conference, huh, *prima*?" Champagne tapped his cigar on the limousine door handle, and the large ash splintered as he addressed Adelita with his best I-really-don't-know-how-the-hell-I-got-here-in-a-big-Limo look.

It was true. The crazy kid that she had known since she was about two years old, the poor cousin that she had watched as he navigated through nine lives worth of reversals. The familiar kid she had seen return and get up long after a champion fighter would have walked away from it all. He really was at the center of today's announcement by Albuquerque's movers and shakers.

V

"Ooohh, Santos! *Sinvergüenza!* On my birthday!"

Santos Sánchez was *El Rey*, the Emperor, the Grand Master of bad timing. *Sin duda*, he could not have planned it worse.

July 15, 1971. Out of high school exactly two months. His old Chevy parked on a quiet street, a couple of blocks from Coors Boulevard, not that far from Pat Hurley Park, Santos decided to break the news to Mónica Vázquez. His timing was catastrophic. On their way to the Route 66 Drive-In to see Zeffirelli's *Romeo and Juliet*, nineteen-year-old Santos Sánchez informed young Miss Vásquez that he had decided that this would be their last date and that she was free to see other guys if she wanted.

"Mónica, listen to me! It's better now than later. I know I'm no good for you. *Soy no mas un vagabundo.*" A thin worry line formed on his thick, brown forehead as he leaned into sincerity the best he could.

"No, you're not, *¡pero sí eres un pendejo!* We've gone around for almost two years, and now you want to break up? On my sixteenth birthday?" Her long, fake eyelashes quivered in the tense air.

A yellow porch light from the closest house on Bluewater Street flickered on.

"See, *que te dije*. I'm no good for you, and this is the proof. Mónica, I don't have a job. I can't take you out

30

to restaurants or anything," he retorted in his a more-squeaky-than usual voice.

"Santos, I honestly don't mind that I have to pack bologna sandwiches for our dates to the drive-in. Or that you have to sneak me in through the trunk. Or that I had to siphon gas out of a car that time we were stranded out on the *mesa* last week. Or that your car door doesn't open on the passenger's side." Her oval face of hurt tilted and her sultry Rita Moreno voice softened while recalling their shared moments of young romance.

"It's just not going to work out in the long run, I know."

Long, awkward pause. Not unusual for dates with Santos. An image of her bully dad glaring at him, violence under the surface, gave Santos the courage he needed to make a clean break. "I guess since now that we're officially broken up, you probably will want to give me that ring back? You know so it won't be there to bring up any memories, huh?"

The slap on his face was so loud that a policeman heard the echo two blocks away. He mistook it for the backfire of a car or a small caliber gunshot. And another porch light went on.

"No way, Santos. I'm keeping the ring, *cabrón*. For one thing, I lent you half the money to get it." She paused. "For another thing, you just might change your mind about breaking up." He tried to ignore her clenched, flashing teeth.

"No, actually, I don't think so."

The look she gave him was Judge, Jury, and Executioner. Another porch light caught both their eyes.

Santos ventured, "Probably you're not in the mood anymore to go see *Romeo and Juliette*."

"NO! Take me home, now! *Vagabundo!*" The fake eyelashes danced a no-nonsense threat.

Santos hunched his shoulders. "Mónica, would you please hand me the pliers? Please?"

The worse-for-wear vehicle that Santos Sánchez drove could not be opened from the inside driver's side without the use of pliers. Mónica was used to that. He stepped out, left the door open, and looked at her quizzically. The look she returned had him buried about nine feet under.

"I know, I know. This damn piece-of-shit car needs a push start, cuz your *pinche* starter went out," she hissed as she got out and positioned herself behind the left-rear bumper, as yet another porch light flashed on.

"Modesto, over at Primo's Used Auto on Fourth Street said he thinks he might be getting in a used . . . "

"Shut up and push, *jodido!*"

"Remember, Mónica, it's got to be going at least fifteen miles an hour before I can . . . " He bit his lip and dared not finish what he was going to say.

Kafloonga Sheeehhnnn! After popping the clutch, the engine snorted to life, one more porch light blinked on, and Mónica dived past Santos into the creaking, squeaking, clanking, grinding, sputtering, wheezy excuse-for-a-car.

Santos pulled the light switch, and nothing happened.

He glanced at Mónica. "Lights?" She immediately reached out through the passenger side window, slammed her light brown hand hard on the fender and the headlights came on at the same instant that the final porch light left in the west-side neighborhood came on, and the excuse-for-a-car jerked forward, leaving the illuminated street.

For the first dozen or so blocks not a word was spoken, and Mónica became more aware than usual of the permanent pungent smell of cat piss that permeated the excuse-for. Whenever the excuse reached its top speed of twenty-eight miles-per-hour, the poor wheel alignment resulted in such a non-stop, trembling convulsion that it halted all but the most necessary conversation.

"I-I-I-I-I-I'm r-r-r-really s-s-s-soorrorrry f-f-f-for t-t-tonight."

"J-j-j-juuuuust s-s-save i-i-i-it, ass-as-assss hole."

Of course, during the final eighteen-minute drive back to the Duranes side street where Mónica lived, the car radio alternated between dead silence and full-blast, *gran-tormenta*, the blaring of electrified *corridos* and rock-and-roll. It went on and off and changed stations with a mind of its own, prodded by the huge, bad-alignment car-quakes.

Adelita's eyes flew open at the first echo of that rattling excuse-for-a-car, even though it was about one and a half miles away. The fourteen-year old's mother, Delfina Margarita Chávez, paused in the middle of her nightly rosary. Yes, it's that poor sister of mine's kid, riding around in that six-cylinder deathtrap, she thought. And then she refocused on the image of Our Lady of Guadalupe on the fresh-flowered altar she kept in a corner of the living room. That poor Señorita Sánchez López stirred in her sleep and was relieved to receive the audible confirmation that Santos' car, and Santos himself, had survived yet one more night out on the town.

Adelita Notebook # 747

Aww, damn it. I was right in the middle of a really cool dream. I think it was about one time before I started school, and Mom and Auntie Linda took Santos and me to the Fiestas in Old Town in June. I remember him and me watching them crown the Fiesta Queen, sitting on a chair with red flowers all around. She had a green ribbon sash and was up in the gazebo, and a Mariachi band was celebrating, their trumpets hailing, the guitarrón thumping, the violins weeping, and the vihuelas strumming wild like rabbit legs racing away on Easter Sunday.

But no, once again that junk Chevy of my primo, Santos, ripped me out of a flowing dream. Again, I wish he would get rid of that joke-of-a-car and get something that didn't look like it could fall apart if Maldito jumped on it.

Ahh, I see by the flickering amber shadows on the bathroom wall that my mom is up, saying her nightly rosary, probably for Lena Carrillo, who has been sick in the hospital. Or she could be praying for Mrs. Elliot whose son got in trouble with the cops again. Or Mrs. Rutledge who . . . but, wait, I know what she's praying for. For my Dad. She never stops praying for his soul, or for me to do good in school. I appreciate her praying for me, but sometimes I wonder if it does any good. Does God even listen? She would kill me if she knew I had thoughts like this sometimes. I could never tell her that I have doubts. Why is there so much evil around, though? Why does she have to work at El Modelo all day, making thousands of tortillas, and still has to take in sewing projects for extra change just for us to break even? I offer to work part-time babysitting, but she just says, "No M'ijita, your job right now is to do good in school." Which I am trying, but sometimes I just don't care.

Well, no more writing for tonight. I've got to get enough sleep. Got another math test tomorrow. Maybe now I can sleep again, now that Santos' car finally shut up. Where was I? Oh yeah, the San Felipe Fiestas, the ancient melody of 'De Colores' in the blossoming old church air.

José Vásquez angrily glanced over at Mrs. Vásquez, who continued sewing the *colcha* she was making to replace the old one on their bed. Mr. Vazquez snarled, "That bastard is returning sooner than usual. If he so much as . . . "

"*Por favor*, José. Please don't start up. Your blood pressure. *Recuerdas* what Dr. Woodard said."

"¡Cállate, mujer! I'm just concerned about my daughter!"

"And I'm worried about my husband and my daughter. *No te preocupes.*" He returned to examining the evidence summary on the Vallejos case.

The only *vecino* unaware of the approach of the Sánchez' excuse-for-transportation was old Mr. Gallegos. That was because he had been deaf for twenty-seven years.

Sounding like an amplified recording of the sounds of all of World War I, World War II and the Apocalypse combined, Santos Sánchez' car pulled up in front of the Vásquez home, and Santos turned the ignition key off. After about three minutes of contentious convulsions, wretched sputtering, some frequent wheezing, and good old-fashioned backfiring, the engine died. Then, just for the hell of it, the glove compartment door flung open for absolutely no reason at all.

Mónica threw the pliers over, Santos opened the door, and Mónica pushed him out of the way and stumbled out of the rusted wheezer. As she dashed into the house, her red blouse blurred in the porch light.

A three-second quiet calm before the storm.

"WHAT DID THAT BASTARD DO TO YOU, MÓNICA?" José Vásquez' voice pierced the Albuquerque night like the car-from-hell on a bad night. "¡José! ¡Cálmese, señor! ¿M'ija, que pasó?"

In between sobs, Mónica groaned, "*No te preocupes, mamá.* I'm going to be alright, but that's the last time I go out with him."

"This never should have happened!" José bellowed as he grabbed his old baseball bat from behind the refrigerator. "I'm gonna hit his head from here to the furthest corner of 4 Hills, in the far Southeast Heights!"

"José, will you stop? Don't make things worse, *hombre*!!"

"What could be worse than that *vagabundo* giving my girl a black eye?"

Mónica's gentle touch immediately disarmed him.

"This? No, Papi. This is just grease from his pliers. No, he might be a *pendejo*, but Santos would never hit a girl," Mónica half-whispered in his defense.

José knew it was true. He let air out of his mouth like a leaky balloon, put the bat back behind the fridge, and reluctantly went back to the paperwork on the Vallejos case. Esperanza went back to her *colcha*. Mónica whimpered as she washed the dark grease from her hands and eyes.

Right before Santos successfully revived the excuse-for-wheels by pushing it down Zickert Road, he heard the final curse in this night of many rounds between him and José Vásquez.

"He's nothing but a *pinche vagabundo*!"

VI

Seven years later Santos reflected on his situation. After bouncing like a soccer ball from one girlfriend to another and finally jumping into marriage like a tetherball that flew off of its rope, Santos found himself settled into one small apartment with one loving and faithful wife and one bewildering road of responsibility spread out before him.

"He's nothing but a *pinche vagabundo!*" Max Martínez' apocalyptic curse tore through the 1978 autumn dawn like Maldito through the gopher field of the San José churchyard.

"*Te dije, M'ijita.* I don't want no daughter of mine staying with that bum!"

Santos Sánchez waited like a Yucca plant planted in the same spot outside the Martínez house where he always stood while Maribel went in to give her parents the bad news that she was, yes, *still* married and generally happy to live with that bum.

"But Dad, he's my husband. And he's so young. He just needs some more time to find himself." Maribel pleaded, half by habit these days.

Santos was stabbed by every word of their conversation, knew everything that his wife's father said was true and felt ashamed that everyone else in the barrio clearly heard the shouted words of truth except for old deaf

Gallegos who had heard nothing for thirty-four years.

"And what? You're supposed to live in that tiny, crumbling *cajón* until he finds himself?

Just divorce him, *M'ijita*."

"Listen to what you're saying, *esposo*." Cecilia Martínez usually had luck calming her husband down, but today she was fighting a losing battle.

Today was different for another, unknowable, sobering reason. Today, at about 9:45 a.m., *La Mala Suerte* chose to make a visit on old Lucero Road, right in front of the Martínez house. It was the unexplainable, somewhat regular visits by Lady Bad Luck that in later years gave rise to speculation about a Champagne Sánchez Curse. Some believed in it, some didn't, but all of *la plebe* in the 'hood still made the sign of the cross when they felt that *La Mala Suerte* was lurking around.

What is it about freak accidents that they always seem to happen in slow motion, like old Viejo Vilmas trudging through the Duranes *caliche* mud after a winter rain?

"God won't send you to hell for divorcing him if that's what you're worried about. Think about it. I'm your father, and I just want what's best for you. Think about it, okay?"

"I won't, Dad. I can't. I love him, and I have to give him a chance."

"You've given him a year; that's long enough. Just get rid of him!"

"Dad! Don't say that!"

Maribel ran out of the house towards Santos.

39

Maldito, who jumped at the sight of anything moving, leaped from Santos' arms and crossed in front of Maribel, seconds before she reached Santos.

At that exact moment, a fast-moving Southwest Heating Supplies truck came bounding through the old dried-*caliche* road. Frightened by the roar of the propane-filled vehicle, Maldito flew from the nest of Santos's arms into the ruts and *hueco* checkerboard that passed for Lucero Road. *La Mala Suerte* silently snickered. The driver swerved out of Maldito's serpentine path and then lost control.

Maribel reached the waiting *abrazos de* Santos as the truck approached the Martínez house. And exploded. And took Maribel's parents, younger sister Marisol, and the family home with it.

The couple fell backward from the blast. Maribel's sobbing was an ocean of sadness in the arms of helpless Santos Sánchez.

Santos' grief was a river of confusion and *gran tristeza* with nowhere to go. *La Mala Suerte* lowered her head and walked off, in her cowardly way. The fog of despair and sadness getting too thick for even her, who did nothing but bring tragedies to frail humans.

Santos wondered to himself "Do curses actually exist?"

Adelitas Notebook #1,209

Some things are just too sad to write about. At least until a lot of time passes.

40

VII

Adelita's Notebook #1,210

So many times I wish that life could start over again, and I could go back to when I first started writing in my little red notebook, or, at the very, very least, before yesterday and the awful explosion that took almost all of the Martínez Family. What do you say to someone if you thought it might be the last time you could exchange words with them? But life never starts over again; no it just goes on again. I don't know if I could still live if I were Maribel. Doesn't God know when life is just too, too sad? He must know. He must.

La Esperanza, the spirit of hope (not the other Esperanza, José Vásquez' wife) dropped in on Maribel and Santos for a quick *visita*, a half-year later, when the blue irises began to bloom.

It was the day that Maribel walked into the Ortiz store, to get some *frijolitos pintos*, and she ran into her Auntie Lupe Casaus. She and Lupe spent the afternoon sipping *cafecitos*. Lupe told Maribel lots of stories about growing up with her mom. At the end of the sunny *tardecita*,

41

Lupe searched her purse and gave Mari a picture of her and Cecilia when they were just teenagers.

One night, after a rough day spent cleaning doctors' houses, up in "Pill Hill," most of those houses located right off of Ridgecrest Avenue, for grocery money, Maribel fell into an indigo sleep and was visited by *La Esperanza* who led her to a lone, small adobe building *en un valle de sueños*. Esperanza disappeared, but when Maribel looked into the *capilla*, there was the spirit of her mother, whispering the words "*Estoy bien* . . . I am all right and so is your *familia*." Maribel awoke to a Monarch butterfly morning, knowing it was true.

La Esperanza intervened on Santos' behalf one stinking asphalt afternoon. Having been pulled over for accidentally going seventeen miles over the speed limit, Santos was about to use his my-speedometer-just-went-out-ten-minutes-ago excuse when Officer Ecklund got an emergency call to a robbery in–progress.

Santos was let free to make progress on future traffic violations as he headed North on Rio Grande Boulevard.

Just to prove that she had a soft spot in her heart, *La Esperanza* wordlessly whispered into Dora Candelaria's imagination that she should suddenly return home to catch her husband, Daniel, backsliding into one of his guaranteed-to-lose poker games. On her mad dash out of the American Legion Hall, Dora handed her bingo card to Maribel, who proceeded to win the next six games in a row. Enough to pay for the traffic tickets Santos had accumulated the week before.

La Esperanza was not, however, making a visit to Santos Sánchez the day he ran into Harvey Friedman and his guaranteed-to-get-rich-damn-quick business plan. Santos only thought *La Esperanza* was hovering close by when, in fact, she was visiting old man Gallegos, who suddenly, temporarily, for about a minute or so, found himself able to hear the speeding cars on Rio Grande Boulevard, which saved his life. Of course, this visit merely balanced out the previous day's visit by *La Mala Suerte,* Lady Bad Luck, who had taken 95% of his eyesight with her.

Santos had already dreamed and re-dreamed their dream vacation to Acapulco. Santos had fantasies about him and Maribel back in Albuquerque, eating steak and lobster dinners at Baxter's Steak House. Santos had visions of moving into a large, new house of their own, with brand-new plumbing. Santos even had daydreams of them cruising Central Avenue in a sparkling Cadillac and being able to also afford the payment, in full, of all of his tickets for different driving violations. The source of Santos' unbounded hopes and dreams was Harvey Friedman and his you-can't-go-wrong-with-this business plan.

Maribel was watching *The Price is Right* when Santos sauntered into the tiny living room and sat in the once overstuffed easy chair that now looked like an anorexic scarecrow because Maldito had scratched through the upholstery and carried off most of the cotton stuffing. The sound of *The Price is Right* announcer abruptly ceased, mid-deal. Maribel sighed, walked over, and slammed her fist on the black-and-white portable marvel and the sound returned.

"Maribel, there's something I wanted to talk to you about."

"... and we'll throw in a brand new Mr. Coffee as a bonus!"

"Mari, listen. Our lives are going to change."

"Mrs. Hudson, let us start Round Two, now."

"Yeah, yeah. Our lives are going to change."

"Don't you want to hear how?"

"You're going to take up robbery now?"

Santos walked over, banged the banged-up portable TV on the back and Mrs. Hudson immediately shut up. It didn't matter, *The Price is Right* was over, anyway. Time for the *Juan David* show.

"No. *Escúchame. Todo serio*, we've gotta move out of this place. We're going to have a new life."

"I guess I'll just go outside and check if any money grew last night on the *algodón* tree."

The fact is, Santos had an atrocious track record in the area of employment and even he admitted that *La Mala Suerte* had nothing to do with that fact.

"I want you to listen to me, *querida*. I'm trying to be serious here."

"I am listening. You're trying to be serious. Would you like cilantro with the beans?" She got up and headed for the kitchen.

"Yes, cilantro, *por favor*. I'm talking about starting a new life for ourselves."

"Starting a new life? You say that every two weeks. How about *verdolagas* in the beans?"

"I think it's time we go into business for ourselves. *Verdolagas* would be fine."

"*Verdolagas* we can afford. Thank God that weeds grow for free."

Maribel pointed through the kitchen door with a paring knife in her hand.

"As soon as we get that settlement check, why don't we, you and me, honey *querida*, why don't we go into business. I'm serious."

Stone silence. That settlement check was the compensation from the Southwest Heating Supply Company for the tragic accident.

"Honey *querida*," Santos said again in a feeble attempt at charm and diplomacy.

"Honey *querida*?" Maribel broke the silence. "Why do I sense a *movida* in my near future?"

A vision of Santos, proud as Atahualpa Yupanqui, but with no admiring Incan subjects around, flashed in Maribel's mind. Santos, with the presence of royalty, but dressed in a Black Cat Firecrackers t-shirt, surrounded by admiring kids from the *barrio* was the image in her memory. Exploding strings of firecrackers making lots of noise and fury signifying absolutely nothing but a huge loss of profits, Santos Sánchez held court on Lucero Road, worshiped by *la plebe* of Duranes for his pyrotechnic (and costly), spectacle.

Maribel glared, like an exhausted, just-spent Fourth of July fountain. "Business? Oh, yeah. You mean like your St. George Fireworks Stand that got shut down last summer for violating the city noise ordinance? After you had blown up what little profits you had squeezed out of the neighborhood hoods?"

Santos snapped, like a delayed firecracker (like a dud) from a string, "Hey, I was forced to give some demonstrations for publicity purposes. Besides, what I have in mind is a year-round business."

"What? So we can lose money twelve months out of the year instead of just three? Business? Oh, yeah. You mean like your San Pascual *Tamales* Stand?"

The summer before last, Santos actually had a thriving, minimal profit-squeezing operation for a three-month run. Yes, workers on their lunch breaks from the City Weed and Litter Department would eagerly line up to buy those tantalizing, unique-flavored *tamales*. *Unexpectedly,* El Viejo Vilmas told Esperanza—Pabloto's wife, not the elusive healing spirit—who told Frankie *El Feo*'s mom, who told somebody who told the Weed and Litter workers that— in spite of the remarkable smoky unique flavor—the rumor was true. Santos Sánchez' primary supplier of the meat for his smoky, succulent delights was La Señora Matagatos, who was rumored to be the leading force behind the stray-cat control for the *barrio*.

"Forgive me for reminding you, Santitos, but you couldn't even hold your job with the city, how are you going to run a legitimate business?"

It was true. Santos' stint with the city Abandoned Auto and Discarded Tire crew was indeed, short-lived, too.

46

"Oh, come on. The only reason I got fired was for rumors."

"Rumors? Santos, somebody at the horse track took down the license plate numbers of your truck. ¡*Pendejo!* What rumors?"

"Honey *querida. Escúchame.* We had just stopped at the track to get some cokes."

"Eighteen miles out of the city limits?"

"So we got a little lost. Besides, the cokes taste better out there. Hey, nobody's perfect."

"Perfect? I would just work a little bit on not being a *vagabundo* or *pendejo.* "

"¡*Ya basta!* Just hold it right there. You're not going to talk to me like that, *mujer!*"

"*Bueno. Perdóname,* Santos, *pero* the bills are starting to pile up. I can't take in any more ironing and . . . "

"That's what I'm trying to talk to you about. Listen, what does every woman in the *barrio* need right by her side?"

"A responsible husband?"

"Maribel! Seriously, what does every woman in the neighborhood dream of having in her house?"

"A new couch with actual springs?"

"*Mujer!* What is every housewife's major fantasy?"

"A date with Al Pacino?"

"*Cabrona, te voy a . . .* "

"Alright, alright! What is our fantasy? ¡*Déjame pensar!*"

"How about being the proud owner of a brand-new Kirby vacuum cleaner? Delivered right to your front door."

Almost a pause.

"Delivered to the front door."

"And how do you fit into this?"

"After I become a big enough salesman, my assistants would do follow-up visits to my customers to see if they would want to buy attachments for the Kirby."

"Your assistants?"

"This is my grand plan for going into business for ourselves. Santos Sánchez, Kirby Dealer, for not only Duranes but the San José and Martínez town neighborhoods and maybe I'd even deliver all the way up to Westgate."

Santos pulled the folded, colorful brochure out of his back pocket and dangled it like *pan dulce* in front of Maribel's astonished face.

"Be the first one on your block to drive a Cadillac! Vacation in the Bahamas!"

"Where are the Bahamas??"

"*¿Quién sabe?* but we could be the first ones from Duranes to go there."

Maribel snapped out of her trance. "I wouldn't mind driving a Chevy that didn't break down once a week. Going to Santa Fe or Taos would be a real vacation for us."

"Great! Now all we have to do is send them eight hundred dollars for my three Demonstration Models, my Training Manual, official Company Uniform, and business cards and this other stuff. Maribel, you and I are going to be in business."

"Eight hundred dollars?"

"Cars! Vacations to places you never even heard of. Dancing all night like rich people."

"Dancing?"

Adelitas notebook # 2, 317

Chicanita, soy Chicanita y tengo mucho orgullo de decirle, de escribirle, de ser una mujer de piel bronceada y de raíces mexicanas.

My hopes and dreams are now manifesting, poco a poco. Something about being in the journalism program at U.N.M. and actually getting my articles on minority students on campus published in the Daily Lobo and yet still remaining true to El Espíritu de Poesía feels just right.

Took my mom to the doctor the other day for some tests. I still don't know what to think.

Is now the time to start praying again? It's been so long; would I even know how? A lot has changed in the last five years. Have I lost a type of humility that used to be part of my character and my personality?

Wonderful time that we had, después. I took Mamá to El Paraguas in the South Valley, after the doctor's appointment and feasted on carnitas y salsa. Today was the first time I noticed just a few small, white hairs, a few canas, framing her lovely face. I wish she had someone to share this all-too-brief candle-of-a-life with. Maybe I think about myself the same way for about three minutes, and then I wake up in reality! La verdad es que I want to be a professional writer!

That goal comes first.

Ahora . . . Quién sabe . . . Quién sabe . . .

VIII

Money in the *barrio* was as rare as teeth in old Vilma's mouth or good sense in Santos' schemes. The settlement check from the accident had been deposited in the Pony Express Bank weeks ago, and it was trying to earn some interest. Maribel Sánchez had made only one withdrawal. In a moment of weakness, vision, pity, foresight, confusion, or a mixture of all of these states, Maribel took $875 out of the bank. $75 of it for some paints, brushes, and canvasses for herself and the other $800?

"*Bueno*, honey, *querida*, wish me luck!"

Standing in the front door, looking like a buck private in the Kirby army of salesmen in his tan and white uniform and cap, Santos Sánchez bid farewell to his faithful wife as he set out, on foot, for one of the first times in his life, to make an honest living.

Salesmanship is hard enough but when you have a reputation as a former cat-meat *tamale* salesman, or a former fireworks dealer with no self-control when it comes to demonstrations, or a former city employee with an extremely poor sense of geographical realities, or an old landscape laborer unable to distinguish between ragweed and zinnias . . . But enough about his more successful schemes, the fact is that salesmanship and Santos Sánchez were about as appropriate a match as symphony conducting and old deaf Gallegos.

"What do you mean you didn't get a chance to demonstrate the Super-slim, Extra-strength, Low-noise model? You've been gone for fourteen hours."

"Just what I said. I didn't even get to talk to anybody about the Super-Slim, Extra- strength, Low-noise model, much less show them the *pinche mugre!*"

"Did you go down Zickert Road?"

"I went all the way from Los Luceros to Vicic, from Chávez Ravine to Rio Grande Boulevard. *Y nada.* Nobody would let me in, even Panzón's mom closed the door on me right after she saw who it was on her porch. Are you ready for this? Magdalena Moya finally answered, after my seventeenth knock, and told me she was too busy drying out *Yerba Buena* leaves and to come back when she was done. It takes five days, at least, to do that. ¡*Qué jodido!*"

"Hmmm. That's not a good sign, Santos. Is it too late to return your Training Manual and uniform and the Super-Slim, Extra . . . "?

"Don't even think about it, Mari. I'm not giving up that easy."

"Okay, okay. I was just thinking that maybe there's some other way of going into business for you."

"No, Mari. I need to actually try this. *Toda mi vida* people have been telling me 'Santos, you need to do it this way, 'or 'Santos, you're no good at this, why not try that?' Since the third grade, I've had people tell me, tell me, tell me."

"Third grade? Mrs. Jaramillo. That's it."

"What's it, Mari?"

"Mrs. Jaramillo. Doesn't she live over on Amador Street? You didn't go over there with the Super-Slim, Extra-strength thing?"

"Mrs. Jaramillo? My third-grade teacher?"

"She'll at least open the door and talk to you. ¿Qué no?"

While he didn't exactly picture himself driving a Cadillac up Central Avenue or sunbathing in San Juan, Puerto Rico. Santos could imagine Mrs. Jaramillo at least opening up the door for him—if for no other reason than utter amazement that he was still alive, or maybe the sheer curiosity about what he was doing with his life.

Mrs. Jaramillo's door slammed shut so loud that old deaf Mr. Gallegos stopped, mid-step, thinking that he heard a volcano exploding. Magdalena Moya, her intuitive powers at a very strong level today, halted her harvesting of *romero* and *manzanilla* and *chamisa* and remarked to herself, "¡*Tata Dios, ayúdalo!* He needs your help, Lord. Thy will be done."

"Aw, come on, Mrs. Jaramillo, this will only take about five minutes."

"GET THE HELL AWAY FROM MY HOUSE, YOU HOODLUM, OR I'LL CALL THE POLICE. I mean it, Santos!"

Apparently, Mrs. Jaramillo's curiosity about Santos Sánchez' current occupation or mode of survival was minimal.

"Come on, Mrs. Jaramillo, I have something to show you."

"Where the hell did you steal that vacuum cleaner from?"

"Shee," thought Santos, "this is going to be a little harder than I expected."

And *La Buena Suerte? La Mala Suerte's* compassionate counterpart was nowhere around. Today Santos was on his own.

"This is my demonstration model, and it's been paid for. All I'm asking is for five minutes of your time. Come on, Mrs. Jaramillo, give me a chance. *Por favor*. Don't you remember about telling us to pull ourselves up by our own bootstraps?"

The anti-burglar chain was disconnected. The deadbolt moved, and the door clicked open.

The shotgun was lowered. Mrs. Jaramillo spoke, "Where did you steal your boots and uniform from?"

"Mrs. Jaramillo! Remember what you taught us about not judging and all that?"

"I also tried to teach you kids about not being careless." She put the 12-guage rifle back into the broom closet. "I always felt that a Catholic education was wasted on you, *pero, ¿quién sabe?* Only God knows what He has planned for each of His children. *Pase adentro.*"

Santos entered the dark, overly-decorated living room. The walls were saturated with photos of former students and old faces that once belonged to the widowed Mrs. Jaramillo. As she busied herself turning the switches on to no less than five table lamps, Santos set the Extra-Strength Demo on the eggshell-colored carpet and the attachments on the lumpy couch. Mrs. Jaramillo spoke as the room lightened up.

"You know, this is an old, old house. One of the original *adobe* homes, here in Duranes."

Santos half-listened as he threw seven handfuls of extra-dark dirt on the floor in anticipation of his sure-fire demonstration of the power of the Super-slim vacuum cleaner.

"Now I have to warn you," Mrs. Jaramillo began as she turned to face Santos and his current foul-up, "this is an old house." It hit him the instant it hit her.

"Where's the electricity?"

"There aren't any electric outlets in this room."

In the previous eighteen or twenty-two years, Santos had generally learned how to land on his feet after taking an unexpected tumble, a trait he shared with Maldito, who survived the most incredible challenges to his life.

Reaching into his pouch, Santos produced a handful of frayed, cut, worn-down, but conceivably-usable electrical extension cords. "No problem. If there's one thing I learned from the Boy Scouts, it was to always be prepared."

"You were in the Boy Scouts?"

"For about three weeks, before I got kicked out for starting Lupe's sleeping bag on fire."

"Never mind. I don't need to know the details."

A walk through the museum of Mrs. Jaramillo's memories featured unforgettable scenes of schoolyard terrorism initiated by Panzón, Franke *El Feo*, Big Mike, Lupe, and Elfego.

Horrible as they were, these incidents always rated inferior to the grief caused by the schemes of Santos Sánchez. There was the time that Santos took on a dare, in fulfillment of requirements for him to hang out with Frankie and the guys, (their part of the agreement only minimally adhered to). He carried out an initiation rite to sabotage the lights for his class Christmas tree. It resulted in wiping out the total electrical power to the school. Students went wild with joy. If Mrs. Jaramillo had the power to unyoke one mad memory from her collection of horror, that would be one that came to mind.

And now, fully grown and coming into his prime, *El malvado,* Santos Sánchez pulled an armful of old frayed extension cords out of his over-stuffed pouch.

"All right, now where is an outlet."

Mrs. Jaramillo tried to block the electrical outlet. Too late.

Santos could no more be detained during his demonstration of the Super-slim, Low-noise Demo model than Maldito could be held from using the back seat of the car for a litter box.

"Alright, here we go." He turned on the vacuum cleaner.

Mrs. Jaramillo interrupted Santos' set-up waltz. "Santitos, do you smell something burning?"

Santos looked up, after putting the special corner-and-small-spaces attachment on the Demo model. "One of your neighbor's isn't making *tamales*, is he? To me, it kind of smells like that."

56

The sparks flew from the demo. The smoke increased. Jaramillo screamed.

Santos blurted out "Quick! Where's your water faucet?"

Never mind. Before Mrs. Jaramillo had a chance to warn him that the innocent teapot sitting temptingly on the stove actually contained soupy, stain-guaranteeing, deep-red chile, he had covered the Super-slim, Low-noise Demo model. And the doily-covered chair; a large area of her favorite carpet; and part of the couch.

"Not tea?" he sheepishly inquired.

Mrs. Jaramillo thought, I'll be in my nineties, and if I don't get blessed with Alzheimer, he'll still be in my thoughts.

"Chile stew." Santos had a talent for stating the obvious that was legendary.

She clenched her hands and bared her teeth.

"No, it's not tea. It is chile stew. It was in the teapot because it warms up faster in the pot than in the pan. It's also not the best thing to use for putting out accidental household fires that could have been prevented."

"No problem. I'll clean that right now."

"No, you won't! Just leave. *Pronto, vagabundo.*"

"No, really. I caused this mess. It will just take a minute to- "

"*¡Vete! ¡Ahora mismo!*" It sounded like she meant it. Just like in the old days.

"*Perdóname, Señora* Jaramillo. I'm really sorry."

"So am I. I knew I shouldn't have let you in the door. Now get the hell . . . "

Mrs. Jaramillo froze, mid-course, as something odd caught her gaze. Not being one to remain distant from his owner, Maldito had apparently followed Santos to Mrs. Jaramillo's house and mistaken Mrs. Jaramillo's front step for a litter box.

IX

"*Vete a la chingada?* Get the hell out of here before I shoot your *cojones* off with my shotgun? You and your *gato* from Hell. That's what your best potential customer told you?"

Sheepish nod.

"*¿Sabes qué*, Santos? Maybe this selling vacuum cleaners idea, even if they are Super- slim and Extra-strength, just isn't for you. How about going back to landscaping with Jimmy Garner?"

"I don't think so, but at least now we're richer in experience."

"*Sí, mi amor, pero* I don't think that will help me pay the bills. I'm pretty sure that I still can't go to El Cambio and buy *chorizo* and *huevos* with richer experience instead of *dinero* like everybody else."

"But you do not see the big picture, *mujer*. What this means is that we can take what we've learned and apply it to this great, no-way-to-lose idea that I just got."

Maribel got more cautious as Santos got less sheepish. "*Fíjate*. Delicious *huevos rancheros*."

"Santos, *querido*, no more great ideas. Why not work with Mr. Garner?"

"No. No more cactuses and yucca plants for me. How about *menudo* and *posole*?"

"To be a businessman you have to . . . "

"Imagine *carne asada con tortillas de maíz*."

"*¿Qué traes? ¿Tienes hambre, hombre?* Do you want to talk or eat?"

"No, this is my idea."

"What? Mexican food? Sorry, but I think somebody else before you came up with the concept of a Mexican restaurant."

She sniffed at the pungent air. "What's that smell?"

"Huh? What smell?"

"Can't you imagine having a regular paycheck to take to the bank each Friday? *Por favor*, Santos, think about going back to Jimmy's Landscaping business."

"No way. I don't want to be hauling railroad ties and volcanic rocks to all those mansions in the Heights for the rest of my life." Sniffs. "Hummm. Does smell, doesn't it? Getting back to my idea. Nobody has a restaurant up in the Heights where you can get a real *chile* stew, real *burritos*, authentic *taquitos*. Call me a genius, but that's where the money is. Imagine it. Chante Sánchez. Our very own business, Mari."

"*Yo no sé*, Santos. We've got to be very careful with that settlement money. I'm already out one thousand dollars for your vacuum cleaner business."

"One *thousand* dollars?"

"$800 for your Demo Kit and then we had to pay for Mrs. Jaramillo's rug, and to redo her electrical system."

"I just know that most people are buying their vacuums and everything else at the Oñate Mall, up in the Heights. Hey, everybody's doing their shopping there, not just the Anglos. They've got traffic jams just to get in there, Mari."

Maribel's resolve to not buy into Santos no-way-to-lose scheme weakened.

"Come on, Mari. Think of the big picture. You could hang your paintings of flowers on the walls for the people to look at while they eat their *frijoles y sopaipillas. ¿Qué no?*"

Curiosity would never kill Maldito, but it sure did a number on Maribel Sánchez' better sense.

"MALDITO? Santos, if that damn cat of yours has gone used our carpet for a litter box ag . . ."

"EL CHANTE SÁNCHEZ."

"Huh?"

"El Chante Sánchez featuring the artwork of Maribel Sánchez."

"El Chante Sánchez, huh?"

"And with the profits? Vacations! More Art supplies! Dancing all night! Faucets that don't drip all night!"

Adelitas Notebook #2,349

Does romantic love, in its unique, seductive way create more words? Or does it destroy just as many? Why am I even thinking, now, about categories of words? Maybe I can fool others, pero a mí misma? No puedo, have to be honest, I'm thinking about the use of words in connection with feelings of attraction and curiosity about besos, besitos tiernos, if I only knew him better, then the idea of little kisses would feel more comfortable. He's in one of my advanced journalism classes – my Exposé and Investigative Journalism Seminar. His name is Antonio, a serious, handsome, and dignified Chicano from Taos, and we got to finally talk during a mid-class break. Drinking coffee in Maron Hall, we discussed how the city's daily newspapers would rarely cover the protests at the Regent's meetings that the Directors of Women's Studies, Chicano Studies, African-American Studies and Native-American Studies had led, in recent weeks, against the proposed cutbacks to the Centers and their programs. Antonio brought up the idea of just starting an underground newspaper, but when I talked about our lack of resources, we agreed that maybe it would be more practical to work within the system to get internships at the dailies and propose campus coverage articles.

Our time together wasn't enough to start finding out a little more about each other personally, but there's always class on Thursday, a couple days from now.

So does the romantic urge kill words? I don't think so. If anything, it stimulates new and more words, just to describe feelings, even if in a superficial way. Does Love create more words?

Poetry, letters, notes, journal entries, poetry, and yes, more poetry (I think that Love is the chapel where poetry is prayed). Yes, country, time period, age, resources, or culture doesn't stop that. Love births more words.

Adelitas Notebook #2,353

With my second cup de cafecito ando pensando, I mean I really wonder if any other soul alive will ever read these words . . . Y con estas palabras puedo pintar sueños. It's true, I could paint dreams with words, but it's also true, each of these words would be like grains of sugar in this, my second cup of morning coffee. Sweet for an instant and then sacrificing themselves to the caramel flavor of the Brazilian roasted bean. Swimming together in the early morning scalding water.
A little later . . .
I don't know about these things called words. La cosa es, much of the time, they don't even work. Do words work for when somebody dies, words to try to describe the indescribable loss – I mean the real I'll-never-see-her-or-him-again? Do they work as the pieces of a eulogy – when, sometimes we stand up there, hoping not to crash into sobs or melt into tears in front of the gathered familia y amigos, compañeros? And the words

lose color like a painting turning into a canvas with tears or mist on it, like the clear nothing; nothingness that says less than the sound of la lluvia on autumn-baked oak leaves. Words at a funeral that say less than the loud finality of tears dripping on the clean pages of my daily journal. There exists a tragedy of words not saying what feelings call for.

Later still . . .

Pasos, pasos. Pasos tranquilos, pasos sagrados. Some steps are sure, but followed by more steps, unsure, trembling steps into the unknown adventure of a new day, an experience even if it's just a journey to the post office to mail a letter filled with lots of letters to an appreciator of letras y pasos y letras y pasos.

§ § §

To anyone who knew him, Santos was going through his regular routine, on a typical unemployed day. Walking to the Ortiz store to see if there was a copy of yesterday's newspaper (that he could have for free, because what was wrong with getting the news late, anyway?). Then a short stroll to Old Town to see if any tourists had dropped any coins on the lawn in front of the landmark sign. But then he stopped in front of the Faustino's barbershop where . . . and he froze in unannounced grief.

It hit him at the most unexpected moments. The loss of his father-in–law and mother-in- law and the suddenness and the utter depth of their departure. It was beyond his knowing how to have to accept, beyond his knowing how to understand, and beyond his knowing how to even begin to try to console Maribel. It was certainly beyond the capacity of words to have any effect on grief.

One cold, April day, it hit him like an unexpected blast of the sun, and he stood there like a paralyzed mute staring at the melting ice-cream cone of reality dripping over his hands, unable to do anything but stare off, thinking about the disintegration of yesterday's world. "Do I have a curse inside of me?" Santos wondered. A seed of Solitude sank to the bottom of his aching, helpless heart.

X

Adelita's Notebook #2,368

After class, the other night, Antonio and I enjoyed a marathon talk, fueled by shots of espresso at the Common Grounds, a coffee shop, where we went back and forth on everything. From whether it's better to reach the masses through newspaper articles or Community Poetry readings, whether it's important to write in Spanish to reach La Chicanada bilingually or in English or to alternate the language. We rapped about whether the Church keeps our gente en esclavitud or whether to follow the César Chávez example of working mano a mano con las monjas and the priests that come out and support La Causa.

We also explored each other's taste in música; he loves rancheras and Carlos Santana, and I told him I like folk music, everything from the canciones sung at Las Posadas to the gentle ballads of Joan Baez.

Then we talked about how many black and brown people we see on campus working as janitors or maintenance workers, cooks, and dishwashers, doing the heavy lifting jales in the library and the photocopying jobs. And how few Chicanos or Blacks or Native-Americans or women actually have jobs like being the department heads, the tenured professors, the editors of the campus newspapers, the administrators at the concert halls on campus . . . the whole vast legacy of colonization.

That being such a Big Topic, all by itself, we parted with a promise to meet next Tuesday again, after class, for more conversation on social class, for coffee, for another chance to find out about some more about our favorite things.

Don Juan de Oñate had brought dozens of families and hundreds of heads of cattle in an enormous colonizing caravan of *carretas*, horses, and pilgrims up from Mexico to what is now New Mexico. The Oñate Mall was a huge collection of clothing, sporting goods, toy, and furniture stores in Northeast Albuquerque. Here, hundreds, no, thousands of families made daily caravans in search of the best prices, and greatest selection of all those things for the house, including brand-new faucets, extension cords, auto accessories and art supplies. And vacuum cleaners. Also, kitty litter boxes. Although you could buy sweet and sour pork, Orange Julius drinks, Coney Island dogs and chile burgers during shopping breaks, one thing you couldn't get there, no, was some decent Mexican Food and some good green chili.

Across the street from the Oñate Mall, a half block

from the freeway exit, was an old, abandoned, former TV repair shop that Santos Sánchez had been looking at for some time. This modest frame-stucco building with the tumbleweed-infested parking lot was going to be transformed into Santos' Chante Sánchez. Santos' other faithful companion, alongside his faithful and innocent wife and, of course, Maldito, was Tykie Mendoza.

"Tykie is your source for used restaurant equipment? Santos, you gotta be kidding. What, do you want: the police to throw a raid on us as part of the Opening Night Festivities and arrest us in front of our new customers for receiving stolen property?"

"Mari, he swears that the stuff isn't hot. According to him, he got all the stoves and coolers and stuff from Ramón Longorio, because he had to move his *familia* back to Chihuahua, *de volada*. Tykie just happened to be in the right place at the right time."

"Right. And next, you'll be telling me that the President of the United States is going to fly in every night just to sample your *chicharrón burritos*. Santos, you shouldn't be buying stuff from Tykie. You know that."

Tykie Mendoza hadn't started school with Panzón, Big Mike, Elfego, or any of the other guys. He transferred to Duranes Elementary in the fifth grade when he was thirteen and had flunked twice before. Tykie's influence made it as impossible for honesty to thrive as expecting old deaf Mr. Gallegos to give opera lessons.

The fact is, when *La Mala Suerte* saw Tykie Mendoza within nine miles of Santos Sánchez, she turned around and headed off in the opposite direction, realizing she wasn't needed and decided to search for some other poor soul to corrupt and torment.

The fact is, standing in the parking lot of the old TV repair shop, next to his loaded-down Dodge pick-up truck, was Tykie Mendoza with the goods.

"Everything you're going to need to make Chante Sánchez a living, breathing, grease- producing and consuming restaurant. Here we've got a couple of industrial-size stoves, pots and pans, a cheese shredder. Hey, I've even got a slightly used cash register. I can already smell those *carnitas* cooking and hear those *chicharrones* sizzling. Shall we unload?"

Santos looked at Maribel, who simply stared at the small mountain of basic restaurant necessities. Maribel silently nodded with resignation.

"Since you're *familia*, I'll let the whole pile go for only twenty-one hundred." His up- turned palm hung in the air.

Santos looked pleadingly, and Maribel nodded. What the hell. At least Maribel had her *comadre* Delfina Chávez, Santos' Aunt, there for encouragement and to lend that gentle helping hand.

Delfina Margarita Sánchez Chávez, devoted friend of Maribel Sánchez, and mother of that promising journalism student, Adelita Chávez, was as faithful as any saint. Delfina Margarita Sánchez Chávez was more than just an aunt or neighbor to Maribel. Delfina was there to listen, advise, laugh with, cry with, question, and pray with Maribel.

Since long before she married Santos, Maribel went to Tía Delfina whenever she needed *consejos* or recipes for the basics, like *enchiladas*. Although her husband Modesto had died when Adelita was only three years old, Delfina always seemed to have the perfect suggestion when it came to relationships, corporeal or spiritual. Oddly, even though Delfina faithfully watched her *Telenovelas* and knew every character's background by heart, absolutely none of her *consejos* in real life, in any way, resembled actions that the protagonists in her Spanish soap operas would take.

Adelita Zoila Augusta Chávez had learned almost every single survival skill from her mother, along with developing an incisive intuition about people. Ever since before she could talk, Adelita carefully watched her mother's interactions with *la plebe del barrio*. Rarely a day passed when some neighbor wasn't at her house, unloading her problems on Delfina, who listened patiently and deeply, went and lit a new candle on her altar, whispered a prayer and then gave the challenged *vecino* what always seemed to be the perfect plan to re-achieve tranquility. Usually, her advice was transmitted in the form of a *dicho* that had been passed on to Delfina from her grandmother. In all things, Delfina taught Adelita by example, and Adelita always followed her mother's advice, especially today when Delfina told her that it would be better if she stayed home and started reading the brand-new, and expensive, books for her journalism classes instead of helping out with the preparations for Chante Sánchez.

"So, Delfina, you gonna show Maribel how to make

those famous, delicious *chile rellenos* of yours?" Santos bellowed.

"*Pos sí, cómo no*? I would do anything to help *mi comadre* Maribel."

"I can see those customers fighting to get in the door, wrestling to see who gets to be the first in line to try those *rellenos y quesadillas, tan sabrosos.* I'm getting hungry myself, just talking about them. I can also hear the music of that cash register ringing like the bells at *La Misión de San José* on Easter Sunday."

"Before we're going to hear that, Santitos, maybe we better listen to the sounds of those *estufas* being unloaded from Tykie's pick-up truck. ¿*qué no*?" Maribel reminded him.

By the time that old Chicano dance standard, *Flor de Las Flores,* blared from the radio in Tykie's truck for the seventeenth time, the crew had pushed, pulled, wedged, squeezed, manhandled, assembled, unwedged, disassembled and re-assembled the essential equipment out of the dented truck and into El Chante.

"I haven't worked this hard since that time on the landscaping crew when we had to unload the Kentucky Blue Grass sod rolls for that big job at Police Chief McCannon's place," Santos weakly gasped.

Tykie cracked another cold Olympia and rasped, "Shit, if I would have known it was going to be this much damn work, I would have paid my cousin Nacho to help us."

"Nacho wouldn't have shown up till tomorrow, you

71

know that. *No importa,* I'm just glad this is done. *Chingao.*"

The front door blew open and Delfina proudly announced, "*Jóvenes,* you have to come outside, *pero pronto,* to look at the masterpiece that Maribel just finished. *Ándelen, chamacos, vengan afuera.*"

Sucking back the last cool gulps of their cheap beer, the guys dragged themselves outside of El Chante to take their first look at the enamel-paint-on-plywood sign that Maribel had been working on while they had rested indoors.

"*¿Qué te piensas,* Santos? *¿Te gusta?*" Mari shouted from the roof where she leaned against an edge of the fiesta-colored five-foot by six-foot eye catcher.

Sure enough. With only a basic color palette, Maribel Sánchez had created a stunning collage of flowers, birds, and children's faces. Not to forget the central four-foot tall inscription, *El Chante Sánchez,* in such an arresting, aesthetic manner that even the speeding cars that were exiting the close-by Interstate exit were honking their enthusiastic, overwhelming approval. Even when the sun had long faded behind the West Mesa volcanoes, and visibility dimmed to a minimum, the warm, still air was punctuated by passing motorists shouts of "Great sign!", "Gorgeous work!", "We love your painting!", etc.

Too bad they didn't love the eye-pleasing sign enough to stop and sample the stomach- pleasing delightful treats that awaited the speeding art-critics-on-wheels.

No. Eight days later Santos Sánchez waited, after cleaning and re-cleaning the kitchen, bathrooms, and dining room, firing up and putting out the stoves. After testing out the savory meals with family and friends (and even a couple of strangers dragged in, against their will). After covering the thousands of parked cars at the Oñate Mall, across the street, with paper flyers announcing Two-for-One Specials This Week Only, Chante Sánchez, Tykie, Delfina, Maribel waited. And waited. In fact, they waited so long for just one car to pull into the parking lot that even Delfina's patience-of-a-saint was taken to its limit.

"*Perdóname, comadre,* " she mumbled to Maribel, "*pero necesito irme.* I'm going to have to get home and make sure that Adelita has eaten something today. *Esa muchacha,* she'll read and read and write and write and forget all about eating."

Maribel nodded her head and thanked Delfina for staying at her post for the past twelve hours.

"I understand. I appreciate you being here for us. You are a true friend. Would you like to take some *taquitos* for your *hija*?"

"*Gracias, pero,*" Delfina humbly declined, "*parecen muy secos.* I think I'll make some fresh ones for Delita when I get home. Call me if you need anything. *Adiós.*"

"*Adiós, comadre.*"

The trio watched the endless stream of thousands of cars speeding past El Chante Sánchez on their way to dozens of stores and the cheap pizza, burnt hamburgers, stale French fries, and soggy salads they could conveniently pay extra money for in the same Mall where they had gotten great bargains on plenty of things (that they didn't really need) but totally blew their budgets on the outrageously over-priced, bland food (that was really convenient, however).

Tykie Mendoza broke the solemn silence like a sudden belch at the 5:30 a.m. mass at San Felipe Church.

"*Sabes qué*, homeboy, I think this might not be the very best location for a restaurant, no matter how good the food is. All those cars are going way too fast to stop, *ese*. If they even tried to pull off into this parking lot they would get rear-ended, for sure, *verdad*?"

Tykie Mendoza's talent for stating the extreme obvious was rivaled only by Santos Sánchez' desire to constantly look at the big picture but his inability to actually do so. The stares that Maribel and Santos gave Tykie were hot enough to heat up the *caldito* on the main stove even more so than the previous twelve hours of gas flames.

"*Órale*. Well, homes," Tykie offered, "I know you probably want to talk strategy with Maribel on what you want to do now. So, I think I'll just leave you two and boogie on out of here. *Nos vemos*, Mari. *Al rato*, Santos."

And just like that, he vanished, like a dust devil out on the early April West Mesa.

Before Santos even had time to think up a small speech related to the bigger picture, a tan Chevy station wagon pulled onto the Chante parking lot and a wild-eyed, blond hippie girl, wearing a peasant blouse and faded jeans jumped out.

"Far out! What an incredible, fantastic creation! That really turns me on!"

Talk about lost in time and space, Mari and Santos

74

thought, as they turned and looked at each other, speechless.

"I'm getting such good vibes off that folk art mural. Hey, you wouldn't consider selling that, would you? I know the Pig Farm commune members up in Taos would be in ecstasy if I brought that back. Those colors make the Impressionists look lame. Far out!"

A half-hour later, Santos finished tying down the El Chante Sánchez plywood, Impressionist-surpassing sign on the roof of the hippie's station wagon.

"You know, my horoscope said that I would be having an extremely pleasing aesthetic discovery today, but I didn't expect anything like this."

"We know. Far out. Listen, it's been a long day for us, so we'll just say thanks and goodbye, okay.?" Santos politely muttered.

"Alright. I want you to know that the Rainbow Family will be forever appreciative. *Adiós.*"

"Yeah, *adiós.* Have a safe trip up north," Mari sighed as she put the $75 payment for her positive-vibrational, Monet-like sign into her purse.

She was reminded of the *old dicho* that she had often heard her *abuelita* tell her when it was important to see the good that can come out of even what seems like something bad, *No hay mal que por bien no venga.*

If nothing else, at least Maribel now had some cold, folding money to get herself some replacement paints, brushes, and canvasses from the art store on North Fourth Street. As the artistically-roofed hippie wagon re-entered the stream of speeding Mall shoppers, Santos dejectedly sat on the warm, gray curb and sparked a stale Marlboro.

After listening to the rhythm of squealing tires, racing engines, and squeaky brakes for a quarter hour, Maribel spoke to her inconsolable husband. "Santitos, *ya es muy tarde*, we should start driving home."

"You go, honey *querida*, I just need some more time. By myself. *Qué pendejo.* I should have figured out that it would take more than a pretty sign to get all those customers to stop. This wasn't the best location after all, no? I'm sorry, Mari, I should have known."

"Shhh. Don't get mad at yourself. Some things are just not meant to be. So, you want to go?"

"No. *Serio*, I need some time to just think. You go ahead."

"You gonna be alright?"

"No te preocupes. I mean it. I'll be fine."

Still, in his aching mind, Santos considered the possibility . . . "It feels like I carry a curse inside of me."

Doubt. A gray cloud looking for a person to depress. Doubt. Damn persistent doubt.

Mari gave him a soft kiss as he handed her the car keys that reflected the final purple rays of the Mission grape-colored sunset.

Time passed by like a handful of tears getting swallowed up by a melting-snow-stream. *Soledad.* No words were to be uttered, no thoughts to be exchanged. Santos didn't even need to raise his hand to try catching a glance of a reflection. Of the reflecting indigo of the cape that some claimed she wore. No. All that Santos needed to confirm the presence of *Soledad* was the absence of all other presences in the purple twilight. No. After all the other people had found other places to be, after even *La Buena Suerte, Consuelo, La Esperanza,* and even *La Mala Suerte* had found other people to visit, torment, seduce, tease, inspire, suggest, please, calm, and protect, only one presence remained.

La *Soledad.* After all had been done and said, after all had gone and come and gone again, Solitude remained. After the rowdy reunions of Veterans of Wars, after the well-wishers left the widowed at the gravesite, after the final goodbye at high school 30-year reunion gatherings, there was that last, patient, uninvited guest, who was still there after any and all last calls . . .

La Soledad.

Adelita's Notebook #2, 371

La Soledad.
Solitude. She is the only one. But she does exist in different apparitions, different faces. Nuestra Señora de La Soledad. She, the quiet suffering Mother who had to witness the scourged, mocked, and crucified Christ.
None can know, ever know, her sorrow. An icon, a lithographed copy of the sad-eyed Soledad is on my mother's altar in her sewing room, touching the east wall, to the left of La Guadalupana.

La Soledad. Solitude.

You see her every year, the first week in June, during the San Felipe Fiestas. Everyone has seen her, but none know her name. She glides like a smoky mist in between the mix of tourists and Old Town natives, singing along with the *mariachi* and *conjunto* bands, and she floats into a pew near the front, yards from the main altar. The air is foggy with her silent prayers; her lips move to the muffled beat of her devoted heart.

La Soledad was the subject of a hundred and eleven paintings done between 1943 and 1964 by Ralphie Moya, and each of these images were bought by tourists from San Francisco, California to St. Martinville, Louisiana. All of the owners of the dark, almond-eyed woman's portraits found themselves especially conscious of her penetrating, yet sympathetic gaze on Holy Thursday, every year.

Another incarnation of Soledad was a student in my *Literatura Hispana* class last year and you were never really sure if she was ever there or not. For some strange reason, when she was gone, which was about every other class meeting, you could never be sure where it was that she usually sat, as no one seemed to be missing. Never speaking aloud in the presence of Profesor Enrique Lamadrid or his Spanish Literature students, it actually felt as though the collective mood of the group was brought to its knees when she walked in late (straggling in tardy every time she attended) and removed her black leather coat, but kept her red bandana on her forehead, over her teary eyes. It was as if she possessed a gravity that brought, to the emotional surface of everyone around her, an awareness of mortality that was awoken only in her presence. When asked, at the last class meeting, who she was, Profe Lamadrid revealed, after checking and double-checking with all present for their class final exam, that the name of La Soledad did <u>not</u> appear on his roster.

And the song that old, deaf Mr. Gallegos was heartily singing, playing his cracked wooden guitar at Fito's, one eerie Saturday night in 1946, the very minute he inexplicably went deaf was called "La Soledad."

XI

Adelita's Notebook #2,374

Last week my cousin Santos opened up or tried to open up, his Chante Sánchez Restaurant, across from the Oñate Mall. Kind of sounds like a good idea, pero pobrecito, just like all those other good ideas that he's had over the years, it flopped. Nobody, and I mean nobody, nadie, dropped by, even for ice tea, to go. It's not so much that, once again, his financial situation is in spin, I secretly wanted this adventure of his to take off and succeed because it could have been good for my mamá. It's no secret that my mom makes the very best carne adobada, stuffed sopaipillas, huevos rancheros, and enchilada casserole in the neighborhood. And that the public, even those who aren't that crazy about New Mexican Food, would have become regulars to Chante Sánchez after eating there just once. Which would have meant that Mom would be in high demand, even after teaching Maribel how to duplicate her recipes.

I know that Mari would have wanted her to be there by her side, most days, to supervise making the chile Colorado, the sopas, and the flan dessert (and also the tres leches pastel) that nobody can make as creamy, as dreamy as she does, even using the exact same ingredients. My mom would have had a serious reason for getting out most days and driving up to Louisiana Boulevard to oversee la cocina and every plato especial that went out of that steamy kitchen. Mari and her love to talk while they work and that would have been good for Mama's soul. It's not that we don't talk; it's just different when we do. The talk between comadres is just different than mother/daughter talk, any parent/child talk, or even friend/friend talk. Comadres can share anything, and do. My mom would have had a rich-smelling, radio-blasting-in-the-background place to be at, día a día. A place.

And a purpose.

§ § §

Smoke. Slowly circling smoke. A tumbling snake of conspiratorial smoke trailed from the hand-rolled cigarette in Tykie Mendoza's oil-stained hand.

Tykie spoke in hesitant, clipped tones as he passed the thin joint to Santos.

"*¿Sabes qué, carnal?* No matter what you try or how hard you try, you're going to end up poor, homeboy."

"*Pues, yo no sé.* Maybe you're right."

"I know I'm right. It's the system *ese*. The *gringos*

just watch out for the *gringos*. Actually, I don't blame them. That's what I would do if I were in power. *Pero te digo, Manito*, it's all one big fix."

Santos finished sucking on the joint and handed it back to Tykie. To get his mind off the harsh, burning sensation in his throat, he studied the barely-visible posters on the small garage- converted-into-an-apartment walls. The defiant image of Che Guevara in bold red and black. The Zig-Zag Man in angular artistic shorthand. An M.C. Escher poster of shifting geometric shapes.

"Maybe." Santos exhaled. "*Pues, ¿qué hacer?* Maybe that's just the way God wants it, *¿qué no?*"

"*¡QUÉ NO!*" Tykie raised his voice and narrowed his eyes. "*Qué NO* is right, *ese!* It's not God's will that we live *como perros*. We live in a *pinche* racist system, and we need to train revolutionaries in order to . . . "

"Uh oh. Here we go with the politics again. Tykie, I don't want to listen to that kind of talk now."

Santos had been through this scene way too many times before. First, they would start out with a couple beers and talk about the good old days. Then, Tykie would flash that pearly white grill of perfect teeth and bring out his stash of marijuana, and the topic of their *plática* would shift to *La Injusticia*. After a few more chilled *cervezas*, they would wind down, easily talking about the most difficult subjects of death, eternity, love, and truth.

"You don't want to what? You don't want freedom? Power over your own life?"

Here we go again, thought Santos as he cooled his

burning throat with the perfect wash from the bottle of Olympia.

Tykie was just getting started. "Hey, what would you think if I told you a way you could earn a couple thousand dollars in an hour. *Una hora, no más!!*"

"No, *ese*. I'm not going to hold up some 7-11."

"No robbery, *ese*. Some poor Chicano pulling a gun on some other poor Chicano having to work the midnight shift. I don't believe in that, man. No, just a little delivery, *jodido*. That's all. And nobody gets hurt."

Santos glanced past the blood-colored hanging light bulb and thought he saw Mr. Zig- Zag wink his eye at him.

"This sounds illegal."

Tykie shot back, "*Órale*, who suddenly made you the Chief of Police? Is it legal to keep *Chicanos* and *Negros*, *Indios y Mujeres* down in the ghettos, the *barrios,* and the rez in institutional poverty? That women should make half the pay of men in the same damn jobs? Actually, that's the problem. It's not right, but it is legal."

At times, Santos would hear echoes of Tykie's older brother Manuel, who had died in some riots in L.A. when he talked like this. Che Guevara nodded his beret-crowned head in agreement.

Santos slowly placed the empty bottle on the wooden, oversized telephone cable spool table and offered, "But the risk of getting caught is pretty high, you know that, man."

Santos knew that Tykie knew the chances of getting popped for dealing were not worth the gamble, but there was a war inside. One side that argued, "*What do you* have to lose, you're already a loser," and another side that argued, "*Come on, pendejo, think about Mari!*" That silent argument inside also included the ideas of "*This is an excellent way to have a secret victory; the hell with the law!*" and "*You fool; do you really think that Tykie is going to bail you out?*"

The fire in Tykie's *panza* overflowed.

"Like the stupid risks you've been taking all along? What is this? Vacuum cleaners? Restaurants next to the Indianapolis 500? *Snapéate*, bro! This little *movida* will get you enough seed money, after a couple deliveries, for a down payment on your own small shopping mall. *Qué te piensas?*"

It was either the Michoacán Gold, the fermented brew, or the combination of the two, but when Santitos looked up at the Escher checkerboard transforming into a pack of geese, it all seemed to make perfect sense. Once again, Santos Sánchez was considering a new *movida*.

Still, Santos cautiously drawled, "*Pues*, I don't know what Maribel would say."

"She doesn't have to know. In fact, if might be better she doesn't. What, do you need her permission to do anything? Be your own man, *ese*."

Something snapped inside Santos. He glared at Tykie.

"Nobody tells me what to do. Not her, not you, not nobody." Santos scowled then growled. "Or what not to do."

Tykie, bolstered by the beer-weed mixture, decided it would be safe to push the issue.

"Take some initiative, *hombre*." Tykie gambled on an opening. "This is your chance to get even with the *pinche* system, homes."

Perfect bait.

"How long would this little delivery take, Tykie?"

"*No más* three, maybe four hours out of your busy schedule."

"Yeah. But I could get busted, admit it."

"Not going to happen. Did I get caught when it came to the restaurant equipment?"

"You swore that Señor Longoria said that that stuff wasn't hot."

"Forget that, bro." Tykie closed his eyes and sculpted with his hand gestures. "I can see it now, can't you?"

"*¿Qué onda?*"

"A new car, Santos. Can you imagine it? One that starts up every time. Even in the January freeze."

Santos almost saw it.

More bait.

"Enough for you to take Maribel out to Baxter's Steak House every Saturday night."

Santos temporarily fell for the illusion, but then caught himself.

"So tell me, *Señor Sabelotodo*, why don't you take this little job?"

"Santos, *te digo*, I've got some other, bigger, riskier

business that I'm taking care of. No time for this. Stick with me, and who knows? Maybe someday you could move out of that little *chante* with the leaks in the roof and the toilet that backs up and the windows that always get stuck."

A new house. A way of making it up to Mari. A way to be independent. A way to have a secret triumph. Bite. Santos was hooked.

"*Órale.* Maybe I will try this delivering business."

"No more smell from the city sewer in your home all night."

Tykie couldn't stop now. Santos forced himself to see it.

"Alright. I'm in."

Tykie wouldn't stop now.

"No more noise of cars from the frontage road."

"I said I'll do it"

But Tykie wasn't taking chances. Tykie had to seal the deal.

"No more packs of *perros* barking all night over on Carlota road. You could be the only *vato* I know, besides myself, that's buying his own house."

"I said **I'll do it**! Dammit."

Pause. Tykie acknowledged with a nod of his conspiratorial head. He opened his eyes and stared hard into the confused, weary brown eyes that tried to focus hard.

"*Órale.* Good move, *carnal.* Now listen. Meet me this Friday night in the alley behind Okie's Bar right at midnight. Park at least three blocks away and make sure that nobody follows you. I'll be in the back by the pool tables. *Órale.*"

In his heart of hearts, Santos Sánchez suspected that the jeweled-over apple-of-a-dream that Tykie held out was rotten to the core, but he decided to take a leap into the nightmarish darkness of dangerous risks. That's part of what happened when you suffered from the tragedy of words not matching the illusions they painted.

Outside, in the corruptible cityscape, *La Tentación* cackled, and *El Gallo* crowed three times in a dejected tone.

Adelita's Notebook #2,378

La Soledad. That's me, now. I talked with Antonio and found out accidentally, and that almost made it hurt worse, that Antonio already has a girlfriend, Luisa Franchini. They've been together for almost a year. He mentioned it, casually, and I found it harder to talk to him. But why should I? It's not like he did anything wrong, anything against me. It's not like it's anybody's fault. It's just that reality hurts sometimes.

They've been together for almost a year. Oh yeah, I already wrote that down, didn't I? He hadn't hidden that fact; it had just never come up before. After all, we're just getting to know a little bit about each other. Still, it would have been consoling to go out with Antonio, and maybe see

some plays at the Little Black Box Theater. Have
coffee and then afterward, afterward . . . I want
to keep him as a friend, but still, there is always
that deep, quiet curiosity,   that   longing,   los
deseos . . .

§ § §

Antonio spit on the sputtering joint and put it out, completely.

Luisa asked, "Why?"

Antonio shot back, "Because this is stupid. Smoking this stuff either makes you stupid or lazy, and I can't afford to be either. Revolutionaries can't afford to be weak, stupid, or careless." He gave her a light kiss. "And neither can you, *mi amor.*"

§ § §

Old man Gallegos took one last puff from his roll-it-yourself cigarette, thought about his friend, Coriz, the Pueblo Indian who grew this tobacco in Santo Domingo Pueblo, and he put it out in his ceramic ashtray. He thought about how few friends he still had alive. So Gallegos said a prayer from his heart for Coriz and then fell into a dream about the last fishing trip he and Coriz took, up near Eagle's Nest, where the air is pure and temptations are far, far away.

§ § §

Frankie Fernández plugged his 1964 Sunburst Fender Strat into the black and cheap bar glittered-Vibroluxe amplifier. He turned the volume and tone nobs, each to seven, allowing for somewhere to go further during his upcoming solos for this noisy Saturday payday night at Fito's. The brittle sound of can openers slicing into thin aluminum cans of cheap beer bounced in all directions of the twelve-by-twenty floor. Rocky Romero unplugged the jukebox midway through Patsy Cline confidently warning that she'd be "Walking, after midnight . . . "

Adelita's Notebook #2,388

My Dance Dream returned last night after three other Dream paths that I hurried on and left. I found myself in a circle of non-speaking, non-smiling Mexica (Aztecs) in a verdant clearing; watching, our eyes projecting Pacific blue light on los Danzantes. And as the dancers thumped on the cool, moist tierra with their bare feet, I saw the vision of creaturitas de abajo being hypnotized. Falling into creature dreams of river dreams and hidden food now awaiting the creatures further underground. And, they left the Place of the Circle of Watchers safe, for at least another year, silently-singing hearts leading.

XII

"Why won't you tell me where you're going? What's going on, Santos?"

"I'm just going out. *Qué jodido!* This is a free country, remember?"

He slammed the door on his way out, more out of guilt and disappointment in himself than anything else.

Maribel knew that something dark and sinister had been occupying spaces in Santos' thoughts and spirit for the last few weeks, in fact, ever since Santos had been spending more time with Tykie. She couldn't figure it out and now decided to do the one thing she actually did have control over. If she couldn't change the world, she could change how she dealt with the world.

On the blank canvas, she started outlining the edges of the cloak of *La Virgen de Guadalupe* with a narrow line of lemon yellow. Before long, she would get to the point of spreading a thin layer of her personal blend of glowing turquoise that would dry into the field where she would dab a handful of twinkling stars.

§ § §

Above the chattering and cruising avenues, in the

vast moonless Burque night, the blinking sands of light slowly crawled on their endless circular dance.

Below the blazing neon Route 66 tourist-scape, the Central Avenue watering holes buzzed with the drunken songs and the speech of seductions, betrayals, political schemes, and devil-be-damned deals. The cry of *La Llorona*, wailing for her lost children could be faintly heard, under it all, echoing from the nearby *bosque*.

Inside cavernous Okie's, past the professor-and-adoring-freshmen and the after-the-big- game-fan meeting rooms, beyond the modest first-date and pizza-and-beer-after-work rooms, and behind the let's boogie all-night dance hall, Tykie lowered his raspy baritone voice to just-audible-above-the-jukebox tones.

"*Te digo, carnal.* There's a whole lot more where this came from."

For the first time ever, Santos flipped through a stack of twenty dollar bills.

Tykie made it seem so simple and free of consequences.

"All you have to do is keep making these little deliveries and before you know it," he snapped his fingers to the muted Motown snare drumbeat in the background, "out of that little small *chante* on *Los Anayas Road* you've been surviving in and into living in luxury."

"I'm ready."

There were diamonds in Santos' eyes.

"Uh huh."

Tykie swept the suds from his thick mustache.

"*Estoy listo.*"

Santos' fingers ached for any semblance of a ring of gold.

"*Órale.*" Tykie sucked on the dying cig.

"Hey, bro, I'm really ready." Santos could feel the steering wheel of a T-Bird with cold chrome wheels.

"Yeah. I heard you." Tykie glanced at the dart board on the wall just to escape the hunter's look on Santos' face.

Santos leaned forward in the music-and-thick-smoke air, "No. What I mean is, I'm ready for the big bucks. As in hundred dollar bills, not stacks of twenties. This is just chump change. What do I have to do to start earning the really big money?"

The money-lust in Santos' voice almost threw Tykie off balance, but he took a chug of brew.

"I wouldn't exactly call what you got there chump change, but I think there's an opportunity for a man like you. A man with a vision. Santos, do you know how to drive a big rig?"

Only a split-second hesitation, Santos lied, "What? Oh yeah. A big rig. I know a little something about them big rigs."

Tykie frowned. "You know what I'm talking about? An eighteen-wheeler? Do you know how to handle one?"

"*Seguro.* I never drove one real far, *pero, tú sabes.* I can handle just about anything if I set my mind to it."

"You don't sound sure. Could you drive a rented Big Rig from El Paso to here?"

"If the price is right, *puedo hacerlo.*"

92

"Don't worry about the *plata*. You free to do this quick run this coming weekend?"

Santos wanted in on this *movida*.

"*Estoy listo*. When do I start?"

"Start by listening carefully."

Tykie shook his head, sobered up, moved in closer, and spoke more deliberately, all at once.

"I've got a *conexión* in Juárez who's got a few tons of Acapulco Gold. Splendid shit, *ese*. But it's got to get here by Saturday night. We need someone to take a rented car out *mañana, muy temprano*, and get the Gold back here by this weekend. You *sure* you're up to this, Santos?"

"¡*Ajúa*! As sure as of anything."

And he was. For now.

Tykie stood up, looked suspiciously around (in Okie's, who didn't, even if they didn't have the slightest reason or excuse to look around suspiciously) and dramatically took a small piece of paper out of his worn leather wallet.

"You're sure, now?"

"*Muy, pero muy seguro*."

"Here's the address of the warehouse in Juárez where I'll, er, where *you'll* be making that pick-up. I'll call you later, at home, after you've thought about this to confirm your participation."

"Tykie, *qué me dices*?"

"Like I said, I'll call later, make sure you haven't changed your mind, and then I'll give you the guy's name and our password."

He glanced over both shoulders. (Who didn't? After all this was Okie's and glancing over your shoulder was practically required when standing up).

"You can't tell nobody nothing about this, *hermano*. Including Maribel."

"Tykie."

Santos raised his hands in a gesture of complete confidence.

"*Bueno, necesito irme.* If you decide you're not up to this, 'ta bien. You can keep up with the small deliveries, like before. *Necesito volar. Al rato.*"

Tykie abruptly shook his hand and then disappeared through the smoke, like a stranger into nothingness. After all, this was the criminal night that blanketed Okie's Bar and Grill. Outside, Tykie wove through the thrill-seekers pounding the sidewalks alongside the endless streams of wooing cruisers.

§ § §

At that frozen moment, Maribel put the finishing touches on the face of the *Virgencita,* and no matter how hard she tried to paint mercy and hope, the face she worked on came out sorrowful and sad. Joy was far, far away.

§ § §

Santos savored his fermented fantasy about riches and power and respect in a lumpy booth in the furthest and darkest back room in Okie's. The room of temptation-rules-the-talk and deals-that-end-in-tragedy.

Adelita's Notebook #2,391

Tragic though the situation seems at times if I can just manage to keep writing through it all . . .

XIII

If there was one thing about the crappy cars that he drove, Santos Sánchez at least knew all of their quirks, tendencies, idiosyncrasies, patterns of dysfunction, and really odd behaviors, needs, and limits. Under the moonless, Mexican sky, Santos sat in the elevated cab of an 18- wheeler like Moctezuma on the Pyramid of the Sun. Inside the *Fruta de Oro* big rig, Santos looked at the complicated set of gearshifts that controlled the truck's transmission and sighed. I guess this is the unglamorous part of the contraband-runners job, he thought.

Only a half-hour ago he was joking, in his limited *pocho*-Spanish, with Manolo *"El Rico" Ramírez* as they shared shots of tequila straight from the bottle. Only a half-hour ago, Santos felt *como un macho* as he and members of the *Alacranes del Norte* drug-gang loaded a couple tons of Gold into the back of the rig. Only a quarter-hour ago Santos had said, *"Ahí te miro. Bueno, bye,"* to 'El Rico' after assuring the veteran marijuana supplier that he had handled plenty of delivery trucks like this before. Only now, Santos sat alone, after taking twelve minutes to start up the diesel engine, presently struggling with how to get his future on its road.

You would think there was a limit to the possible combination of ways to grind the gears of the transmission of a semi, but no. Santos spent the next twenty minutes playing variations on a theme of crunching metal.

Finally, the *Fruta de Oro* express crawled out of the abandoned Juárez warehouse only to jerk, bump, cough, hesitate, screech, hop, and jump its way through the awakening streets. Early- rising fruit-and-tourist-crap vendors could vaguely hear the diesel-muffled curses emanating from the truck driver's seat.

"¡*Pero qué jodido*! ¡*Pinche buey*! Stay in gear, you stubborn son-of-a-bitch. Damn big rigs. *Como me molestan*."

Meanwhile, several hundred miles north of the scene of the magnificent driver-vehicle- mismatch, Maribel Sánchez placed her cup of steaming Bustelos coffee on her creaky work table and began the time-dissolving ritual of starting a new painting. After a sip of the strong black *cafecito*, Mari glanced at the Woolworth photo booth image of Santos and decisively scratched a couple of curved charcoal lines across the pure, linen canvas.

§ § §

At the same time, a few blocks away, Mari's *comadre*, Delfina, had begun her monthly ritual of re-arranging her always-evolving *altar*. In gratitude for his help in finding a vinyl record of 'El Mosquito' by Eddie Dimas and the Upsets that had been lost for over three years, Delfina moved the plaster statue of San Antonio almost dead-center on the wooden table and placed the still-fresh irises in front of him. Because of the intercession of San Ysidro, the much-needed rains had begun earlier this summer, so Delfina thanked him, dusted off the foot-high painted piece of pine and put the image next to San Antonio. *La Guadalupana's* constant protection of her beloved *comadre* Maribel was acknowledged by Delfina's daily offering of fresh-cut marigolds. 'Fina was still angry with San Cristóbal for not having watched over her cousin Porfirio's return trip to California, so the brightly-painted *retablo* of Cristóbal had been removed from the altar and forced to spend a week of banishment in Delfina's linen closet, facing the wall behind the towels and the band- aids.

Delfina's daughter, the bright and ever-observant Adelita, was way too excited to sleep, and her imagination was working overtime as she stared at the ceiling, thinking about her current journalism classes. Words had always been her passion (even before that little Red Notebook); she used to go over the sounds of words in her head before she could write them down on paper, in essence, writing before her hand could follow). Words had always been her consolation.

Words had always been her focus of interest. 'Delita had written more stories, finely-crafted, about more subjects than any other budding writer for every issue of the school newspaper at Valley High, but tomorrow she would see her first article in the *Daily Lobo*, the student newspaper at the University of New Mexico.

Although Adelita could hear the muffled sounds of her mother's altar renewal taking place in the room next to hers, it was the very idea of learning what real newspaper reporters did and how they did it that kept her awake this evening. Professor Roberto Romero. His very name created images in Adelita's mind of the learning of the tools and the demeanor needed to walk right into the office of the editor of the *El Paso Sun* and say "Got your letter, and I'm here for the interview if you really want to bother with that. You know I'm the one you're looking for, why not just show me my office and we'll get started right now." Or something like that.

Maybe, just perhaps, she would consider putting in her first couple years gaining experience at a smaller newspaper like *The New Mexican*, located in Santa Fe. Of course, she could always stay in town and begin her career at the *Albuquerque Journal.* Then there was the afternoon paper, the *Albuquerque Tribune,* with a smaller circulation, that sometimes allowed more freedom for new reporters to do human interest stories. And then, again, there was always the even smaller, all-Spanish weekly, *El Hispano.*

§ § §

Santos gulped the luke-warm *cafecito* he had picked up during a swift pit stop in Truth or Consequences, after being flagged right through the Immigration and Customs check-stop outside of town. The white letters on the sign said: Albuquerque −180 miles.

Savoring a mouthful of warm java, Maribel dragged

a camel's hair brush of pthalo-blue acrylic paint over the charcoal guideline. With a wider brush, she scooped up a fingernail's worth of titanium white that she blended with the blue to create a striated pattern on the slowly-disappearing off-white canvas.

§ § §

Martyr's violet was the color of the long-stemmed cosmos bouquets that Delfina dipped into the vase in front of St. Jude, the patron of hopeless causes. Her silent prayer was for that *vagabundo* husband of Maribel, Santos Sánchez, who, she reminded St. Jude in the lifting of her heart in petition, was also her faith-challenged foolish nephew.

§ § §

Then, again, Adelita could always be a big fish in a small pond by starting out at the *Socorro Sun*. On the other hand, spending her time working on major articles on the boys' basketball teams' win over the Bernalillo Tigers didn't exactly seem glamorous or an appropriate use of her critical thinking skills at analyzing and articulating society's ills at the local, as well as international levels. Neither did the prospect of writing about the recent flower show at the County Extension Agent's Expo seem all that challenging, but getting published had to start somewhere.

§ § §

South of town, where the desert heat pulsated in waves from the pavement, a black Lincoln was parked near the intersection of South Broadway and Rio Bravo. This far out of town, this late at night, the only vehicles that whizzed by were driven by priests on emergency calls, interstate-hopping criminals, insomniacs, or truckers. Lots of clothing, furniture, tire- and food- delivery trucks. Oh. And amateur marijuana smugglers.

By now, Delfina had replaced the beeswax stubs with fine, tall replacements and was increasing the golden glow in the room with the spread of the silent flames.

§ § §

Albuquerque - twenty-eight miles. Santos barreled north like a bat out of Carlsbad Caverns at dusk.

§ § §

Maribel's fine-line sable brush was pushed to create an unsorrowful look on the emerging brown-red face but succeeded in only more sorrow with each deliciously colorful dab.

§ § §

Of course, Adelita could always propose a few looking back in history articles and then write about the failure of the government to protect the linguistic and cultural rights of the people living in the southwest before the U.S. stole one-third of Mexico's territory. She pondered. Naaww. That might be just a little too political for even Profesor Romero. But, whoa, Antonio would be impressed.

§ § §

"What time did you say he should be arriving? Estimated, of course." The gravelly voice from the driver's side inquired.

"My informant said that the estimated time of arrival for the shipment was Saturday night. Late. Just be patient, José."

The two occupants in the smoky Lincoln squinted as they stared south, into the endless desert highway while Patsy Cline declared in her tiny radio voice that her search for love would extend into well after midnight, out in the moonlight.

Delfina exhaled a breath of surrender and turned from her pulsing shrine.

Adelita's thoughts clouded as her eyelids fell.

Maribel's brushes rested as she blended the paint with her thin, nurturing fingertips.

Santos' gas-pedal foot lifted as he read "Albuquerque City Limits" in the distance.

The narrow eyes of the mountain lion and the snake, *puma* and *víbora,* widened as they focused on the approaching headlights of the miraculously on-time, on-schedule, 18-wheeler rolling along the asphalt ribbon that was once called El Camino Real. The gears ground and screaked as the rig slowed but didn't stop at a stop sign.

"What did I tell you, Special Agent Vásquez? This summer's supply of Acapulco Gold just crossed into the city limits. Courtesy of Santos Sánchez."

XIV

The *víbora* and the *puma* shot glances back at each other and then straight ahead.

When Santos made the decision to get his future on the road, the future for everything and everyone around him changed.

The lawyer sitting in the passenger's seat in the dark Lincoln had plans of his own. And that *víbora*'s plans meshed with those of the Special Agent in charge of Vice and Gang Activity sitting in the driver's seat. The lawyer spoke first. (Lawyers usually did.)

"Yup. There goes Santos Sánchez in a *Fruta de Oro* truck just like I told you. Poor sap. Somebody should have told him that *Fruta de Oro* went out of business over five years ago. Anyway, word on the street is that only part of that cargo is oranges. The rest is a fortune in a slightly more valuable commodity, in street terms. I think that falls under Vice and Gang Activities, don't you, Special Agent Vásquez?"

"I've been waiting to bust this punk for years, but I never really had anything on him. Who's the source of your tips, Giovanni?"

Tony, *the Snake*, Giovanni, was a narrow-eyed lawyer whose practice had always been less-than-successful and who was not currently beneath doing anything to make a buck. Ever since José, *the Mountain Lion,* Vásquez quit the Albuquerque Police Department for a position with the local F.B.I. Office, he met people who were really professional or had integrity, but Tony Giovanni certainly was not one of them.

"Never mind my intelligence sources, José. They're reliable, I guarantee my future, and yours, on it. Hey, at least I heard about this. You should have better contacts than me on what's going down around here. Isn't that your job?"

His look seethed *chíngate cabrón abogado.*

"You damn lawyers think you know everybody's business, from Arresting Officer to Warden, huh? I can't just go out and bust somebody based on some last-minute, second-hand information. You should know that. I want to make this bust stick when it actually happens. I've waited too damn long for this opportunity."

The snake eyes widened. Tony needed this *movida,* or he would have to close down his excuse-for-a-law-practice-office over on Gold Street and have to call Saul, his ex-brother-in-law, and beg for some work.

"I didn't drag you all the way out here just to watch the rattlers leaping on field mice, Vásquez. I didn't find out about the truck that just whizzed from some old ladies' *mitote.* I did my research."

José despised Tony, (not just for being a lawyer, but for being himself) but if he had something on Santos, then it was possible to find *una fuente de paciencia* within himself. So, he drew on that to help him achieve the bust he had only dreamed about for years.

"I'm telling you, this Sánchez kid just drove in with a big enough supply of smoke to rival what passes through the doors of the *A Mi Gusto* bar every *Cinco de Mayo.*"

Vásquez drank from his internal well of patience and let Giovanni ramble on.

"This is the plan. You bust him, I come forward and offer to represent him. This is gonna be a cake walk, *qué no?*"

Vásquez hated it when Tony mispronounced, or otherwise butchered up Spanish words and phrases with his annoying New Jersey accent that even distorted English so badly that often José had to ask him to repeat himself. He also hated it when this small-time, fast-talking bastard scraped his dusty heel against his freshly-washed dashboard. The hell with patience.

"Just as long as that *pinche vagabundo* ends up on ice, that's all I give a damn about!"

"José, José, ya gotta trust me with this."

"I'm trusting you with my reputation," the revenge-filled agent responded.

José thought to himself Good God! That's like saying I trust you with the knowledge that the world is round. No telling what he could do with that while claiming to represent his clients from the Flat Earth Society. You never knew what this damn lawyer would do with what little he knew.

Roadrunners, field mice, scorpions and rattlesnakes all went scurrying. José's angry outburst had surprised even himself. After a wordless eternity, the persistent lawyer in the black pin-striped suit ventured a question.

"Is it just me or are you taking this just a little too personal?"

"Too personal? Just what the hell do you mean by that?"

"I mean, we bust this street punk, get some investment money, tax-free, end of story, right?"

"I could care less about the money." Vásquez felt like getting it off his chest. "I just want to hang this Sánchez *pendejo* by his balls. That's why I'm playing along here."

Vásquez felt like he had just admitted to a long-held secret resentment that had weighed down his heart for years. Which he had. To the stinky breath, smirking lawyer whose perspiration now reeked of cheap whiskey.

Well, nothing for me to do here, *La Mala Suerte* thought to herself as she headed south for a long vacation. Things would go to hell in a hand basket without any assistance from her.

The darkness in the black car in the moonless night turned 100 degrees darker. Revenge would wait no more.

Drawing on his limited cross-examination skills, Anthony Salvatore Giovanni inquired, "Vásquez, why do you have it in so bad for this kid? What did he ever do to you?"

Maybe talking about it more would release some of the pressure, keeping him from taking premature, reckless action.

José began, "When Mónica was sixteen years old . . . "

"Mónica? Your only child?"

"When she was just an innocent teenager . . . "

"Oh, no. I can see this coming. Don't tell me. When Mónica was sixteen, this Sánchez character . . . "

"Let *me* recount the story, *jodido*."

"Alright, José. Sorry. I'll shut up and listen. I won't say anything else. I promise to keep quiet; after all, this is your story. You should be the one to explain it, in every detail."

So shut up then, José thought.

"After all, what do I know. This is something that you went through, not me."

Stupid son-on-a-bitch.

"You've apparently been carrying this around for years. It's your right, no, your duty to tell it and tell it precisely like you want to."

"As good as Mónica was to this kid—they knew each other, growing up, and had dated for over a year—that bastard turned around and broke it off with her and broke her little heart. She was never the same after that. I think she really cared for the pathetic bastard."

"Heartbreaking." The lawyer part of him, along with the investment schemes side of him, rested temporarily. "You know, José, I never had kids, but I imagine when they hurt, you feel their pain as much, if not more, than they do, at times."

Even the most conniving creature on earth was

capable of some limited capacity for empathy. How surprising, José thought to himself.

"Even more, I say. Aw, what the hell, they were kids. They made mistakes, just like us."

Funny, Tony thought to himself, I don't ever really think of myself as having made mistakes. Oh well.

Then Vásquez revisited the *coraje* that the very mention of Santos' name brought out in him. "Still, that bastard treated her like dirt."

Before Vásquez had a chance to get blinded again by thoughts of revenge, Tony Giovanni, the master of re-direction, spoke, "Listen, José. As you well know, the real prize is not gonna be some trophy for trapping this rookie driver for *Los Alacranes*."

"*La Familia*," José corrected him.

"*La Familia*? I thought *Los Alacranes* . . . "

"*Alacranes* are the Mexican connection, but their counterparts here in the States are members of *La Familia*."

"At any rate, you've got to see the big picture here, Agent Vásquez. Do you know how much cash will be confiscated during the arrest of Sánchez and company? Do you have any idea?"

"Not exactly. No. Nobody knows."

"My point. Exactly. Nobody, but nobody knows exactly how much cash our rookie driver will be holding. After his business is concluded, we move in. You know our suppliers here have a pretty consistent habit of shorting out their distributors. After our bust, some of that cash could probably get lost in the shuffle, don't you think?"

José's second mind told him that revenge was a bad business, but his first mind said that it would feel good just to get back at Santos. In all his years in law enforcement, José recalled, I have never before allowed personal feelings to so deeply get the best of me. Screw it, revenge feels good right now.

"Claro. Some of that green stuff with Ben Franklin's face on it will probably disappear into thin air as they say."

The smile on José's face revealed his realization that he could make some fast cash and get revenge at the same time.

"Whose word are they going to trust? Our hard-working, dedicated, respected Special Agent Vásquez?" the under-nourished and over-alcoholed alcoholic lawyer hissed.

"Or some fool loser who can't even drive without grinding the shit out of the gears on an 18-wheeler?" the weary and compromised Special Agent offered.

Darkness covered dark.

XV

Maribel was sitting in the kitchen sipping some extra-early morning coffee when the creaky door announced the arrival of the prodigal husband.

"Oh, honey *querida*, I didn't expect you to be up already."

"I'm not. I just never went to sleep last night."

"Maribel, I told you I had some business to take care of."

"My husband's been missing-in-action since early yesterday morning, and I'm supposed to just sleep like a baby?"

Pause. A gentling wave passed through Mari, for no good reason.

"Well, you look okay. Are you really okay? I have something to tell you."

"I'm fine, as good as I've ever been. And I have something to say to you. Maribel Sánchez, things are going to get better."

"Santos, would you please call that damn Tykie and tell him you're back. He kept calling over here about every five minutes last night. '¿*Ha llegado el Santos*? ¿*Todavía no*?' What's so damn urgent with him?"

"Maribel, you can start packing. Not too long and we're moving out of this tiny apartment. And we're getting a new car. You're going to finally get a washer and a dryer."

"Santos, never mind about that. I'm happy in this tiny apartment as long as I can count on you to be here and help."

"The hell with this place and the hell with this life."

He spoke fast and fervently as he tried to find the zipper on the small backpack he held.

"All my life people have treated me like a bum and a loser. 'Santos got in trouble at school again.' 'Santos struck out and lost the baseball game for us.' 'Santos has him and his wife living off that settlement from the Southwest Heating Supplies Company disaster.' Well, no more. Now I've done something on my own for us."

Like a fisherman displaying the perfect rainbow trout, Santos proudly fanned a roll of fifty-dollar bills.

A wave of shock mingled with suspicion passed through Maribel and was reflected on her face.

"No. Oh no. This is a business *muy malo*, Santos. We can't have that going on."

"This is just the beginning, Mari. First, we'll get a new car. Then we're moving into a new place up in the Heights, and that's just the beginning."

"No! This is why Tykie kept on calling here, *verdad*? No, Santos. Yeah, I wish you had a good job, and we had more money, but not that way."

"*¿Pos, qué quieres, mujer?* I would think that you would be grateful that I'm doing something that will get us ahead, for once in our lives. This *movida* will just be temporary, just to give us a new start, ¿me entiendes?"

"What is it? Drugs, no? Huh? That's it, isn't it? Yeah, I know that Tykie. This has something to do with *drogas*, doesn't it? No way, Santos, I'm not going to let you get us involved. You're not dragging the baby and me into some illegal *movida*."

"It's just temporary, I said."

Then he shook his head as if he had water in his ears.

"Wait, what?"

"What?"

"No. Before that. What did you say?"

"What, what did I say?"

"Baby. What baby?"

"Oh."

She looked down at her paint-spattered jeans.

"Finish what you were starting to say. I heard you say the baby and me."

Gentleness and grace returned to Maribel as an inner voice in Santos told him to shut up and actually listen to what Mari had to say to him. They gazed into each other's brown eyes.

"Santos, the reason you've got to settle down and just settle for an ordinary job . . . the reason I haven't been feeling well in the mornings . . . the reason you're going to have to walk away from this bad business with Tykie . . . Santos, *corazón mío*, I'm pregnant."

"*Mi vida*. Why didn't you tell me?"

"You were too busy with this business with Tykie, and, I don't know, I wasn't sure until yesterday. And you

113

were gone. I went and saw Dr. Aranovsky, and he said I'm due in about seven months."

Gentle *abrazos* and soft kisses. Whispered words and light-as-light thoughts. For the blessed couple, *La Tranquilidad* spread her wings of light in the gift of a crack in time.

And Esperanza cooked while Delfina altared and Adelita journaled.

José studied old cases as *El Rico* wheeled and dealt as Panzón ate a dozen *enchiladas de chile colorado* all by himself.

Professor Romero changed his lesson plans to reflect the changing situation on campus as Tykie smoked.

Giovanni late-night lawyered and plotted as San Rafael protected old Mr. Gallegos walking up and down Beech and Amado and the other dusty roads of the barrio of Los Duranes.

Even Maldito pawed a silent path past the old *capilla* where Father Galli said morning Mass and counseled souls.

As porch lights were extinguished, this evening, for the briefest of nights, everything and everyone was *contento y tranquilo. En toda Nuevo Mexico*, enchantment was weaving in and out of *sueños y abrazos. Chicharras* chattered in the ancient cottonwood trees and crickets sang a song of peace.

XVI

Adelita's Journal #2508

The serpentine coil of transparent steam hovered over the cup of my eggnogged coffee, and for about three minutes, I honestly felt content to my core.

If I actually become a professional journalist, will I have moments like this in my future?

Imagine that, sitting at my desk in the Tribune City Desk department before everyone else arrives to offer their fair share of story pitches, their contributions of vocal and typewriter cacophony, an almost musical chaos of voices competing with the clacking of keys. They will describe last night's and early-this-morning's world of births and deaths, school-closings-due-to- snow, hints of political scandals about-to- break, the latest news on movie director Robert Altman's "Nashville" project, in collaboration with Screenwriter, Joan Tewkesbury, the health of the economy, the macro and the microscopic, the evil and the holy, all the streams-of-life that feed the canvas of the Tribune.

But I might have that perfect cup of coffee forty-

five minutes before the writing, describing, rewriting, slashing, adding, misspelling, respelling, rereading, revising, intoxicating playing-with-words that could be my source of making a living in the future.

And even if it worked out, being a Real Reporter, would I get tired of that after ten, maybe twenty years, and then wish that I'd been an impoverished poet instead? Who pays poets to write? Yet who feels satisfied with writing assignments? Even if I got paid? Is there a middle ground? Could I be a full-time Newspaper Writer with enough energy and desire left at the end of the day, the week, or the month to still want to write about my inner life? The world of myself or Mom or Auntie Linda or cousin Santos or old man Gallegos or La Soledad or La Buena Suerte or Saint Jude or San Rafael, or to write about those paintings that Maribel is working on. Art like hers, now that can inspire a holy mosaic of words, I think.

§ § §

It wasn't that working at the R. & T. Fireworks Company was difficult, it was just plain boring. The most exciting change in routine, throughout the eight-hour day, was getting to leave work to pick up the South Valley's hottest *burritos* from Kathie's Carryout. The change from unceasingly stuffing plastic bags to unloading the supplies truck came in a distant second, in the favorite activities category. But, for about five hours of his eight-hour day, Santos Sánchez stuffed clear plastic bags with an assortment of smoke bombs, whistlers, snakes, sparklers, and a variety of sparkling cones. Oh, there was some variety in that; different amounts of the pyro- technical treats in the A, B, C, and D packages. But, for the most part, it was just grab a plastic empty, put in the appropriate cardboard backing, place the assortment of fireworks in their pre- designated place in the bag. Then, use the electric staple gun to seal the top of the R.& T. Fourth of July assortments.

After the first couple hours, when Santos would think about the previous day and night, and then he mentally calculated and re-calculated how much the minimum-wage job would be reflected in his Friday paycheck, Santos's mind wandered into the strange, uncharted territory of the meaning of life. His thoughts became as restless as a riderless horse. He thought about how things might have turned out very differently if, for example, his mom had met somebody different and his dad would have been someone else, maybe a man who never left his wife and kid. Or if his father had been treated more fairly by his dad. And if his grandfather had been treated . . . These thoughts multiplied in the fertile imagination of Santos Sánchez until it occurred to him, contemplating the wide, wide world of ancestral combinations, that had his mom met and gone out with, say, Calixto Balderrama, he might have ended up with *El Feo* or Panzón, as his brother! Oh, brother. Just the thought of that. *Qué chingao!*

What would one different parent have made regarding how he thought? Would he then only have half the great mind that he now possessed? Would his mind have ended up even more argumentative with itself than it was now? Just the thought.

What would his life be if he had done what his Valley High School counselor suggested: go to the local technical-vocational school and get trained in auto mechanics. He might have gotten superb at fixing cars and making repairs at the new Pep Boys that opened up on West Central Avenue. Of course, had he followed that path, that would have meant that he would be working, side by side, with Panzón, which would probably mean going to La Casa Grande bar after work every other day, for just a couple *cervezas, no más.* Yes, Santos himself might now possibly have found himself tipping the scales at about 245 pounds, well on his way to advanced alcoholism and/or diabetes with about four Driving-While-Intoxicated convictions under his wide leather belt.

Had I gone with Elfego to Califas right out of high school, Santos thought, I might have pursued a career in Chicano rock music. Playing rhythm guitar in a group like Malo or Tierra, enjoying the success of a regional hit like *Viva Tirado – Part 1* or *Don't Let No One Get You Down.* On the other hand, Santos ruminated, I could also now find myself playing *La Bamba* for the ten-thousandth time at an East L.A. graduation party near San Alfonso's Catholic church, or at a *quinceañera,* close to Garfield High, so bored out of my mind that I would have to make mistakes

118

on purpose or change the lyrics to keep from going totally insane. "*Para tirar la Bomba . . .* "

Or I could have ended up somewhere in between the oppressive big time or the creative, but the penniless local-scene status of musicianship. Like Frankie Fernández did with that perpetual gig at Fito's, playing standards with the West Ella Band. The creative spin that he added every weekend, changing out his solos, rewriting lyrics—many times on the spot. Often, giving different arrangements to old hits through his somewhat constant steady flow of invited guest artists like Cisco Montoya, Wayne, Ish or Craig Callahan. The music always remained fresh in Frankie's artistic hands.

To take his mind off the fact that he would make a minimum of thirty-two round trips to the back room to replenish his supply of small Mt. Vesuvius Cones, Santos speculated about how his existence on Earth might have been radically changed had he decided to become a priest, like Father Galli had suggested to him during Santos' occasional visits to St. Edwin's Church in the South Valley. Of course, he would have had to attend college, then the seminary for over eight years, curtail (or completely cut out) his drinking and smoking, search his soul, confirm a calling from God, take a vow of chastity, poverty, obedience. Nawww. Not in this lifetime.

His untamed heart had to fight to keep from totally losing it, and possibly ending it all one crazy day. Coming into work with a blow torch and blowing up the entire R. & T. fireworks bunker—and himself, in the process. All this in a spectacular, but unprecedented, explosion of frustration and boredom, Santos thought about how important it was for him to hold this job for the sake of the baby.

Maribel thought about nothing but the baby. When she washed dishes, she thought about how, in less than a year, she would be sterilizing bottles. When she ate her morning oatmeal with honey, she thought about how she was eating for two people. When she slept, as she drifted into colorful, safe journeys with her San Rafael, and her gentle, on-going conversation with her mother, she wondered if she was dreaming for two.

Santos daydreamed while dumping dozens of whistlers and small cones into their respective bins, about how life might have turned out different if he had only joined Lupe in taking some classes at TV-I right out of Valley High School. Maybe, like Lupe Leyba, he would have learned some basic typing, sharpened up his composition skills, and then transferred to the University of New Mexico. Lupe stuck with it long enough and, after earning his Bachelor's Degree in political science, got into the U.N.M. Law School, graduated, passed the Bar, and now defended lots of the local guys (many from Duranes) in court. If only, Santos thought.

What a brilliant intellect, Adelita pondered, if only he would use that great mind of his to help *la gente* more. Adelita had mixed feelings about Professor Roberto Romero. Oh, he was proud of his background. Spanish, he called himself, sometimes Hispano, and every once in a while, while in a sudden radical fever, Chicano or

Latino. In class, he would often refer back to the old days of his youth, fighting and partying and loving in his old Martíneztown neighborhood. He even proudly identified himself as *un mestizo*, the only one in the whole journalism faculty, but Adelita was bothered by the fact that Professor Romero seemed so absolutely focused on success, at any price. When it came down to it, Adelita felt, he spent more time with his college cronies than his old *vecinos* back in Martíneztown. Still, he had what she wanted. A total and deep understanding of the power of words to shape and steer public opinion.

After a few weeks in his Advanced Journalism classes, Adelita was impressed with Romero's extensive knowledge of the history of the printed word in the world; and the state. Turns out Romero had worked for the *Las Vegas Optic* shortly after getting his degree. He had researched, written, and edited his own stories, worked on increasing circulation of the small weekly newspaper beyond the geographic limits of that small, Northern New Mexico town. And he had won a few awards for a series of reports he did on topics ranging from heroin addiction to efforts by local Chicanos to get Land Grants returned to the original heirs. As impressed as she was with the amount and quality of actual experience he had, in addition to his book knowledge, it still bothered Adelita that Romero's connection to La Raza seemed behind him. It lived like old war stories related by a detached *veterano*.

§ § §

Back in the trenches, buck private Santos Sánchez restocked ammunition, er, smoke balls, into the musty, dusty old pine bin at R. & T.

Adelita's Notebook #2,509

Maribel's paintings, based on her memories of when she lived in Jarales, and used to walk in the jaral in late July, the straight green shoots aiming their thin green fingers upward in praise to the nurturing ramas of the sun. Mari's depiction of golden rays inspiring and meeting the emerald rays of nature in full summer-ecstasy inspire my riffing-on-words, and I feel, with each poetic burst, a connection to a sister artist.

Life cannot be too easy for Maribel, being married to Santos. Oh, pobrecito Santos, still struggling as he always has for identity, stability, security, and for that elusive state called being comfortable-in-your-own-skin. We must all go through that, though some of us suffer more than others. I have days when the most haphazard and wandering riffing in my journal feels so infinitely more meaningful than completing some of the journalism class assignments for Prof. Romero: Interview Someone In Your Neighborhood sounded so good as a title. But Prof. Romero constrained us by limiting the question and the approach, and I realized it was ruined for me. We only could ask about the source of livelihood and participation in the local economy. I had already chosen Magdalena Moya as my subject, and the questions I had in mind were: Tell me more about these songs, estas canciones en Español that you have always sung but now have found out may have roots in old Jewish modes. That one alabado that los viejitos used to sing in the San Felipe Church is of Turkish origin, isqüe. And why do you think it made it all the way to our little corner of El Nuevo Mundo over 300 years ago? What about the effects on our soul when we sing the old songs?

But no, Prof. Romero wanted us to go into depth about the local employees' opportunities for a livelihood available to our neighbors. What? Like the privilege of working as check-out clerks, stockers, and carry-out boys for the Piggly Wiggly and Furr's food chains? And talk about chains. How about the fact that the corporate owners, like Winn-Dixie, are using documented union- busting tactics on the recent strike by the workers here? I actually asked, out loud, in class, if we could take that angle of investigation, but the professor snapped at me that I'd never get that inciting piece past the editor, so why waste my time?

So what are we practicing? Safe

journalism? (Antonio's radical ideas are starting to rub off on me. Hmmm.) A lifetime of writing about good little worker ants who are born, go to school, get married, have children, get jobs, get old, retire, and then die, and then their children do the exact same thing?

I want to write about people who change history, take control of their lives, expose corruption, and help people live the freedom that we are lucky enough to enjoy. To me, Freedom of the Press doesn't mean being free to write beautiful compliments about the local extensions of the large corporations who try to run over rights to unionize that our grandfathers fought for, men who worked for the railroads, and so on. Yes, I'd rather write about the real world labor relations. And when I'm done with that, write about my ideas of human interest. Articles about those whispered streams of hidden culture that flow through our veins. Our rivers of memories, the ancient Ladino chants of the Sephardim, the Judeo-Spanish songs that flow through our Mestizo souls.

XVII

Things could only go so good for so long.

Sure enough, one super, extra-boring day, Santos absolutely had to mount a major rebellion against the tedium of stocking, restocking, sorting, arranging, organizing, bagging, and boxing small, medium, and large cones, whistlers, smoke bombs, and Roman candles. He wasn't sure whether his discontent came from the stifling, airless, windowless environment. Could it have been from spending time with only one other non-communicable fellow worker who was still a mystery to him after laboring side by side all these months? Santos wondered if it was the mind-numbing tasks or whether it was the growing resentment that he felt towards the boss, Mr. Fisk, and his sons, and the new Cadillacs that each drove. Whatever it was, or the combination of all of the above, one afternoon at 5:05 p.m. he drove straight to the Casa Grande Bar.

He knew he was playing with temptation by stopping there and then threw *carne* to *los perros* as he proceeded to chug three ice-cold Tecates, one after the other. Unconcerned about the dangers of mixing drinks, Santos ordered up a Cuba Libre. He had heard Tykie talk about that particular combination of rum and Coke through the years, but this was the first time he actually tried one. Just for the hell of it, Santos then had the bartender bring him a Kahlua and crème, which he drank way too fast, barely tasting the dark flavor in passing.

A strange thing happened while Santos sat on the bar stool, losing himself in the mild dazzling colors of the back-lit bottles of liquor. As Santos stared at the glass-portioned handfuls of Ouzo, Bacardi rum, Melón, Cherry Brandy, etc., he became vaguely aware of the continuous plaintive ballad that strummed and moaned in the background.

It wasn't a needle stuck in the groove of a scratched vinyl 45 or that somebody had drunkenly pressed C-23 about nine times in a row on the old Imperial Jukebox. No. Somehow an electrical short, mechanical malfunction or cosmic intervention, (or all of the above) resulted in the Casa Grande music box serving as the mystical source of Bob Dylan's constant mourning of *Knocking on Heaven's Door* for a straight half hour. As the old cliché goes, it was like something out of the movies. Mortality and blind pride danced in *La Tentación's* favorite corner, yes, Temptation was present for a penitent destination.

The intoxicating scene to a short movie came to an abrupt end when Santos turned to gaze at the old movie poster of TinTan and Mara Felix and, instead of focusing on the bigger- than-life images of betrayed love, Santos found his eyes locked into Tykie's are-you-ready-for-a-real-deal stare.

Tykie strutted over, a glowing Marlboro in one hand and an ice-chilled rum and Coke in the other, his *chuco-suave* smile a sparkling pearl that grew as he approached. A machine-gun burst of words. Pure guilt. Some condemnation. A dash of self-pity.

The masculine scent of sweat and the old leather of Tykie's bomber jacket around Santos' tense neck filled the air.

"*Órale, Señor* Sánchez. *Hace mucho tiempo* and I never hear from you. What's going on? Too good to give your old *camarada* a call? Just forget about me, huh, *ese*? Oh no, wait. I get it. You're making so much *feria* at that *jale* at the fireworks company that you don't need your old *carnal* Tykie anymore, huh? No, it's all alright, don't say nothing, homeboy. I get the hint, bro. I'll just park my sorry ass over there with the rest of the untouchables who aren't worthy to talk to the too-good-for-low-life-bums like me, huh? *'Ta bien.* I'll just leave you to enjoy your, what the shit? To enjoy your little Kahluas here?"

The resentful grip on Santos' necked loosened.

Santos cautiously directed Tykie to the seat next to him by gently pushing his elbow to table level.

"*Siéntate*, bro. I never said I was too good for you," Santos slurred. "I'll buy you a drink, Tykie. *Vamos a platicar.*"

Tykie swept Santos' hand away from his side.

"No, Santos. I understand. You got your thing going *a todo vuelo.* You and your old lady *y todo.* You don't need to even be seen talking to your old *carnal.*"

"*Todo serio*, Tykie. I was going to call you. I mean it."

"No, forget it. You and Maribel got your life going

well, and hey, don't feel sorry for me, Santitos. I don't need nobody's damn pity. I don't want to waste your valuable time."

Santos slapped the table. "Sit down, man. I'll get you a drink."

"*No te preocupes*, I brought my own. But if you really mean it, we could talk *por un ratito*."

Within a half hour, Tykie Mendoza had managed to buy the two of them three more rounds, tantalize Santos Sánchez with more tales of easy money and painless fun, and to get him to admit that he was bored to tears and murder from his job at the R. & T. Fireworks Company.

The smoke got thicker, the laughs grew wilder, and the pair became careless, joining the loose crowd of a dozen jukebox jiving, harmonizing, nonsense-joke-telling revelers. What the revelers didn't know was that Tykie was publicly celebrating his re-recruitment of Santos into his *Los Alacranes/La Familia* network. What the drunken mob didn't know was that Santos would not be returning to R.& T. tomorrow, or ever again. What Santos didn't know was how large and deep a price, in a head-splitting, stomach-threshing hangover, he would suffer over the next two days and a half.

Tykie, with some assistance from a couple of anonymous, free-drinks recipients, shakily stood on the cigarette-burned, solid oak bar, and raised his *Cuba Libre* to the stars outside. This particular highway-to-hell party was about to reach its deliciously disastrous crescendo with a rum-driven ecstatic declaration from Tykie Mendoza.

128

"*¡Afuera! ¡Afuera para un anuncio!* Everyone outside for one last toast and one last, special *trago!*"

In an unusually obscene display of bold extravagance, even for a big show-off spender like Tykie, he handed over a fistful of twenty-dollar bills to Tantalus Kronos for a case of champagne for his announcement. History was being made. At the Casa Grande, 90% of the drinks sold were beer, tap or bottled. 7% of the liquor consumed was whiskey and 2% wine. That last 1% was champagne and moving a bottle of champagne was so rare that Tantalus had to wipe the dust off the cardboard box after he pulled it out of a forgotten corner of the walk-in cooler.

Outside, in front of the bar, where Central Avenue temporarily curved South, just a couple blocks from the Rio Grande, the party reached its peak. Bathed in radiant Route 66 neon, Tykie Mendoza stood on the hood of his black Cadillac, one hand raising a bottle of Cold Duck and the other arm around the barely-standing guest of honor, Santos Sánchez. The crowd drunkenly circled the car in the fools-in-paradise parking lot, and self-quieted through the chugging of shared bottles of bubbly and then tightened around the obsidian-black throne.

With the magnificent sound of the Central Avenue late-night cruisers like a background symphony of engines, horns and 50's rock and roll on the radio, Tykie's voice rose above the street beat.

"*¡Escuchen, todos! Quiero decir que* I am very proud to have been friends with Santos Sánchez for the past twenty years!"

129

Loud drunken roar.

"I am proud to have known you *por casi toda mi vida.*"

Santos reply was on automatic pilot.

"*El orgullo es mío, carnal!*"

Drunken loud roar.

Tykie refilled Santos' glass and raised his voice even louder over a passing Impala blaring *In the Still of the Night.*

"And I just want to publicly celebrate our friendship."

The roaring chorus interrupted with such a shout that, miles away, in the shadow of the concrete water pump house that stood like a massive volcano, old deaf Mr. Gallegos felt a shudder.

"*Espérate*, people, wait a minute. I want to not only celebrate my friendship *con mi camarada* Santos, *pero* I want to celebrate our continuing partnership in our home-owned and operated little Mexican *conexión, ¿qué no?*"

The drunken choral approval was accompanied by the simultaneous sparking of about a dozen hand-rolled cigarettes of Mexican-grown, but home-distributed product.

In a final burst of intoxicated *gritos* tearing through the marijuana clouds, Tykie bellowed, "¡*Salud!* ¡*A la vida loca!*"

"¡*A La Vida Loca!*" Santos echoed.

"¡*A mi camarada!* ¡Santos Sánchez!" Tykie grinned

Then, Santos spoke. "*Espérate*, homeboy. Not

Santos anymore. *Chále, ese.* From now on, you can all just call me *Champagne* Sánchez."

And the inebriated crowd spread the word.

"¡*Qué viva la fiesta!* ¡*Qué viva la vida!* ¡*Qué Viva* Champagne Sánchez !!!"

Adelita's Notebook #2,617

Antonio couldn't (or wouldn't) meet me for coffee tonight. He ran out of class as soon as it was over, so I went to see The Seventh Seal, an Ingmar Bergman movie showing at the Campus Basement Theater.

How do these guys, the film directors, come up with their stories, I wonder? Do they keep Dream Journals?

You sit in the center of the seventh row, and you're actually the closest to the screen of the twelve or seventeen heavy-jacketed students who have sacrificed being caught up with assignments and the comfort of shelter on this cold windy night. The still chilly air in this theater matches the black and white Norwegian winter projected on the flattened snow screen. A knight, and his reluctant squire companion return from the Crusades, their hearts seem defeated, their very souls on a final pilgrimage. You are walking beside the weary travelers in moments, haunted like them by the same low-

voiced messengers of mid-life and mid-winter despair. You momentarily feel a parallel with the alienating journey through the lonely tomb of a university library, where ideas and counter-ideas are packed and stacked on wood and steel shelves. So you think escape will come tonight at the underground campus movie theater.

You wonder where this Bergman got the idea to show the wailing Penitents, in all their regretful, resentful parade of misery through the once-festive village? You are reminded of the faithful few who likewise repent and walk in procession to the sonido de los esqueletos in Northern New Mexican hamlets during Lent— from Abiquiu to Santa Rosa, from Pecos to Villanueva. The path to purification, you are reminded, is an open invitation for all on our way back home, in the near-midnight, near-freezing, muffled air.

On my way to the all-night drugstore for aspirin, I drive past a crowd who holler and howl at the moon, each other, and who crown a fool in their drunken ritual. A sheer abandonment to Bacchus, the unthinking adoration of the tomorrow-penitent, now-whooping crowd, out there making pendejos of themselves in the midnight hour. It's a morality play unfolding in the mid-evil parking lot of a cheap cantina known as Casa Grande.

XVIII

The Fall of Champagne Sánchez shifted into high gear unlike the old Chevy he was currently driving that could never shift into third. It went into second only with some coaxing and a terrible gnashing of gears and would frequently jump out of reverse every other time he tried to back up. But all that was about to change.

First came the fact that he was fired from the R.& T. Fireworks Company, the first employee that they ever had to let go in their seventeen years in the South Valley. The Official Reason was because of a pattern of tardiness, but the real reason was this: with the huge hangover that he came in with every Monday morning, the Mystery of the Mispackaged Bags was solved, evidenced, proven, solidified, shown, and revealed. Mr. Fisk gave him a B package of fireworks with his final paycheck. Half of the pyrotechnic samples were duds, and when he lit a large cone, Maldito scurried by and tipped it on its side. Champagne's attention was momentarily captured by a passing motorcyclist, and the ferocious sparks started the straw *Bienvenidos* welcome mat on fire. But of course.

Champagne's renewed partnership with Tykie found expression in the purchase of a new Cadillac—white, since Tykie's was black and they couldn't, not in the Duke City, have the same color. Champagne managed to earn three speeding tickets, two careless driving tickets, and a failure-to-yield citation that he immediately received driving home from the Cadillac dealership.

This rapid descent to more dangerous levels of personal hell paralleled the growing distance between Champagne and Mari. Now six months pregnant, Maribel's nesting and nurturing instincts dominated her every thought, prayer, and action. She withdrew from her entrepreneurial husband physically, emotionally, psychologically, and spiritually. One day she made a decision for the growing child she carried.

"Santos. I'm going to make this very simple. I'm not angry, and I don't want you to get *agüitado, pero* I've decided either you move out or I will." Her very calm tone underscored the seriousness and finality of her decision. "If you want to stay here, fine. I'll move in with Delfina. She already said it would be all right with her. I'm not going to have my child anywhere near this evil drug business. *Es una cosa muy mala, es del Diablo, y tú lo sabes.*"

In her mind, Maribel could hear the lyrics of that old song *de cumpleaños,* 'Las Mañanitas,' and now she fully understood one *estrofa,* in particular . . .

"De las estrellas del cielo, tengo que bajarte dos,

una para saludarte, y otra para decirte adiós . . . "

("And from the stars in heaven, I need to bring down two of them for you,

one to greet you, my love . . . and another to tell you farewell . . . "

He barely won the battle to hold back his tears as he

packed up his clothes in several old Tecate beer cardboard boxes. She cried silently. On his way out, he paused by the front door, looked down at the cat's litter box. Maribel gently lifted Maldito from the couch and placed him in Santos' arms. Looking into Santos' eyes of misery, Maribel whispered as she made the sign of the cross on his forehead. "*Te quiero con todo mi corazón*, but this can't go on around our baby. You'll be in our prayers. May the *Virgencita* watch over you and *Tata Dios* over us all. Call me every once in a while to let me know you're all right. *Con cuidado*." And with that, Santos was cut adrift in a sea of temptation and illusion.

XIX

"Why do some men act so foolishly? Delfina, *comadre*, he's not even thinking!"

"Ah, *comadre*. You just answered your own question. Sometimes men act foolishly because they don't think! Sometimes women don't think either, but mostly, I believe we do. Actually, *a veces*, the men are thinking, but only about five minutes ahead, or enough for that day. Hand me that towel, would you, *comadrita*?"

Maribel placed the frayed *toalla* in Delfina's outstretched hand and continued. "But it's been a couple weeks, Delfie. I thought he would have learned his lesson by now, quit that dangerous business with Tykie, and gotten an honest job and come home."

"Sometimes," Delfina responded, as she dried the *reredos* behind the tabernacle, "a person needs to hit bottom before they actually learn their lesson." Delfina carefully descended the short step-ladder. "Is the altar dry yet?"

Maribel touched the swirled, holy marble. "*Sí, comadre*. I'll get the linen cover." Maribel respectfully lifted the pure white cloth out of the old Altar Linens cardboard box and handed one end to Delfie.

They then carefully unfolded the linen cover with embroidered borders and centered it over the altar, precisely the way Father Galli liked it, just like how they had done it every last Saturday of the month for the past seven years. Somehow, the rotation of *mayordomos* never actually took place at *La Capilla de San José* the way it was supposed to, so Delfie and Mari ended up being the primary caretakers of the sacred *adobe* chapel year after dutiful year.

Why do men act so damn foolishly? Adelita Augusta Zoila Chávez thought to herself as she placed a fresh, pure white sheet of paper in the black metal Remington typewriter on her desk. But she opened her journal and began to write in it instead of starting her assignment.

Adelita's Journal #2,705

Professor Romero has the potential to spark his own modest revolución on campus, but he always stops short of giving los estudiantes permission to use the written word as a weapon against las injusticias. "You have to be objective in your reporting," he always reminds them. "Don't let your emotions ruin a good piece of journalism." Does he think that he'll lose his precious teaching post if he dares tell his classes about the role of the press in social movements? Why won't he mention the bravery of hombres como Carlos Magón Flores whose words still are remembered by los pobres de México? Meanwhile, the anglos

y los vendidos among our people who control the
media here in our country pretend to be objective
and even-handed while ignoring or discounting
our history and our contributions to society.
César Chávez was organizing farm workers
down in Las Cruces last week, and that story
barely made it to the bottom of section D, page
16 of the local Albuquerque paper. ¡Qué gacho!

Why do men act so foolishly? Esperanza Vásquez stared at the carved-out hollow in José's chair where he did all the hard work of examining evidence, after hours, at home, for no extra pay. Today was supposed to be his day off, *pero, no. Tan cabezón* as he was, José just had to meet with that sleazy *abogado* Giovanni on some extra secret case coming up. And that stubborn fool had canceled their day trip up *to El Santuario de Chimayo* that Esperanza had planned months ago.

Aw, *no importa*, thought Esperanza, I'll just make the best of this day by writing Thank You cards to Onésimo and Neomí Fréquez and Johnnie and Bárbara Medina for the gifts they brought that *mula* husband of mine for his surprise party last weekend. He didn't deserve it, but Esperanza had organized a small *cena para celebrar* his fifty-fourth birthday on Saturday. The visit from the friends that he had from the fire department and their compassionate wives was worth it. Any time you did something out of compassion for somebody else, it was always worth it, whether they appreciated it or not.

Esperanza signed both of their names on the cards she had found at the Sunshine Market this morning.

¿Por qué son los hombres tan pendejos? Doña MariLuz shook her head, squinted her pilgrim-violet eyes and sighed to herself as she gathered the discarded Budweiser bottles and Olympia beer cans and put them in a black plastic bag. She usually cleared the field in the misty cool of the morning, close to one of the irrigation *acequias.* She crisscrossed the small patch and said prayers of thanksgiving to *Tata Dios* and then harvested *las hierbas.*

MariLuz pulled out her hand-sharpened knife and began cutting the tops of the yellow and faded-green *chamisa* plants. MariLuz had a *vecino* or *cuate* or *comadre* in mind for each and every herb that *la tierra* gifted her with. "*Gracias, bendito Dios, por estas plantas tan buenas.* These will be good for Señor Gallegos when he gets his usual winter *dolor de estómago* in December." MariLuz's deep-soul prayed intentions for each fortunate recipient of her teas, salves, *parches,* and homemade ointments accompanied the process, from gathering to delivery.

"*Comadre*, did you ever think of leaving your husband, maybe even leaving this city or this state to get away? So there would be no chance of ever seeing him again?"

"*Muchas veces, comadre.* About every other week."

Maribel was so shocked at the revelation that she

hesitated. "*¿De veras, comadre?* But I thought you were always happily married."

"Every couple, even the closest, in fact, especially the closest ones, the ones *que son enamorados*, every couple goes through hard times. And, yes, every couple feels like calling it quits, sometime. And separating. And maybe leaving town forever."

"So what kept you and Modesto from ever breaking up forever?"

"Faith. Faith in our marriage. It's different from our trusting in the *Santos* or Our Lady or having faith in Our Lord, but it's still a kind of faith." Delfina put the cloth down and stepped back a couple feet. "*Mira, comadre.* Look at the *Santo Niño's* eyes. They're shining again, *qué no?*"

"*Sí, comadre.* That's so strange. The baby Jesus' eyes always seem to follow me. No matter where I'm standing or sitting in the chapel."

Just then the friendly New Mexico sun sliced through the cloudy indigo sky and passed through the small stained-glass window. It encircled the head of the plaster statue of the Holy Family behind the altar. Maribel and Delfina were ambered in the honey-glow of quiet reverence. "*La Santa Familia, comadre.*"

"*Sí, comadre,*" whispered Maribel, "*La Santa Familia.*"

Adelita's Notebook #2,715

Magdalena Moya sang me all the way to la casa de la Doña MariLuz, and I hummed along. The curandera, Doña MariLuz, is her sister. We walked into the sage and lavender-scented medicine room and I spotted an egg on the worn cloth on the table. Magdalena then left me alone in the flickering candle stillness. She said she had to leave because "Today I have to go meet with a man who says he has some letters that he thinks were written by my father. If they were, they might answer questions that I've had for over fifty years."

What questions, I wondered, but poof! She was gone. Magdalena often disappeared as quickly as she appeared. She brought me to Doña MariLuz because, after una plática with her last week, she said that I showed signs of being cansada and espantada. She may also have told her I felt the strain of carrying a full load of classes. The weight of knowing that my mom is sick, although we still have to wait for the outcome of yet more tests. And the burden of feeling like I am stuck in Student Hell, not free to take on a full-time job, yet wanting to put into practice a lot of what I had already learned in my journalism class. All of the above was taking its toll on me.

The moment Doña MariLuz floated in, I felt covered, protected, understood, and empowered. She asked me questions about myself, mi mamá, mis pensamientos, y mis sueños. She rubbed my shoulders with her healing fingers. Her voice was a summer breeze of soothing tones. This was unique Woman Wisdom put into practice.

"Bendito, bendito, bendito sea Dios; los ángeles cantan y alaban a Dios," she hymned in front and behind my heart. Her whispered Spanish prayers surrounded us both like a scentless smoke. In adoration and praise, she invoked an ancient petition for the fright to leave my body ¡En Este Momento! and my fear gently peeled away. It was a soothing beginning for a spiritual cleansing.

Doña MariLuz didn't pick up the egg to rub it on my belly like she often did with the babies that she ministered. Instead, She lifted white turkey feathers from her red-clay vase and began her limpia of me by gently fluttering away the espanto from the top of my head, off my shoulders, away from my elbows, and out of my legs and feet. Doña MariLuz took a small chunk of charcoal and placed it in her green and gray clay ahumador, her incense burner. She added small pieces of copal, a sacred resin from trees in Central America. When the lumbre from her match caught the piece of charcoal, the copal sputtered and released its soul-awakening aroma that blended and then covered the most delicate perfumes of lavender and sage. The copal infused the whole room con respeto y paz. Using the feathers to brush the circling smoke on my face and chest, I re-connected to Nahua strength and the Aztec traditions. The limpia invisibly stripped layers of worry and fear from me like last year's skin from a snake.

I breathed deeper and slower. Doña MariLuz offered more muted prayers to El Padre, El Hijo y El Espíritu Santo, and made manifest my intentions and impulses to be re-centered, balanced. My heart felt utterly calm. Before she walked out of the room, she placed my feet on the wooden floor. They felt strong and ready for the next part of my jornada.

I have no idea how long Doña MariLuz left me in the medicine room, but peace was mine again. Before I entered the vida de la ciudad air outside, I prayed slow words of gratitude for the healing hands of MariLuz and the compassionate singing of Magdalena Moya, Doña MariLuz's sister, as well as God's present-day incarnation of the spirit of San Rafael for this gift. It was a day of pure unfolding Grace.

XX

A hot dagger of pain brought Maribel back from a golden dream of Sunday driving over the *mesa* with Santos. Her child was kicking, harder than ever, so she stepped into the kitchen, lit the pilot light, and put a teapot on the blue flames as she searched behind some plastic Kool-Aid cups for a plastic baggy of *yerba buena.*

"*Tranquilo, niño. Cálmate, por favor.*" The young mother-to-be stroked her swollen belly and then hummed an old lullaby Delfie had reminded her of, earlier today.

"*A la Ruuuuu, a la rrruuuuuu, a la me. Duérmete, niño lindo, en los brazos del amor, mientras que duerme y descansa, la pena de me dolor.*"

The kicking stopped. The water boiled. A cricket now rested. Maribel gazed at the picture on the refrigerator. Her Santos.

"Ah, Santitos. *¿Dónde estás,* my poor, mixed-up vagabond? Are you doomed to wander forever?"

§ § §

The white, unwashed Cadillac zig-zagged, back and forth, across the deserted avenue, the radio singing an old 50s East L.A. ballad. It was 4 a.m. The *xoloitzcuintlis* barked.

At the corner of 12th and Central Avenue, the *víbora* and the *puma* smiled sinisterly in the sick-yellow light from overhead. The glimpse of the partied-out driver in the Caddie made the previous three hours of silent waiting worth it. This drunken dance was about to end.

"I say bust him tonight. Now. He's gotten careless enough to have something valuable in the trunk of his new Caddie."

"You think so?"

"I know so. Go on, José. Call it in."

"This isn't just anybody to me, Tony. Remember that. I'm not going to take the risk of him not carrying anything."

"He's carrying. He's careless enough. No risk. I promise you. Call it in. Now."

José Vásquez slowly removed the voice-piece from its dashboard cradle. A tiny voice emerged from the crackling static. "A.P.D. Special Communications Channel. Password, please."

"Acknowledge. Puma calling in. This is Puma."

"Acknowledge Puma," the static echoed. "Who can I connect you with?"

"Can you put me through to Officer Gallagher and Officer Cruz?"

"I'll try. You sure they're on midnight shift?"

"I'm sure. Go ahead and try them."

"Hold on," the distant voice crackled back.

José tapped his hand to the scrambled chaos while the *víbora* sucked on a stinky Camel filtered.

The Caddie crawled past the Dog House neon, heading West, and Santos, for no other reason than to keep from nodding out, turned the sunshade down. A 2" by 3" faded photo of Maribel fell to the floor.

Gallagher was heading East on Central, just passing the empty Casa Grande parking lot when Special Agent Vásquez's matter-of-fact voice came through.

"10-4. Gallagher here. Can I help you?"

"Yeah, Jerry, this is José Vásquez. Listen, There's a dirty white Caddie, '72, chrome rims with a front vanity plate that says *Champagne*, heading west on Central. Looks like a definite D.W.I. You in the area?"

Gallagher grinned at his partner in the passenger's seat. Eddie Cruz. "Yeah, José. You still got every cop's beat memorized, I see." He winked at Eddie who shook his head and guiltily gulped his last bite on a freshly glazed Golden Crown Donut. "Tell me, José. Are things really so slow that they've got you guys casing out cruisers on Central Avenue?"

Crackle. Feedback. Static. "I never really left the streets, Gallagher. You'll find that out if you ever actually get a promotion."

"Alright, alright, Vásquez. Don't rub it in."

"Actually, I've been after this particular cruiser for a while. The reason I'm calling is I highly suspect that he may have more than just a case of warm beer in his trunk. I'd appreciate it if you'd suspect that, too, and give me a call. Okay?"

146

"You'll hear from me in a bit."

"Let's go to work, Eddie." Gallagher flicked his half-smoked Marlboro out the window and gave the cruiser some gas.

§ § §

Like a slow boat half-tangled in moss in old Tingley Beach, the white Caddie barely crossed the intersection of Central Avenue and Rio Grande Boulevard as the traffic light turned red.

"Oh shit," Santos drooled to himself as he squinted into his rear-view mirror. The cop car that had just passed him in the opposite direction was, sure enough, making a U-turn and his cherry-red top was flashing bright, busted red. So close to home. So not far away from *la ley,*

Santos grumbled to himself as he chugged warm mouthfuls of brew and ditched the bottle under his seat. There was no way to get away, he thought, so I'll just play the nice guy and take my chances. The Caddie floated into the Safeway parking lot with the police cruiser on his bumper. Santos heard a muddled mix of voices and static but couldn't decode the exchange.

"Vásquez, Gallagher here. The suspect is pulled over. If this indeed ends up being a big deal, don't forget to give credit where credit is due."

"I never forget my roots. I'm still connected to the streets, you know that. Don't worry, man, the Chief will hear all about your impeccable work."

Flashlights in their hands, pep in their step, and grins on their faces, Cruz and Gallagher approached the Caddie.

"Well, if it isn't Albuquerque's own Champagne Sánchez, crawling through our deserted streets this early, lovely morning."

Santos just kept his cool and stared straight ahead. Gallagher made exaggerated movements with his face, sniffing loud and long. "What? That wouldn't happen to be an illegal substance that I smell, would it? Officer Cruz, you smell that marijuana, too?

"Think I do."

Santos nodded. "Okay, you got me. I did run a red light, somewhere back there, Officer, and you should give me a ticket."

"The red light? No, don't worry about that. If I were you, I'd be more concerned about this odor of an illegal substance that I smell. Officer Cruz smells it, too."

"That's right. Something smells illegal."

Gallagher grinned. He was only warming up. "Alright, Mr. Sánchez, would you please step out of this vehicle."

"Hey, I admit it. I've had a few beers, but weed? No way. I don't smoke it, and you don't really smell that. You couldn't cuz I haven't."

"You confronting a peace officer in the midst of his duties, Champagne? Officer Cruz, would you say that this subject is being confrontational?"

"I guess you could say that."

"Hand over your keys and step out of the car right now. No sudden movements, you understand?"

Not quite sure of what was happening, or why, Santos handed his keys through the window, opened the door, and leaned against the captured Caddie in a confused haze.

In his mind, Gallagher could already hear praise from the Chief. "Champagne, I have suspicions that you're transporting an illegal substance in this vehicle. You agree, Officer Cruz?"

"You could have suspicions of that. Yeah."

"I do believe we're going to have to inspect the trunk of your vehicle, Champagne Sánchez.

"What!"

"Hold it, right there. You don't want to be charged with disorderly conduct, as well, do you, punk?"

"Well, no, but you can't just search without a warrant."

"Or obstruction of justice? That's a pretty serious charge, buddy. Now let's co-operate and take a look inside that trunk." Gallagher dragged Santos by his collar to the back of the dirty white car.

"But don't you need a warrant to search?"

"Cease and desist, buddy. Officer Cruz, does it appear to you that Mr. Sánchez is obstructing justice again?"

"It could appear to you that way."

"Okay, okay, I'll co-operate." Santos was overwhelmed, but he got the picture. "Here are the keys."

In the distance, a vague mournful cry echoed from

the Rio Grande. *La Llorona?* Crying for her lost children? Moaning for her lost innocence. Santos knew her well.

"Well, well, well. What do we have here? Officer Cruz, does that look like a dealer's stash to you?"

Nestled in the corner of the trunk was a black leather briefcase, an armful of marijuana in plastic baggies, and a handful of white powder in plastic baggies.

Cruz observed, "That couldn't be just for personal consumption, Officer Gallagher." "Nope," Gallagher grinned again, "looks like somebody's little business venture is just about to be closed down. Permanently. Handcuffs, please, Officer Cruz."

The cold steel tightened around Santos' wrists as Agent Vásquez' unmarked car flew onto the scene.

"Evening, Officers. Need any help?"

Now smiling way too hard, Gallagher held one of the white powder baggies like it was a dead rat. "Actually, is your lab open twenty-four hours? Do you think your guys could run a quick test of this stuff?"

Vásquez walked over, snatched the illegal white rat, and peered into the dark trunk.

Walking away with the briefcase like it was his property all along, José spoke over his shoulder on his way back to his car. "Good work, boys. I'm going to put in a special call to the Chief, personally. Excellent police work."

"Excuse me, sir," Gallagher shyly began, "shouldn't we get Polaroids of the crime scene with all of the seized articles, in place, in the subject's vehicle?"

"Gallagher, how long you been with A.P.D.?"

"Eighteen years, sir."

Vásquez whistled. "Eighteen, huh? And you still haven't made lieutenant?"

"No, sir, still trying, though."

"Well, you just get some good Polaroids of those bags of weeds and baggies of undetermined content. I'll be talking to your boss in the morning about your remarkable police work. And about your long overdue promotion."

"Yes, sir." Gallagher escorted Agent Vásquez and his new briefcase to within earshot of Santos and Officer Cruz. Vásquez chuckled as he passed the rapidly sobering vagabond leaning against the cop car as Cruz body-searched him. Vásquez whispered to the back of Santos' head, "Hey, *vagabundo*. Looks like your wandering days are through, Champagne, you no-good *pendejo*."

As they drove off, Officer Gallagher could swear that he saw prominent Defense Attorney Tony Giovanni in the passenger's seat. Strange.

A promotion would be nice, Gallagher thought. This midnight shift is driving me crazy.

XXI

Rrrriiiiinnngg. Five in the morning. Maribel was already up, and she caught the phone on its first ring. She knew, instantly, what this early call was about. And sure enough. She listened as Santos, somewhat sobered up and slightly sobbing, described how his bad decisions, poor judgment, rotten luck, and strange circumstances had landed him in jail. His Caddie had been impounded, and he faced drug possession charges and was unable to get bonded out anytime shortly.

The Fall of Champagne Sánchez continued big time.

She listened. Barely cried. Held her hand over her kicking child and whispered a tearful goodbye and hung up the phone. Maribel leaned against the doorway awhile. "Oh, Mama. Daddy. *Qué tanto yo quiero que* you both could be here. To see your grandchild. ¡*Ay, Dios mío!*"

The baby gave one last *patada* and fell asleep.

Maribel found her voice again. "*Ya basta*. No more, no more. I'm not crying anymore tears for you, Santos." Touching her stomach, she added, "*Niño*, it's going to be just you and me."

Peeling the last veil of last night's dream away from her thoughts, Maribel walked into the bedroom and just stood, in reverent silence before her Altar of Memories.

Her simple version of Sacred spots all over the world, from El Santuario in Chimayó to the healing spring in Lourdes, both places where people go for communion with loved ones, ancestors, saints, and the Divine. Gazing at the small black and white photograph of her dad and mom on her personal altar, Mari lifted her heart in a silent prayer without words.

Women make altars, simple and fancy, small and large, personal and public. Bringing order out of chaos, finding strength in stability, endurance out of arrangement, Maribel was connected to spiritual women warriors. Mari's rituals, lighting candles before the dark, old photos, offering flowers and sweet smells, sprinkling blessed water on the cloth under the pictures and the old letter.

Her comadre Delfina had shown Mari how to set up her woman's altar and design her personal woman's rituals. Delfina told Mari it was the way they kept the world from coming apart.

XXII

Adelita relived the early-morning conversation with her mother as she bounced in her seat in the diesel-stinking, early-morning bus on her way to the city jail. She remembered Delfina's anger and disappointment with "that *sobrino flojo* of mine" after her sister, Linda Sánchez López had called about Santos' current free-fall from grace. She recalled the shocking news that her cousin had gotten busted for drugs and would probably not be going home for a very long time. Adelita had told her mom the exciting news that she would be starting a four- month internship this morning. And guess what? She would be doing most of her work out at the city court and jail complex. Before last night, she had expected everyone there to be a stranger, but now she knew someone who would be in residence: Champagne Sánchez.

Adelita pondered the *dicho* that her mom had told her as she left the house this morning. "*Mi hija, no olvides que 'Poco a poco se anda muy lejos.'* Always."

Adelita knew that every step to her goal, no matter how small, did count. She remembered her mother's blessing as she left the house this morning—way too early on such a brisk day. She was jerked back into reality by the abrupt stop of the city bus in front of the city jail.

She exited the vomit-smelling public transport

and went off to look for Professor Romero and the other journalism students who would be there for their first day of orientation.

Adelita's Notebook #2,814

"Hello cold-steel real world, Goodbye poetry." Maybe. We'll see. Well, the change might turn out to be not so severe, but my guess is that in the next couple of months I'll be writing a lot more about the facts and less about the feelings of things. There will surely be a radical difference in my immediate circumstances, my environment, the images before my eyes. The tragedy of words bound to the service of 'just the facts, ma' am.'

I'll still be recording my thoughts and my impressions in my journals, but after spending the afternoon at the city jail, sitting through our orientation, I know that I'm going into a scary world I've only read about or seen in movies, and only in glances at that. For most of the rest of the semester, we'll be meeting on campus once every other week to read our summary papers, condensed reports of the stories that we'll generate from our time spent with inmates at the central local lock-up facility.

The first sense-awakening shock is the sick, ever-present smell of stale urine. It permeates everywhere in the jail except maybe the Check-In desk near the front door. The other thing I'll have to get used to is the cold echo of steel-on-steel, the threatening reverberations in the gray air, everywhere, even in the Briefing Room, where I sat with Professor Romero and the six other students. That unceasing clanging constantly always shook from every corner of the cold bunker, the noisy, steely scrapes sometimes finding their way in through the heating vents.

And it's cold. It feels like an old, left-over deep freeze that somehow is never thawed by the heating system. Wherever you walk or sit is the lingering cold of a concrete and steel world.

At orientation, Sargent Maldonado went over the list of contraband: no weapons of any kind can be brought past the Check-In desk, of course, but also no potential weapons, including hand combs, silverware or plastic ware, metal jewelry, popsicle sticks, the list goes on. The rules also require that we submit to a pat-down when entering and leaving the Day Room areas where we'll interview inmates. We are not to pass or receive any notes whatsoever and the violation of this, and any other facility rules, even just once, will result in our expulsion from the intern program. And possible criminal charges.

When we talk with inmates we are to do so at a volume level audible to the accompanying guards, and topics are restricted to family background, basic info about the offenses that they are charged with, but no discussion of legal strategies, etc. That is the domain of their lawyers, or in most of these cases, their public defenders. We are told that we might be able to listen in on future conferences between the inmates and their legal help, but that will be determined by the jail staff at a later time.

Obviously, no cameras can be brought in, but if an inmate wants to give us a drawing or other piece of artwork, it might be accepted after being reviewed and inspected by the Community Liaison Officer. I learn that, in their free time, many of the men and women (17% of the incarcerated are female) work on a type of image-making indigenous to jails and prisons. The basic tools are pencil, pen, and their "canvas" is a handkerchief or torn pillowcase. They create drawings of peacocks, roses, butterflies, views of jail cells and prison towers, images of watches, clocks, and hourglasses, depictions of loved ones based on small photos, and the crucified Christ. These paños, as they are called, are affirmations of hope, images of despair, and creations from imagination in a tattoo-like style. Most of the paños are created for family members, and the small size of the handkerchiefs allows them to be folded and mailed in standard-issue jail envelopes to sons and daughters, husbands and wives, or girlfriends and boyfriends.

The universal, human artistic impulse survives even in the clangiest, clingiest, noisiest, coldest, echoist, stinkiest environment.

I'll be back, along with the other interns, next week when we will be given our first tour of the jail.

XXIII

La Memoria stood behind Santitos, embracing him in her weighty shadow, and she whispered into his first mind. In his deep humiliation, hers was the only voice he could hear.

You watch as the greasy-black limousine drives away, transporting Warden Eichwald and Parole Board Member Ned Hutchinson out through the iron Penitentiary gates. You back away from your window, the outside world, and return to the reality of your cold, lime-green cell door where your hand shivers as you lean against the solid, dead, enamel-coated bars. Your fatigue from the previous day's humiliating processing catches up to you, and you lie on the smelly, stiff mattress. Your body, limp as a wet cigarette, melts into the smell and the stiffness smooths out your rag-body. The banging echoes of cruel doors slamming on the cell block transform into the regular beat from that railroad car that you once rode to Barstow, your five-year-old head protected by your mother's Jergen's lotion-scented arms.

The journey to California to reunite with your father, the *vagabundo* Eddie López, was unsuccessful, but you remember how much fun you had discovering the enchantment of blending colored pencil shapes on the unnumbered pages of a spiral notebook, a gift from kind Auntie Consuelo for your exciting train ride.

You remember waking up in the middle of an unmarked night, the steady roll over bumpy tracks tickling the inside of your stomach. The train whistle was a black metal snake's lonely desert cry, and the passing distant lights silently faded and crisscrossed like the fireflies you heard about in a story your mother, Linda López, read to you the week before.

The week before, when an uncle you had never previously met, Ignacio López, from Oxnard (another strange California name) suddenly showed up for a three-day, tear-filled visit with your mom and a gift of colored pencils for *el chamaco*.

There was one perfect four-hour stretch during Uncle Nacho's stay. They drove into old Tijeras Canyon and made a surprise visit to Tinkertown. To not even know that such a place existed and to then be there, within an hour, crawling on the old Route 66 two-lane blacktop through a pine-tree wilderness. Before the dust from the parking lot had even finished settling, you wandered through the waist-high, hand-carved wonderland called Tinkertown: a-turn-of-the- century, hand-whittled world of cabins and miniature saloons, of wooden cars and horses, of sudden door-opening outhouses and embarrassement!

Laughter mixed with the calming smell of sawdust in this amazing, every-corner-filled-with-a-mystery hand-built civilization of bears stealing food from picnic baskets, a black and red railroad emerging from a mountain, a matchstick barrel of tiny roses. There was also the sense of no-longer-real time, of school-forgotten, of gloves and

160

not-needed sweaters, and of arguments disappeared into . . . where?

The cruel metal door clanged like a dull bullet to the brain. You hear "I need a doctor; I'm bleeding again." from a bitter soul in the cell bellow. The stench of rancid piss and rusted iron mixed with stale cigarettes and dried vomit.

Looking up at the ceiling you see the scraggly words carved into the ancient concrete.

Murió Juan González aquí, 1966, and *Los River Rats Controlan*. And *Rifa* and *Mi Vida Loca*.

And you feel sore now as you stand on the smooth ash-sprinkled concrete. You realize that this isn't a dream. The solid concrete, the lime walls, and this sickness inside and outside your shivering body that are not going to go away anytime soon.

This isn't the place of pleasing images created by color pencils; this is the place of haunted and haunting images created by color pencils. Here, in here, so very stuck and so very totally in here is where you are stuck. There is a bitter soul-deep scream every seventeen minutes to remind you.

You talk to yourself to keep from going crazy, as a way of trying to explain your situation to yourself. What you do is, you start with repeating your name to yourself: "I am Santos Sánchez, I am Santos Sánchez, I am Santos." Then you remind yourself of where you've recently been. The last several months. The Casa Grande Coronation. The night of the bust. The quick 'hearing.' The booking into jail. The transfers.

Was it a curse that got me here?" you ask yourself. No. From now on all of my thinking must be truthful if I am going to get out of here. No, it was my stupid mistakes that got me here. Carelessness. Trying to cut corners. I got myself here, and I will get myself out.

You repeat your goal. "I have to survive to get out of here. I have to get out of here. I have to survive. I have to hang on to me."

XXIV

He could have dealt more easily with the loneliness of no one else in his cell than with the presence. Champagne had to deal with the sinister presence, however, the all-knowing ghosts of *La Memoria*. Those *fantasmas* never slept, rested, or shut up for even five damn minutes. No, the worst part of the next few years was already becoming apparent, and it would be ugly. It knew too much about him, it said too much, and it said it all very accurately. The worst part of Champagne's second mind was that it was just as strong and loud as his first mind, the one he thought he had the most control over; the one that found itself toe-to-toe with a formidable adversary.

This business of having *La Memoria* interrupting all the time would have to be dealt with *pronto, pero cómo?* How do you defeat a presence without angering it and making it turn on you? The last thing Champagne wanted was for this pissed-off, *pinche* voice to be yacking at him in the middle of the night when he tried to find a quiet corner *en la tierra de los sueños.*

Chingao! One of the worst things about the infernal squawk box inside was that it had his same tone of voice, vocabulary, and patterns of speech. The damn thing was just like his one and only voice except for the fact that it showed no control, no pity, and worst of all no class or mercy. It just recalled every stupid thing that he ever did in his life and replayed it back to him on a Route 66 Drive-In big screen through the loudest JBL mid-range speakers and bottomless woofers you could ever imagine. And replayed it. And replayed it. The damn thing never ran out of batteries, energy, vitality, or *ánima*.

The tragedy of words when you don't need them.

This morning, of the first full day at the Santa Fe Penitentiary, *La Memoria* took him back to that way-too-fast-to-catch-it-all episode that occurred when he was booked into the city jail. It was mainly a blur of being pulled out of his Cadillac, being pushed against the police cruiser, jerked over to the curb and shoved inside the police cruiser. Then yanked out again and dragged through the booking offices, one fact remained standing—like a lone bugler at a grave site—that briefcase. As way-past-drunk as he had been, Santos clearly recalled that when the clerk at the booking station had made an inventory of all of his possessions at the time of his arrest, the one thing missing was the briefcase from the trunk of his car. *All* of his cash.

Champagne's *tesoro* was mysteriously absent from the list! ¡¡*Ladrones*!! *Cabrones!* *Me robaron, estos cabrones*, he had thought at the time, and he clearly remembered now. No, Officers Gallagher and Cruz and Special Agent Vásquez had made a big deal about the presence of the illegal weed and the heroin in the trunk.

But the briefcase? Mysteriously disappeared. And unmentioned.

§ § §

Adelita stared at the un-sipped cup of joe before her and recalled the desperate look on Santos' face that morning, weeks ago, at the city court and jail complex. Her reporter's instinct haunted her, in that there's-more-to-this-story way that bothered her, more and more now that she had time to reflect on it. That night, that protest, that Santos Champagne Sánchez. That *primo* of mine. Something was definitely wrong when she, Professor Romero, and the other six journalism interns were touring the complex. They had paused at the place in the Booking Area where the clerk had the inmates sign for their possessions at the time of their arrest.

"Where's that briefcase, you thieves?" Sánchez sounded sober enough for that part of the intake process. "Where's all of my cash, dammit?"

The underpaid, sleep-deprived Inventory Clerk glanced back at the typed list on the dirty counter. "One wallet, containing twenty-seven dollars in cash and some personal photos, one Phillips screwdriver, a spare tire, a flashlight and, not to forget, a quantity of high-grade heroin and marijuana. This, Mr. Sánchez, is a complete list of items found on your person and in the trunk of the vehicle you were driving at the time of your arrest."

Adelita broke from the journalism group and took a few steps forward on the scuffed concrete. Yes, this was her cousin Santos Sánchez, the one and only, the one whose

165

wife was good friends with her mom and who could never get his life together.

"Adelita, could you please rejoin us here, prisoners can sometimes act unpredictably."

"Morning, Professor." The way-past-retirement-age deputy crackled. "Could you please take your interns upstairs to Metro Court, now?" He leaned over and whispered. "We might end up with a situation here, and we can't guarantee the safety of your students. Upstairs, please."

"No problem, deputy."

"I had a briefcase *bien lleno de plata* in that trunk and you bastards stole it." Champagne's voice resonated with sobriety, anger, and creeping desperation.

Adelita sensed Champagne's clarity and honesty about this one fact. She knew there was more to it.

"Adelita? Upstairs with the rest of us, please? Now?" Professor Romero cajoled.

"Sir, this is the full inventory of all the articles found and confiscated. Now you can fill out form 91-d if you feel that there has been a mistake."

"I've been robbed! *Pinche ladrones. Me robaron.* Where's my money?"

Professor Romero was now emphatic. "Miss Chávez, let's keep up with the rest of the group so you can get the whole picture of how our justice system operates."

"I think I just got a picture of how our justice system works," she declared as she turned from the sight of Santos, emptily staring at the Inventory Clerk's deserted window.

166

§ § §

Antonio *Tony* Giovanni lit his one expensive cigar. "And there," said Special Agent José Vásquez, "between the white powder and the evil weed . . . " Several dozen $100 bills fell from his hand to the fat, sienna-colored couch next to Giovanni.

"José, what did I tell you? Huh?"

"You were right. These guys don't believe in banks. They actually do haul their cash with them everywhere they go. *Qué pendejo. Qué vagabundo.*"

Tony cracked open the bottle of Single Barrel Jack Daniels that he had saved for a day like this. Using his weathered, monogrammed hanky, he wiped the dust from a couple of chipped Reno, Nevada, whiskey glasses and poured shots for himself and his partner. Before raising his glass, he flicked the switch on the intercom to his secretary. "Valentina, make sure I'm not disturbed for the next half hour."

The uncomfortable silence that followed was an indication that Giovanni's secretary was either on her typical forty-five-minute coffee break, her customary two-hour lunch or that she hadn't even bothered to come in today, which would be difficult to notice, given the current circumstances of Tony Giovanni's floundering law practice.

As his hand grew weary from holding the almost-clear shot glass suspended in the air, Tony made a quick toast. "To the success of Gato Negro Productions."

José responded," To our new partnership. To our new investment opportunities." Gulping the whiskey like it was a club soda, Vásquez cut to the chase. "It's too soon for another shopping mall. Look at how the population is growing in Burque. I say apartments. That's the place to invest."

"Sure." Giovanni sipped and gagged. "The San José Complex. Now that's got a nice ring to it, huh?"

"Yuh." Tony rarely drank and was temporarily speech-impaired.

"Or we should be fair about it. *Órale*, pues, Giovanni is Johnny in English and José is Joseph. How about the J & J Apartments?"

"O . . . O . . . Okay."

"And how bout we name the swimming pool after Sánchez? After all, without his financial assistance, it would not be able to happen." Vásquez respectfully tapped that briefcase.

§ § §

Adelita sipped at the luke-warm coffee as she closed her memory of that morning, weeks ago, in the jail.

§ § §

Santos edged away from his cell window to the empty desert. He sat on the lumpy excuse-for-a-mattress. A strange quiet descended like dust settling on a window ledge, a blanketless mattress, or a shell-shocked man at the first of hundreds of days.

Then *La Memoria* came to him. At about the time he quit chasing it, it came at him. It reminded him of how Maldito would snuggle up to him only after he acted (and really felt) indifferent. The key. The way that Santos Champagne Sánchez would do his time without letting time do him was through his self-mind control. On this desert-still morning, he had the insight that would get him through. For these few pre-pandemonium moments, his second and first minds were reconciled. All arguments ceased. His thoughts were few and pure and united. They were as orderly as Maribel's pictures on the *hielera*, Delfina's *santos* on her *altar,* and Adelita's journals on her nightstand.

Santos Champagne Sánchez resolved that he would, from this day forward, remain on friendly terms with his mind and that this relationship would be his *fuente de fuerza.* The tamed thunderbird inside his head would be on his side, from now on.

And then, as a couple fingers of first-born daylight wrapped around the steel bars, Champagne fell into a thick, rapturous sleep.

XXV

The hummingbird sucked the last red drop of sugar water from the feeder outside the window and darted away. Adelita reached into the cabinet overhead and chose the clear jar filled with the dried green leaves.

"*Y luego, ¿qué pasó, M'ijita?*" Delfina asked as she entered the kitchen, padding along like a kitten.

"Mamá, when I saw cousin Santos, they had him downstairs at some little office, and he was yelling that they need to account for some briefcase of his money that was taken at the time of the arrest." Adelita's spread fingers tore through the morning air.

"Delita, you can stop right there. *Te lo juro*, I've never seen anybody go through money like Santitos Sánchez." Delfina's face held her sincerely justified stare.

"He sounded *muy sincero*, Mamá. I believed him. They stole from him, I can tell."

"I'm sorry, *M'ijita*, but Maribel is going to be here any minute now. Do me *un favor* and make the *té de yerba buena, por favor?*"

"*Sí*, Mamá, but I know his rights were violated. Something is terribly wrong." They heard a short, sharp knock. "Come in, Mari. The door's not locked."

Adelita turned on the gas under the kettle and

looked for the strainer. She had been making this stomach-soothing tea since she was five years old.

"*Comadre Delfina, que bueno a verte.*"

"*Comadre Mari*, come in. *¿Como estás?*"

Waddling in like a hundred and ten pounds of *chorizo* in a seventy-five-pound rubber glove, Maribel settled into the sofa, "Oh, *tú sabes*. Pretty good for a *panzona*." Mari wrapped her arms around the watery mound in front of her. "The doctor says only about two more weeks. *Ya mero, comadre.*"

Delfina placed her hand over Maribel's hands. "*No te preocupes.* Your delivery is going to go smooth, I can feel it. And I will be here for you. *Cualquier cosa.*"

"*Gracias*, Delfina. I've always been able to count on you." Adelita came in and handed them each a hot cup of tea.

"*Mil gracias, Adelita. Lo agradesco mucho. Oiga, comadre,*" Mari continued, "*ahorita quiero ir a la capilla* to light a candle for Santos. *Vas conmigo?*"

"*Por supuesto*, I'll go with you." Delfina took her cup and blew the steam off the top.

"Tomorrow they're going to have another hearing, and I just don't know what's going to happen.

"*Como te dije* if there is anything I can do . . ."

"Well, now that you mention it, Santos' lawyer said something about a plea bargain, whatever that is, *y yo no se qué tanto.* Anyway, that's supposed to be the best way to go, *quizás*, so they say, and so tomorrow I need to go to the courthouse."

Delfina shook her head. "You can't go so close to your time."

"Are you sure?"

Blind-siding them both, Adelita declared, "I'll go for both of you. *No hay problema.*"

They were both so surprised that they didn't know what to say. So the two *comadres* just sipped on their *yerba buena* and blinked their appreciation to her.

Adelita nodded. "I'll be there for the hearing. Mrs. Sánchez, you can't be going out to court, and Mamá, you need to stay close to her, especially now. They are letting me attend hearings, as part of my internship. I'll tell you afterward what happened."

Maribel and Delfina stared over their cups. Delfina broke the silence. "Can you believe it, Maribel? A woman news reporter from our neighborhood? I am so proud of you, *M'ijita.*"

Maribel frowned like she couldn't believe someone would do something so nice for her. "Are you sure?"

"I'll be there, and you'll be at home, resting for your baby."

Mari smiled. "Delfie, you are so blessed, having such a good daughter."

Delfina gave Adelita a big *abrazo.* "*Esta chula es mi mundo entero.*" She hugged her again. "My whole world."

Mari stood up, quickly, wobbling like a water bed. "*Oiga,* Delfina. I hate to be in such a hurry, but I would like to get to the chapel early so I can come back home early."

"*Vamos, entonces.* Let me just get my car keys."

While Delfina got her purse, Maribel looked calmly at Adelita, unspoken questions in the carmel-coffee eyes of both women.

"I'll see you right after the hearing and tell you what happened. But, no matter what, *debes quedar tranquila.* For your baby." "*Sí. Todo para el niño.*"

Delfina spoke over her shoulder as she briskly walked out the door, not wobbling at all, those days being in the past. "Adelita, *M'ijita*, I'll be back soon. There are some *frijoles y chicos* in the fridge. *Con Dios.*"

"*Adiós*, Mamá. Mari."

"*Con Dios*, Adelita."

"*Con cuidado, M'ijita.*"

Adelita glanced back because she thought she saw the hummingbird returning. No. Then she noticed the picture on the refrigerator and saw, really saw it, for the first time in years. Her father, 'Moe, 'Modesto Chávez, his strong *brazos* around her mother, protecting her, at least for that moment when the picture was taken. She thought about that damn Korean War and the devilish heroin that came back with some soldiers to their homes and what it had done to families, far away in time and geography and about how unfair it all was.

"Oh, Daddy. I never even got to know you."

The humble intern reverently made a sign of the cross on the window with her finger. The hummingbird, now invisible, hummed a prayer into the wind.

Adelita's Notebook #2,847

What's the best way to give someone you love bad news? Is it more merciful to tell them the painful truth right away and then mask the shock by following up with some other information that could maybe distract them a moment? Or is it better to give them the truth just a painful spoonful at a time, trying to stretch out the reality, in hopes of diluting the heart-penetrating reality? Does there even exist an effective and humane way to comfort, console, relax the person by speaking about some positive, grounded and grounding truths? Or to use sympathy that will hopefully, temporarily, put them in a position of some power and stability before you have to push them somewhat off-balance when following with the reality of loss and hurt?

I'm stuck not knowing which approach, which words, in which order, to tell Maribel that things did not go well for her husband. That things are bad and are probably only going to get worse. That he's been railroaded, misrepresented, jacked around, isolated, wronged, ripped off, fooled, rejected, taken advantage of, hated, and disrespected. That's just what happened at the latest court hearing for Santos. What is yet to come?

The Fall of Champagne Sánchez is now an uninterrupted free-fall with lawyerly help.
Like the gravity of evil got a helping hand it really didn't need.

XXVI

Champagne awoke from his stony sleep to the jarring yell, "¡*Levántensen, cabrones*! Get the hell up for morning court, *pinches bueyes*."

Chicanos were not only the majority *aquí en La Pinta*, as prisoners, but were over-represented as prison guards and officers.

Damn, thought Champagne, just when I was in the middle of a dream about . . . what was that dream? The gentle image of Maribel in their house, painting a hummingbird on a small canvas. It all melted like snow on a cruel, hot August afternoon. The guards rattled their thick cherry-wood sticks on the bars while rasping out wake-up insults, and the wary men inside stirred. Some rattled back like rattlesnakes, protesting the leather boots that held them down.

It all starts now, Santos silently told himself. I have the power to choose. I can let those cruel, unfeeling bastards get to me, (which is their underpaid job, these days) or, if I want to come out of this hell, purified and stronger, instead of burnt and bitter, I can choose to not overreact in this atmosphere of fear.

I'll just stare at those dozens of names scratched, scrawled, and scribbled on the gray wall over me, he decided. I won't even look at the loud mongrel as he passes my cell with his clipboard and badge. Martínez. Quintana. Yazzie. Mitchell. Espinoza. All these signatures. All these *placas. Mi Vida Loca, Tata Dios, Mi Refugio.* RIFA. Jesus Saves. Warden Bromberg Sucks. Make your time work for you. Yeah, that's it. That's what I'll do. Conally? Where have I heard that name? Conally. Shit. Of course. In an instant, Santos was mentally back in that chaotic courtroom. The day of that fateful sentencing. The day that this sleazy lawyer, who offered to take my case because "my heart is with the *plebe* in the *barrio* who don't have anyone in their corner." Mr. Big Heart stood next to me before a Judge Conally.

"I understand fully well that this is your first arrest for possession of a dangerous substance, but the quantity was large enough to lead me to the conclusion that your primary intent was the sale and distribution of the heroin that was seized." Conally's voice boomed.

"How can you say what I was going to do with it?"

"Also I'm taking into consideration that you have a string of arrests for Driving While Under the Influence."

"I've stopped drinking, your Honor."

"Santos, don't interrupt the judge," his lawyer whispered.

"And given the pathetic state of your present circumstances—no visible means of support, a chronic unemployment history—I believe society needs to teach you a lesson."

"I'm gonna change, I swear. I'm going to get

my education." "Counsel, will you please restrain the defendant?"

Santos' big-hearted lawyer put his hand around his shoulders and spoke urgently, "Don't piss him off, Mr. Sánchez. He'll just make your sentence harsher."

"When are you going to start defending me, isn't that your job? What does my employment record have to do with the charge?"

The judge boomed louder. "Since you have freely entered into a plea agreement, admitted guilt to the lesser charge of possession of a controlled substance . . . "

"Just control yourself and smile nice at Judge Conally," his lawyer whispered.

"¡*Qué chingao!* He hates me. Look at him."

The judge descended like Moses coming down from the mountain.

"I hereby sentence you, Santos Sánchez, to a term of not less than two years at the New Mexico Penitentiary with the full maximum term of five years suspended, pending quarterly good behavior reports. I will also allow credit for time you already served while awaiting this sentencing,"

"Two years? Can't you appeal?"

His lawyer stood.

"Thank you for your leniency, Judge Conally," Mr. Charity and Compassion stated.

"Thank you? For what? Are you nuts?! Can't we appeal?"

"We could, but it's not a good idea, Mr. Sánchez.

Actually, two years is not bad. We made out better than I expected."

Santos snorted. "We? What's this *we*? I'm going to be the one behind bars in that shitty little cell, not you!"

The lawyer put his hand on Santos' arm as if he was trying to calm a child.

"I'm going to be out here continuing to work on your behalf. Making sure those good behavior reports are sent in on time to Judge Conally. As well as filing in all the other paperwork needed to support your case."

Champagne Sánchez kicked the podium in front of him and loudly mumbled: "Shafted by the judge and shafted by my own lawyer."

He was deeply disturbed by the calm manner displayed by the no-fee lawyer who claimed to be always in his corner. Santos pushed the papers on the podium to the floor. Screw his pro bono services. There was something really rotten that couldn't be hidden by the out-of-style, imported, gray Italian suits worn by Anthony *Tony* Giovanni, Champagne Sánchez's public defender. And Champagne was going to have plenty of time to find out just what that was.

Back at the urine-scented, cold metal cage, a gray-uniformed bully barked, "Name and number."

"Santos Sánchez. Number fifty-two, one eleven."

Adelita's Notebook #2,874

To be without a name, what would that be like?

179

How do our names make us who we are?

I've only ever been Adelita, and I can't even put myself in a world where I would be called by another name. Yet, somehow, some people manage to get by doing that. How about being called a number and not a word? By now, Santos has a number that he has to respond to get past certain doors, receive his mail, buy handkerchiefs, pens, pencils, and paper or to get in and out of the Day Room.

If I had to choose a number to be identified by which one would it be and for what reason? Maybe our birth date is our second name. After all, we all easily remember that set of numbers. What if our number became our first name and our word name became our backup name?

I know that people sometimes must adapt to being called by new names, like people in witness protection programs, where they live in new towns, get new jobs, are assigned new names, live new lives. Still, I bet they react immediately whenever they hear the sound of their original first name.

Naming has changed in our century. I was named after my great grandma Adelita Cruz.

She was a strong, proud woman who used to help out on the family farm near Sousal. Will I meet my Grandma Adelita in some future Heaven? Will people call each other using only their first name? Most of my aunts and uncles, many cousins, all of my grandparents and great grandparents were named after the saint on whose Feast Day they were born, or after the major saint whose Feast Day was closest to the day they were born. I wish we would keep that tradition going on within nuestra cultura. If we knew that we had to live up to the Saint that we were named after, wouldn't it be less likely that we would make decisions that ended up in sorrow, in court, in prison?

XXVII

His scream announced the realization that he was now in a whole other world. His little yell of pain caused her to smile and giggle uncontrollably.

"Here, Mrs. Sánchez, do you have him now?"

The nurse cooed as she handed the *canela*-colored newborn, kicking, to his mother, Maribel Sánchez.

"Oh, *mi hijito. Ya no llores.* Your *mamá* has you and will never let you go. Don't cry too much. You handsome little boy. Eeee, *Qué guapo.*"

Maribel glowed and hummed an old *canción de cuna* to the crying singer in the white blanket cradled in her arms.

As the nurse dutifully placed a couple more pillows to support Maribel's back, she asked, "Have you and his father decided on a name, Mrs. Sánchez?"

With no hesitation, Mari declared, "José Rumaldo. His name will be José, after his grandfather, who, *qué lástima*, he will never know. And Rumaldo, after his good uncle, who he will also never meet. But they were good men. And so will you be, *mi hijito querido.*"

And then José Rumaldo started up with his little cry that reminded Maribel of the *borregos* on her Uncle Máximo's sheep farm, near Old Town, years ago.

"Oh, Josecito, it's going to be alright. *Ya no llores.*"

Adam and Eve must have come up with some other names for each other. Did their names ever change or evolve throughout their relationship? I wonder how long until they called each other by the same first name consistently. Were their grandchildren's names similar to their own? Were their own names close, in sound, to words they assigned to rivers and trees, mountains and sky? They lived way before our modern saints, so how did they refer to their own elders or wise women or wise men?

I got to talk with Antonio, after class the other day, a rare opportunity these days as his Intern Cohort group members are spending their research/writing time at the Veterans Hospital out on Gibson Boulevard. He told me an interesting story about names. Apparently, the artist Salvador Dalí always had an obsession with identity and his name. First of all, being named Salvador, meaning savior, would carry a lot of expectation in itself. If that wasn't enough of a burden, it turns out that his parents had a baby before he was born who was also named Salvador, but who died at birth. This must have been really weird to deal with. If he had been named Federico or Antonio or Pablo,

how different would his life had turned out?
Could a country change its quality and style of
leaders by naming a large percentage of their
babies Salvador or Mary or César or Xochitl or
Cleopatra or Rey?
The things we'll never know.

XXVIII

"You make a noise, you're dead. Make a sudden move? Dead meat. You tell anybody later on? *Te mueras.* You want to live, you listen carefully."

Santos stared directly into the fiery brown eyes that were five inches from his face and immediately spoke, silently, to his own second mind. First, this is survival here. We're together on this, so feel no fear. Second, don't even react after he pulls the knife from your throat and gets up off of your chest, which he will after his message has been delivered. Third, once the immediate danger has passed, think about how you will prevent being this vulnerable in the future. Santos' friendship with his mind was passing its first serious test. He would survive.

"*Soy* Louie Mascarenas. *Algunos me dicen El Joker.* I'm your new cellmate. *Bienvenido.*"

And greetings and welcome to you, too. Santos' sarcastic second mind thought. But, of course. *El Joker.* Now that's the perfect nickname for someone who awakens his new cellmate with a three-inch shank, tight on his jugular. Rule number four, always sleep with your back against the wall with a new roommate like Louie. Sorry, '*El Joker*'.

"*¿Qué tal*, homeboy? I didn't do anything to anybody, Joker."

"Not here *en la pinta*, homie. That much is true. But there's this little problem of a missing briefcase *de dinero*. Remember that, Champagne?"

"You can call me Santos since we just met. Now about that briefcase. How did you hear about that?"

"*Ese*, everything that happens out on the street, we know all about it here, an hour after it happens. You knew that even before getting here, *que no*?"

"Uh, yeah, I knew that. *Me robaron. Te lo juro.* It's true. The Feds ripped me off when I got popped. *De veras!*"

There was more pressure on the handmade blade on his neck.

"Don't matter to me if the Tooth Fairy took it to cover some old gambling debts or if you bought your lady a little cabin up in Taos. *A mí, no me importa*, but the Familia asked me to deliver this message: either get them their money back, and soon, or you start working off your debt. Or . . . "

Santos felt his neck sting, and a trickle of blood flowed into his ear.

"*Suéltame. Órale*, message received. Louie, stop!"

Louie wiped the blood off the shank onto the lower part of his cement-colored pant leg, where the dried blood of other encounters had made a pattern like small flaming arrows.

"Nothing personal, Champagne. I just do what I'm told. Message delivered."

Louie hid the crude knife under the pillow-side of his mattress.

186

Choosing his words carefully, Santos said, "*Sabes qué*, Joker, the money in that briefcase was all mine. I wouldn't steal from La Familia. I'm not that stupid."

Without even turning to face him. Louie answered, "Hope you're not thinking of stiffing La Familia. El Patrón can be very cruel when it comes to payback, *ése*."

Santos chose not to use any more words. The tragedy of words, any of them, being utterly useless in some situations. From now on, not only would he have to do a better job of watching his back, he would have to choose his words carefully, be careful when to use them and when to use silence, be selective with whom he ate his meals, and get some new friends. *De volada*.

Adelita's Notebook #2889

Last time I wrote about the possibility (the likelihood?) of people's names possibly influencing their path in life or their character. But Santos? Hmmmmm. Not exactly saintly or holy these days, but he is innocent, I believe, of much of what he is being blamed for.
Huh? Oh no, could it be? The Adelitas were the revolutionary women who actually picked up pistolas and went to stand with their men in the revolución in Mexico. I think I'll just stick to picking up a pen and doing my bit for La Causa, for justice in my own style.

XXIX

"What a true friend *tu eres, comadre*." Mari's voice was slightly hoarse but contented.

"Shhh. *No hables, comadre. No más hay que quedarse aquí, muy contenta.* You stay lying down and I'll bring you the baby. *Creo que tiene hambre, ay, que este muchachito.*"

"Oh, he's always hungry. Bring him over."

Delfina had treated her *comadre como una reina*, and her help made it easy for Maribel to relax into the first few weeks with her *hijito*.

"*Pues qué, cabroncito*, he loves to kick. *¿qué no?*"

"José's done that ever since I was about seven months pregnant. He's as restless as . . . " Mari stopped abruptly.

"As his father? As restless as Santos?"

"*¿Sabes que, comadre*? It's hard. I try not to think too much of him so I don't get upset. I don't know what to do to keep from thinking evil thoughts."

"*Comadre* Maribel, *creo que* the best thing would be to think mainly about José."

She gestured to the feisty, kicking infant who swallowed his mother's milk with innocent abandon.

"When you're with José Rumaldo, think only about José. Think about Santos only when you talk to him on the phone or visit him. *Creo que sí.*"

The womanly spell was broken by the clang of the telephone.

"Do you want me to answer that, Mari? I could tell them that you're very busy *ahora*."

"No, it's alright. If you could just bring the phone over here. Hey, maybe I finally got lucky, and they're calling me to be on *The Price is Right!*"

They giggled. "Hello?"

"Maribel Sánchez?"

"Yes."

"*Escúchame bien, porque* I'm only going to say this once. Get word to your *esposo* that if we don't get our money back soon, his family might have some accidents."

Maribel Sánchez tried to break from the cold-steel *mordida* that shook her. Mari's face was a blood-drained numb picture of fear. As lonely as a starless sky.

"Mari, *qué pasó*? Tell me!"

"This friendly warning was brought to you courtesy of the Director of Communications for *La Familia*." The ominous drone from the phone could be heard across the room.

"¿Mari, *por qué estás asustada?*"

Maribel hung up and poorly-acted as though she just hadn't experienced her heart being crunched by the threat. She swallowed.

"Oh, it's just a stupid wrong number. *Comadre*, will you stay with me all day today?"

"*Pos supuesto*. Not only today but anytime you want. Now, put your attention back to this hungry little *payaso*."

Delfina's sweet smile helped. Mari was able to breathe and move freely again. Her milk flowed warm and sweet again. The bitterness faded. The fear dissipated. The little innocent gulped his milk.

Delfina began singing her soothing, ancient song.

"Como la pluma en el aire, y la hija ya perdida, la huérfana desvalida, pierde la honra y el decoro. Óiganme, mis amigas, estas lágrimas que lloro."

(Like a feather in the air, this long lost daughter, for the helpless orphan, honor and respect are lost. Listen, my friends, to these tears that I cry.)

XXX

On the door to Professor Romero's secluded office in upstairs Maron Hall was a poster of fictional newspaper baron Charles Foster Kane from Orson Welles' 1941 film *Citizen Kane.*

"Come in, door's open."

Adelita brushed past a file drawer on her right that held a photo of Emiliano Zapata. It overlooked everything in the crowded room like a disturbed conscience, his *Indio Mexicano* eyes finding injustice in all of the other images of people, poverty, and politics.

Professor Romero seemed as though he was half here and half preoccupied with one of those emergency faculty meetings.

"Adelita! My last appointment for the day. How nice," he gushed. "*Siéntate aquí.* So, tell me about your investigative reporting experiences with your intern assignment."

He quickly muttered as he scanned a paper on his desk.

Looking up, he managed to add, "Let's see. You're doing the piece on . . . you're working on . . . "

"The Santos Sánchez story."

"Huh? Who? Oh, yeah. Guess I didn't succeed in changing your mind about that."

"No, I didn't change my opinion. That's the subject I want to stick with."

She sensed his preoccupation.

"So. Story's dead, right? Arrested, court, time spent awaiting his sentencing, then his sentencing. Now he's doing time in the joint. So the story's dead. Why not work on something else?"

"I don't think the story is dead, has been told, or is finished. First of all, I don't abandon famil . . . , err, I mean Santos Sánchez is an interesting subject; second of all, there's more to his story than the drug dealing episodes, which I will admit he himself confessed to. Didn't you always teach us that what makes us real investigative reporters is showing the person behind the prejudices, the image, the reputation? The human being behind the face, the poverty, the politics?"

Silence in the professor's office, and for a moment, in his preoccupied mind.

"During his processing, Sánchez claimed that a briefcase of money seized during his arrest somehow mysteriously disappeared."

"Right. We should believe a convict's claim that the cops took the money? They all say that."

"They *all* say that? Wasn't it you, just this last week at a seminar, who advised us to always dig deeper when we hear 'As is believed' or 'Commonly known' or 'They all say'?"

Silence in the professor's office, his mind, and Emiliano Zapata's Winter-night black eyes locked on a Teachable Moment.

"When I asked the arresting officers how much

heroin was found in the trunk, I got three different answers on three separate occasions."

The Chávez blood in Adelita was getting warmed up.

"Those cops deal with dozens of cases. You expect them to remember every detail?"

"Well, you expect us, as novice reporters, to 'get every little detail,' correct? *Qué no?*

One says they read him the Miranda Act. The other doesn't seem to know, for sure."

"What's your point?" Romero stood up.

"Well, just for starters, if he wasn't read his rights, we've got yet another case of a double-standard of justice when it comes to the treatment of a Chicano from the North Valley."

Ouch, that had to hurt. Professor Romero had grown up in the North Valley and had shared more than a few examples of double standards during his youth with the class.

"Get off your Civil Rights soapbox, Adelita! As a professional journalist, your job is to cover stories about people that society has an interest in."

Her blood boiled. She stared at the Professor with her intense cinnamon Chicana eyes. She was facing him, toe to toe.

"As an investigator, you told me to 'Get the whole picture,' to follow all the facts, no matter where they lead, whether we like it or not."

Romero turned away from her unblinking gaze and frantically pointed to his favorite poster in his office, an old Berkeley Free Speech Rally announcement.

"A free press is the cornerstone of democracy, Miss Chávez. Yes, investigations need to be made. Yeah, stories have to be written, but, please. Can't you devote more energy and talent toward somebody that we should care about? Someone who really matters?"

Her heart halted. It leaped from boiling to frozen in a split second. Her voice was ice.

"This story matters. Santos matters. To his family. To his friends. And to his North Valley community . . . the sacred place of his roots."

Emiliano stared down at them, also unblinking, firm, and just. Adelita turned to leave. But Zapata's *campesino* face stopped her.

She turned and noted, for the record, "By the way, if they did steal money from Santos Sánchez, maybe that's why he couldn't afford a real lawyer who would have done his best to keep him out of prison. Kind of like how your own Uncle Mario was not properly represented during his time in court, on that trumped-up charge, that he had committed fraud when applying for a bank loan but had failed to reveal a previous bankruptcy. The one that his father, with the same name had been forced to go through, years before."

Romero's anger boiled over. He crumpled the paper in his hand and slammed it into the trash basket.

"It's shameful to think that lawyers could have such power over us *plebe* from the *barrio*, don't you think, Professor Romero? The old song is right. We are like the 'feather in the air and the long lost daughter, our honor,

194

and respect taken from us' aren't we, Profe?"

At times like these Profe Romero wondered if it was best that Adelita had not changed her mind about her pursuit.

The truth opened the eyelid that had held so many tears that Professor Romero had damned up over the years. But he said nothing. Adelita was sure Emiliano Zapata would have said: Damn this system, damn the power they have, damn the way that lawyers could rob us and our fathers and our fathers' fathers of our honor. Leaving mothers and wives home to cry.

"Santos deserved to have representation by anybody but the so-called, self-described people's lawyer, Tony Giovanni. Everyone, I assume even you, knows that *pinche cabrón* would sell out his own mother for a cheap cigar."

You could almost see the tears that never fell, in public, from Emiliano's compassionate eyes.

XXXI

Tony Giovanni, the excuse-for-a-lawyer who sometimes worked for nothing, which was exactly what he was worth, leaned over his desk and tried to speak in a voice with a semblance of authority.

"Valentina, no calls or interruptions. I'm in a business meeting for the next hour or so."

No response from Valentina, his loyal secretary, who was likely back home, probably waking up just about now.

"A community of interest. Our slogan precisely describes what Gato Negro Productions is all about. Not to forget, *diversity* of investments is going to be the key to keeping our interests profitable."

Somehow, Giovanni always sounded like he was telling a lie, even when he wasn't, and even when speaking to a small group like the sleazebags gathered to conspire in his office.

José, the Federal Agent, stopped the nervous tap of his foot and gestured with his cigar, "Tony, cut the bullshit speeches. What's your point?"

Tony plucked a piece of crusty green chile off his wrinkled pinstripe suit and pompously retorted, "My point is that we get some help in diversification. José, I've asked Mr. Henry Puente to join us and to start managing all of our real estate for us. He comes highly recommended."

Puente could pass for Giovanni's cousin, especially the dead look in his eyes. He cracked open a black leather notebook.

"I promise that Gato Negro Productions will see a significant return on all investments I make on our behalf."

He even talked like Giovanni.

"Mr. Puente, this is Agent . . . er, uh . . . "

José's eyes flashed.

"Mr. Puente, this is my business partner, Mr. Vásquez."

"Actually, you look familiar, Mr. Vásquez. I know I've seen you somewhere before."

Yeah, like in the crowd at the scene of that suspected arson incident last week at the city supply warehouse, thought Puente.

José tried to smile and offered a cold, limp hand.

"*Mucho gusto*, Sr. Puente. Yeah, I think I've seen you at some Hispanic Chamber of Commerce meetings."

José wiped his nose with a handkerchief to hide his smirk. Yeah, or probably that was you a couple years ago who acted innocent when some suspected counterfeiters were caught operating out of one of your sleazy downtown offices.

"Probably something like that."

"José, if it's alright with you, I thought we should give Henry the go ahead and let him hire a manager for the J & J Apartments."

"Less headaches for me. All I care is that I get my cut at the end of each month. Go ahead, Henry, get us a manager."

Just don't hire one of the convicted check forgers that I've seen you hanging around with.

Tony's concerned face loosened and he grinned as he turned the upside-down chart right- side-up on the easel at his side.

"I'm proud to announce that our city bonds are up 400% this quarter. By the way, the insurance money from the strange, mysterious fire at the city warehouse will be coming in soon."

José couldn't stop his eyebrows from rising in undeniable approval.

"I'll continue to monitor our actions in the stock market."

José nodded and almost smiled. If there was one thing that Giovanni lived for, it was for Vásquez' approval. If there was one thing that pleased Vásquez, it was when things went, more or less, as planned. In other words, profitably.

José Vásquez exhaled a small cloud of cigar smoke and rasped, "New cash flow shouldn't be a concern for Gato Negro Productions. In a couple days, we're going to be moving in on Tykie Mendoza."

"Mendoza?" Puente inquired.

"An old friend of Champagne Sánchez has been quite active lately, fronting on the streets."

"Champagne Sánchez? Didn't I just read an article in last night's *Tribune* about him? Claims he had a bunch of money stolen from him when he was arrested or something like that." Giovanni grinned. "Now who's going to believe some small-time convict in the Santa Fe Penitentiary?"

He gave José and Henry their half-filled shot glasses as he raised his full one. Dust flew in five directions from Giovanni's crumpled suit.

"To the future of Gato Negro Productions."

They swallowed and gasped like a chorus. Vásquez managed to squeeze out a grin, "To diversification and a bright, profitable future. Give us your money and we'll guarantee you large dividend, even if we have to steal it for you!"

The unholy trio laughed heartily as the people's lawyer refilled their glasses. Halfway.

XXXII

She carefully gathered each and every dried red petal that had fallen from the geranium plant in the window in Maribel's room and put them in her pouch, for the traditional disposal, later on, outside.

"You must always keep red flowers in your house to absorb the pain and sorrow, any *sentimiento de tristeza*, and then call me when the petals fall off."

Doña MariLuz, Magdalena Moya's sister and the *curandera* of the *barrio*, would later take the contents of her pouch and bury them by the big ditch.

Whenever anyone found themselves in need of physical, mental, emotional, or spiritual healing, Doña MariLuz was there. Most of the time people didn't even have to call her. Luz's intuition was so strong that she would show up early one morning at the afflicted person's doorstep with an armful of *yerba buena*, a faceful of tranquility, and a heartful of prayers. By the afternoon, one of her *vecinas* or *vecinos* would be well on their way to health.

Oddly, no one could ever recall watching her take care of her own needs; no one could remember ever seeing her eat or sleep or rest. Yet she was as present and as reliable as the sunlight. Another thing, she never refused the offer of a cup of coffee. It was as if she breathed it in, anytime.

"For the sake of *el niño*," she gestured toward the

sleeping infant, "you are not to think about that threat on the telephone. You should spend some time, *cada día*, doing something that you like. *Por ejemplo, te gusta pintar, ¿qué no?*"

Mari nodded her head.

"*Bueno. Debes seguir pintando.* Maybe start painting *algunos de los santos*, ¿eh? I could always use a 'traveling San Rafael', for my *visitas. Chiquito.* Just something I could carry in my pouch as I make my visits. *Si puedes. Y después*, paint a San Rafael for your own altar and, maybe *de vez en cuando*, some more so that I can give them to your *vecinos. Pero no olvidas, esto no es un mandato*, just do what you can when your *corazón* moves you. Only do anything you do out of love. And then, remember, whatever you do always comes back to you seven times."

Strange, Mari didn't remember telling Doña MariLuz about the threatening phone call or that she liked to paint and that it relaxed her. She just *knew* things.

"*Otra cosita*, Maribel. Don't let anyone stare too long at Josecito or he might get the Evil Eye. Keep him somewhat covered when you go out."

"*Gracias*, Doña MariLuz. I will take your *consejos* to heart."

After finishing her cafecito, Doña MariLuz Moya blessed Maribel, José Rumaldo, as he slept, Adelita, and their house, as she exited. She walked back down quiet Los Anayas road, serenaded by the birds that included her in in their shared song as she followed her heart to the next needy *vecina*.

Adelita's Notebook #3,001

Antes de la madrugada, there was a gentle knock on the front door that I recognized, and Mom invited our curandera, Doña MariLuz, inside for a pre-dawn cafecito. Although I could barely hear their muffled, melodic voices, I could sense Doña Luz's consoling greetings and prayers, her caring questions and healing advice for Mamá. After about a half-hour, the violet dawn brightened to a blanket of blueness and Mom knocked on my door and asked me to join them for special out-of-Christmas-season bizcochitos and their second cup of coffee con canela and friendly plática. After asking me to make sure that Mamá kept up with her daily three cups of oshá tea with honey, Doña MariLuz urged me to gather up the dead red petals from the geraniums in my window and from my mom's room. She took them away on a regular basis.

Even dead and dried, the geranium petals were the same bright red color of the woven belt that Doña Luz always wore to protect herself, like all 'people of the red'. "Bad always hates good and good always fights evil," she would sometimes remind me as she walked her rounds from house to house. No one walked these enchanted high desert roads more than La Doña.

And she always had something for someone, who needed that very object or word just then. It varied from the sometimes lithographed, ocassional hand painted images of los santos, to the small bags of oshá or yerba buena tea, to the rarely silent, barely spoken, and often-times sung prayers for the well-being of our bodies, minds, souls. Doña MariLuz was a one-woman army of angels, a billowing cloud of angelic intentions.

It's true about good repelling evil. I actually used to see characters like Rocco Ávila or Carlos Mascarenas crossing the street when they saw her coming. Every time it was the city council election season, Louie Villa would visit her and bring cash and food donations. She would turn around and share them with others. He knew that without her support, he wouldn't get a single vote from the precincts in our neighborhood.

Marcella Trujillo would go to Father Galli to have him bless her Christmas tamales before telling the vecinos that they could buy all they wanted for Las Posadas and for after Midnight Mass celebrations. First, though, Marcella would have Doña MariLuz pray over the corn mix before she stuffed the corn husks with the masa-nested chile-marinated pork.

Doña MariLuz was such a strong presence that the one year that she was sick with the flu, 1951, everyone noticed that she didn't make it to La Misa de Gallo. She got lots of Christmas day visitors, many just to confirm that she hadn't died because, after all, she never missed Mass.

Doña MariLuz was as much a part of our days and years as the cuatro temporadas, as much a part of our ditch-veined corner in the city as the sweet scent of hopeful lilacs in the spring, the sounds of babies wailing and toddlers screaming in the streets in the summer. Children still had innocent eyes that could see wings on MariLuz, our walking angel with a pouch filled with dried flower petals under the morning's blue blanket sky. The maroon bag with the blood-red petals leaves could be seen getting smaller with every step. Strange, after a while, the tiny pouch, tied to MariLuz's red belt, seemed to float higher and higher in the distancia.

Adelita's Notebook #3, 011

A late-century electric Gypsy, he stood center stage. He was commanding reverence, and shimmering notes spun from his 1957 Fender Stratocaster guitar. They washed over me, as I ventured in, a couple hours after the sky had purpled into night. The light melodic snow of the tunes plucked from Frankie's electric

Strat scattered and bounced off the walls of the Triangle Bar, a twelve-minute stroll from the university. So this was the famous Triangle Bar, one of the best-kept secrets in the student ghetto, the polar opposite in size and noise of Okie's, that other famous labyrinth of meeting places.

It had taken me weeks to get up the courage to make this mini-pilgrimage. After all, I hate bars, rarely drink, and I really don't have much time to nurse a beer and listen to live music, but my reporter's curiosity led me to see if there could be a mini-article here. I needed a break from the heaviness and stress associated with following the fate of my primo, Santos, running into one wall after another when it comes to our correctional institutions.

I wandered in about six o clock, finally deciding to give in to my three-year-old curiosity about this three-sided mystery box of a building located on a triangular strip of land where Central Avenue met with a couple of other University streets. The apex pointed to the west of the city.

Much darker than I had imagined, the lack of light made the crimson jewel on Frankie's Deluxe Reverb amplifier shine all the brighter. A glowing Marlboro sat on a metal ashtray on his amp. It was picked up by this master guitarist, his Pendleton-shirted arm swift and sure, and he brought the cig up to reveal the

205

serious concentration on his face as he pulled on the acrid tobacco. He was a chiaroscuro of the hungry musician, with roots in the Barrio de Los Duranes. He put the cig back in the ashtray and his face faded in the dark. His strumming came up with a soulful rendition of *Inner City Blues* Chicano-style. I was mesmerized. So this was the famous Frankie Fernández, that even Tía Linda knew and bragged about, saying, "That vato is going to go somewhere with his música, some day."

In this forgotten watering hole a few of the hip professors chose to meet with their favorite students, informally, to say the things that they couldn't say in class, to be the people that they couldn't be on campus. I had heard whispered in the rushing crowd outside his office that Professor Romero was often one of them, but apparently not tonight. I checked each of the seven other, cigarette-lit faces. No, not here tonight. Each of the seven others stared up at the guitarist, bass player, drummer, and the keyboard player on the minuscule bandstand, framed by Christmas lights, and each fell full under the spell of a confident guitar solo followed by Frankie's sincere plea for social justice.

I wondered, have I picked the wrong media to move people? When Frankie sings *Don't it make you wanna holler*, it makes me want to, and then

I want to follow him out to the corner of Central Avenue and Girard Boulevard and protest for all the world to hear. What can my series of articles on men and women in jails and prison, for charges big and small, just and unjust, change in the public opinion? Still, I know, in my heart of hearts, that some, like Frankie, are meant to be the modern trovadores. Others (like me?) are determined to write the story down where it can be read from here to Santa Fe and Taos, from here to Belen and Truth or Consequences. The audience for the written word is still numerous.

Waking out of my reporter's wandering thoughts, I find the famous Frankie Fernández sitting next to me. "I've got ten minutes in between sets. Can I buy you a beer?" I nod. He does. We talk fast, but only about music and words, and then he's up on the mini-stage again. I wave goodbye and thanks; he mouths the words "Come back!"

The pleading electric ballad plays over in my mind as I step out into the honking, chilly air. In my mind opinion I riff on words like a Be-Bop vocalist riffs on blue notes. So much to sing, so much to say about truth in art, the art in truth telling, and the music in both. The victory of words used as poetry and sounds alchemized into the music of power.

XXXIII

Seeing the big picture in the State Penitentiary for Santos meant realizing that mobility was one of the keys to survival. Mobility meant contacts. Contacts meant information and potential friends. Information meant strategies and some potential friends became real friends, but the key to it all was mobility.

Champagne immediately volunteered when an opening came up with the St. Dismas Prison Ministry. He had not violated any rules, gotten in any trouble—at least not any that the administration knew about, anyway. He had not given any guards any shit, complained about the food, or put out any bad vibes during his first few weeks of incarceration, so he was put on the A-list for a volunteer slot.

Having been raised Catholic, Champagne was conversant in basic Christian beliefs and symbols and, since attending the Official St. Dismas Ministry Training Sessions, was reading the Bible for the first time in his tumultuous life. Understanding it was another matter, but he noticed that his comprehension increased radically the more he read, especially the New Testament. He was actually consoled by some of the passages that he understood and, on more than one tortured evening, fell into a healing sleep after reading about Jesus, The Good Shepherd, and the Flock.

He wasn't the only one. Some of the other guys in the joint read the Bible and started attending services, and, in between shanking each other to near-death, sometimes tried to repent.

There were some things about Pastor Roger that puzzled Santos, like the way that Roger looked at him suspiciously whenever Santos talked about going up to *El Santuario* every Holy Week, or about asking for the help of San Antonio when things got lost. The other thing about Pastor Roger that Santos found curious was the way that the Pastor kept on about how important it was to give back, to tithe, to give that ten percent, but it seemed to Santos that Pastor Roger wanted to make sure that the St. Dismas Ministry leader didn't get around in anything less than the latest Cadillac. Yeah, Champagne observed the vehicle of choice for Pastor Roger while looking out his window one afternoon as the Pastor drove up past the main entrance, all eight cylinders humming under the hood.

Champagne decided he could put up with the thinly-disguised anti-Catholic (and sometimes unchristian) comments and that he could tolerate Pastor Rogers's fixation on funding so that he could access the mobility afforded by participating in the St. Dismas Prison Ministry.

Monday morning was Champagne's first unchaperoned Bible Distribution Round, and he felt pumped. Oh yes, this walking around from cell to cell, from cell block to cell block, from building to building, with the occasional leg of the journey under the bright desert sky suited Champagne just fine.

Light-hearted, Champagne pushed the heavy cart through the walkway outside each stinkin' cell in Cell Block B, pausing briefly every six feet.

Champagne lightly stepped up to the next cell and displayed his best got-religion grin.

"Praise the Lord, my brother. How about a free Bible?" Champagne proclaimed from ear to ear.

"Praise my ass, punk." Mad Dog Montoya bellowed back. "Get the hell out of here."

"Escaping the fires of hell is exactly what I had in mind for you, Montoya," Champagne countered as he confidently reached in between the bars with the thick paperback.

"How 'bout it. If you just read St. Paul's first letter to the Corinthians, you could see . . . "

"Read my *culo*, Sánchez. If you don't get outta my face in about three seconds . . . "

Champagne's disappointment showed in his resigned shrug.

"I understand, Montoya. Maybe some other time. You're just not ready yet."

"Over here, homeboy. I'll take one of those."

The friendly voice came from Archie García, the gentlest, amiable prisoner Santos had met, the charming Garcia doing time for a triple-murder.

"Maybe if the man sees that I've found religion, I'll get to walk around this place three days a week like you, huh?"

Champagne nodded, haltingly, "Uh, I don't know.

You'd have to get on the A-list first. But listen, bro, you read this and take its message to heart, and you'll know what true freedom feels like."

"Don't know 'bout true freedom, brother, but I'd be happy just to get out of my cell and over to D and C Blocks every once in a while."

"Hey. Psst. Hey. Sánchez."

Champagne could smell trouble with that simple *Psst*.

"Think you could talk to Spider Saiz over in . . . "

"Gotta go, Archie. I'm running late. *Al rato*, ese."

"Praise the Lord, Champagne."

Champagne's hand was 90% through the cell bars when he looked up into the purely contained rage in the scarred face of Ramón Valdez. The expert torturer had cut Champagne's hand with his razor-sharp shank so fast that it didn't seem humanly possible. But, then again, it was Ramón, who, it was rumored, practiced cutting techniques on his own face when he had no other flesh available.

The guttural murmur from Valdez sounded like a bullfrog on its dying breath.

"Don't waste your Halleluia Rap on me, brother. I've got one last warning to you from *La Familia* regarding your outstanding debt, or you're going to wake up with some of your body parts missing. *Me entiendes*?"

The fold over his left eye quivered. He meant business.

"I understand. You want to let me go now?"

Valdez released his tourniquet grip on Santos' hand, and the bleeding began.

"*Tres días, baboso.*"

"Gotcha. *Ay te watcho.*"

"You get us our money, or you won't be facing me, chump. It'll be Mad Dog Montoya taking a chunk out of your ass."

"*Lo entiendo muy bien,*" Champagne fought the urge to rapidly retrieve his arm through the bars and acted like the gushing gash was just a scratch.

Santos wiped the blood off the Bible. And the bars of the cell. And off of his unpunctured hand.

Some days with the St. Dismas Prison Ministry were harder than others.

XXXIV

On his creepy-crawly way into the office, he noticed that the secretary had not arrived yet. So what else was new.

Actually, what else that was new was the old disgusting mold on the old piece of pizza leftover from a wanna-be attorney's business meeting. The mold was so ancient that it had dried out, flaked, and started to break down. Not very appetizing at all. The potato chips, long abandoned on the dirty paper plate, had gone beyond stale and could now be placed in the category of aged-past-edible. But not quite fossilized. What were once Ritz crackers, were now a poor memory of their former selves. No, I think I'll pass on those antiquated wafers.

Feeling a need for a liquid of any type, he examined the remains of a long-ago-toast to investments in the shot glass. No way. Whiskey may be better the more it was aged, but if you combined the cheap cigar ashes and weeks of dust and the occasionally drowned fruit fly, these particular remnants of Jack Daniels just wouldn't satisfy.

No, this was downright disgusting and unworthy of him, so the fat cockroach quickly exited the office of the city's sleaziest lawyer, Tony Giovanni, running out full-speed under the door and unfed. Out in the hallway, Tony fumbled in his pockets for a key.

A couple of cheap cigars later, it was time for business to get under way. Tony Giovanni leaned over his cockroach-free desk and pressed the button on the intercom.

"Valentina, we'll be in a meeting. No calls or interruptions, please."

Not likely.

Valentina was not about to interrupt her mid-morning nail-polishing ritual to acknowledge her boss' request or even his presence.

Giovanni cut to the chase and described what needed to be done and what didn't regarding the central objective of the Gato Negro Productions group.

"Henry, we've got to keep our overhead to a minimum."

Puente looked up, noticed the curled piece of pepperoni in Giovanni's sleeve, and saw that it matched the dried ketchup on his coat pocket. He said nothing.

"We're not in the business of taking care of people; we're not a charity. We're in the business of . . . well, business. Making a profit and avoiding taxes, whenever and however, we can."

José thought about the mountain of paperwork he should be chiseling at and snapped, "Tony, cut to the chase."

"Right. Henry, the operative words when it comes to the J & J Apartments is 'tax write- off,' in spite of what those tenants who whine about heating and lousy plumbing think."

"Tony?" José impatiently spoke.

214

The undercover agent always felt uncomfortable in a business suit and out of the street clothes that he did most of his work in. Puente, used to his three-piece suit but concerned that he would have to get it dry-cleaned after only a half-hour spent in this pigpen, spoke up.

"I've got it. So we should keep expenses to a minimum. I'll tell that manager to be too hard to get ahold of."

"Exactly. Raise the rent on a regular basis and take every tax break we can get. You understand perfectly."

Amazingly, Valentina interrupted her vain self-maintenance to cut in with a message.

"Mr. Giovanni, there's a certain Richard Hidalgo on the phone. Says it's urgent."

Puente looked at the *puma* who looked at the *víbora*.

"Hidalgo? Oh, yes. Valentina, put him through on line three. Excuse me, gentlemen, I've got to take this call."

Valentina blared shouted back, "I can't put him through on line three, because it got disconnected, just like line two. You didn't pay your full phone bill after the warnings, Mr. Giovanni. You can talk to him on line one, or at least until they disconnect that one, too."

"This is Giovanni. Uh huh. Why, yes, that information would be very appreciated."

Giovanni looked at José, nodded his head, and grinned. "How much? Oh, let's say you can count on 500 dollars cash. Good. Hold on."

He grabbed a pencil out of an old soup can and wiped off the stinky tomato sauce.

"Thursday night. At the A Mi Gusto Bar. Got it. We'll be there, and thank you very much. Huh? Oh, yeah. Your payment, sure. Meet me at The Barelas Coffeehouse on Friday at lunch time and I'll take care of you. Yeah. Thanks to you."

Smiling, like he had just finished a big plate of spaghetti carbonara, Tony Giovanni walked over and put his hands on José's shoulders. José wiped away the small clump of dehydrated artichoke heart that fell from Tony's sleeve.

"Some valuable information for us, Mr. Vásquez. That was one of my contacts there, out in the field. Turns out Champagne's old friend, Tykie Mendoza, is going to be involved in a big deal going down on Thursday night at the A Mi Gusto bar. I was told to expect that he'll be holding lots of cash, in addition to all the illegal stuff."

"Lots of cash, you say?"

"You thinking what I am?"

"Gato Negro Productions expands. Now we'll have more than just a bunch of sleazy apartments as assets."

"Now that's what I call looking at the Big Picture," Giovanni boasted as he munched on one of the roach-rejected Ritz crackers.

XXXV

"And that's why it's over, Santitos. I have to think about what's best for little José, and as long as you're in all this trouble, it's not safe for him. I'm sorry, Santos."

And with those last, sobbing words, Maribel stood up, walked away from him, out of his life and out of the Visitor's Center to the waiting car where Delfina held little José Rumaldo Sánchez.

Santos just sat there, trying to make sense out of something that could never make sense, to his way of thinking. For the safety of their son, Maribel was separating from him. Santos felt like yelling, cursing, and kicking, but as he glanced over at the guards within hearing distance of the inmates and their wives, sons, daughters, and sisters, his second mind reminded him.

"Survival, Santos. Remember, I'm your best friend. Let's keep it what way."

After listening patiently to his mind, Santos replayed the shocking image in his mind: a goddamn brick crashing through the front window! Splintering the peace at three in the morning! Causing Maribel's heart to race and José Rumaldo to be *asustado* without knowing why. Those *pinche* bastards. Mad Dog Montoya was right about *La Familia's* connections to street soldiers. Someone on the outside was starting to deal some payback, and his wife and son were the innocent targets. Enough. I'm doing something about this. *Ahora mismo.*

Calmly walking over to the guards, Santos mused on the Bigger Picture, and he began choosing and arranging his words carefully.

§ § §

Santos made sure he sat at the metal table with his back to the wall and had a clear sight for a quick escape to the side should the need arise. He offered Montoya a cigarette. Declined. Alright, that's okay. Deal with it.

The usual loud racket in the Day Room of Cell Block B lowered a few decibels to a steady murmur of curses, laughter, and guarded verbal exchanges. Accept it all.

Montoya, Valdez, and Jessie Villa were playing a game of Monopoly with molded toilet- paper structures that substituted for the houses, hotels, and game tokens.

Without looking up, Montoya snarled, "Sitting here without your down payment could be dangerous to your health, Champagne."

Montoya squinted through his cigarette smoke.

"Don't start jerking us around, Sánchez. *Si estás listo,* just slip your money under those Community Chest cards there, and I'll promise to keep Valdez on his leash."

Champagne's mind told him not to even glance at Valdez should any fear enter his soul and accidentally get expressed on his face.

Focusing on the scar on Montoya's cheek, Santos

admitted, *"No tengo dinero, pero tengo una idea.* And my idea is this: I've got a counter-offer that *La Familia* will be interested in."

"You want me to shank you myself? Right here and right now? *La Familia* demands *respeto."*

Montoya shot up from his chair.

"Espérate, carnal."

When Valdéz spoke, all inmates in the Day Room instinctively shut up, listened, and watched every move. More out of fear than respect. Even old Rick Morgan, who had been doing time for so long that he got to work in the kitchen, among other privileges that he enjoyed, listened carefully.

"Let's hear what the Champagne man has to say."

He shook the die and moved his toilet paper top hat Monopoly piece past Jail.

Breathing resumed in the Day Room, as well as the usual menacing murmur.

"Gracias."

Santos sent a message from his second mind that no sweat should appear on his face, and his body obeyed. He continued, his sweat-free face staring straight ahead.

"I don't have the money, you say I owe you, but I'm willing to work off any debt you say I owe *La Familia.* Anything, for as long as it takes. All I ask is one condition. That *mi familia* is left alone. That's the only thing I ask. You call off your street *soldados,* and I'm yours."

"Keep talking." Valdez conceded as the twitching in his lower lip slowed.

"You're aware that I've got mobility. Because of my work with the St. Dismas Ministry, I get to make the rounds of all of the cell blocks at least twice a week."

They were attentive. Eyes met cold eyes. There were possibilities.

"With my mobility and access, I could make deliveries and pick-ups for *La Familia*."

"*Chale ese*, we already got delivery boys. What do we need with you?" Montoya scoffed.

Valdez' sudden chokehold on Montoya's throat cut off both his air supply and his blood supply. Valdez loosened up his hand that held the choice between death and criminal life and gave Montoya a moment to let the blood flow back to his brain to allow for a thought or two. Valdez showed the rest of his prison gang that he still always held the upper, life-deciding hand.

"Montoya, *cállate la boca*. We're listening to Champagne's offer because a growing operation has growing needs. I'll make any decision about taking on new soldados or employees. *¿qué no?*"

"*Claro.*" Montoya whispered. Air and blood were rushing again.

"I'm still in charge of distribution, if anyone needs reminding."

Montoya and Villa avoided the sparks from his eyes.

"*Órale*, our operation demands total and constant access to the whole population. *Estoy pensando de algo.*"

He looked at the ceiling and leaned back so his chair swayed on its two back legs.

"*Perdóname*," Santos dared, "but while you're thinking, let me share some good news along that line."

Valdez' steel chair lurched forward, and the front legs hit the floor with a snap.

He stared at Santos, "*Háblame.*"

"Turns out that Warden Eichwald likes my recipe for *tamales*. Starting Monday, I'm also going to be working in the kitchen. I'll have total access, most of the time, including time for meals. We got a deal?"

Valdez did something he only did when either he was going to stalk somebody, or he was genuinely pleased. He actually smiled for the first time in five years. He extended his hand to Santos. Villa and Montoya looked at each other in shock.

"*Órale*, Champagne. I think we can make arrangements for that debt of yours to be taken care of. On the installment plan."

Still no sweat, Santos looked him straight in the eyes as he shook Valdez's hand.

"And my family gets left alone."

"Your wife and kid will be left alone as long as you're working for us. You've got my word. We're in business, and you get an insurance policy during our deal."

Valdez smiled again as he looked down at Montoya and Villa.

"So tell me, you got a recipe that calls for certain ingredients for *chile rellenos*?"

"*Más firme que la chingada.*"

"*Sabes qué*, Montoya," Valdez quipped, "I believe

we just bought us unlimited access to Boardwalk."

Valdez tossed the dice with glee.

"*Gracias*, Valdez." Santos stood up, then slowly, confidently, and triumphantly walked over to an unoccupied table with an old newspaper. As he strode over, he silently congratulated his second mind. Your family is safe. You'll know more about the strongest gang here in *La Pinta*. And, finally, you'll have some cards of your own to play.

XXXVI

Tossing a spoonful of fresh cream, a pinch of nutmeg, and a touch of brown sugar into her steaming cup, Adelita walked over to her usual table at the Common Grounds Coffeehouse and sat before Professor Romero. He stared at the pages before him.

She broke his spell, "Did you like it?"

Romero slowly lifted his head to respond but she cut him off.

"I know. Rule #1. It is not a question of liking or not liking."

He sipped his latte and nodded.

"You're learning, no doubt about that. This piece is well- written; it's finely crafted, indeed."

"So? The problem?"

"Look around you."

She did. Mostly students, a few independently-minded high school seniors. A few middle-aged would-be novelists frantically scratching in their journals. Mainly the college kids.

"Do you think that anybody in this entire crowd would be interested in corruption at the State Penitentiary?"

"If they care about how their tax money is being spent, yes. Ten dollars a pound for hamburger meat?"

Just getting warmed up, she barked, "Construction

contracts awarded nine times out of ten to Warden Eichwald's businesses."

"College students don't pay much taxes," he snapped.

"They don't care, Adelita."

"Well, they should."

"But they don't. That's a fact."

Each took the time to breathe and sip, Italian and Hazelnut.

He swallowed and started again.

"Adelita, your investigative skills are tops and your intuition leads you into some new, unreported areas."

She continued breathing.

"Not to worry. You've got an A in my class, guaranteed."

She gulped some more of the dark-brown brew.

"I'm just saying that you can't forget the context in which you're writing. Hey, the *Daily Lobo* is just a small campus paper. Keep the interests of your audience in mind."

Adelita pushed a strand of her long, straight hair behind her ear as she forced her lips together, trying not to blow it with a comment that would just anger Romero. At that moment, Adelita made a decision. No matter who or whatever the hell he blabbed on about, she would keep the caliber and integrity of the articles in her portfolio in mind. Besides, she was now getting some positive feedback from the head of community outreach at the *Tribune*; they wanted her to write another guest column. She sat back and decided not to bring that up to El Profe at this time. Let him read the article when it came out. A pleasant surprise for him and her fellow interns.

Leaning in, he spoke in a hushed, hard-boiled cub-reporter tone.

"Keep this under your hat, but I heard that the coffee prices are going up by five cents a cup here, next week,"

"Really?"

Adelita put a finger to her tight lips and feigned shock and surprise.

"I also heard that the Regents are reducing the size of the student seating section for next year's basketball season."

"You don't say?" Adelita opened her mouth in a perfectly-scandalized 'O'.

"Now here's a lead for you. I heard a rumor that they're going to get rid of the free parking lot to make way for the new Business College administration offices."

"Heaven forbid!"

Adelita wrinkled her brow in absolute disgust.

He grinned magnanimously.

"Keep in mind your audience."

She looked at the table to their right and spotted Kiko de La O, the unofficial editor of the unofficial newspaper that unofficially had some influence around town. Only a couple hundred students on campus ever read the irregularly-published underground newspaper, *Las Noticias de Aztlán*, but she secretly admired their *coraje* for doing what they did, against all odds.

She again silently recommitted herself to her

profession. She decided that this prison corruption story was worth pursuing even further. Delfina Chávez's daughter also inwardly promised that she would somehow, someday, help her mother's *comadre's* estranged husband (her cousin), and anyone else of society's forgotten, in the name of *justicia*. Just not outwardly until she was ready. Just not this minute.

Adelita's Notebook #3,100

Mystery and tears were left there, back in the dream, left back there where they belonged. Still, Adelita turned over a blurry image in her mind and wondered if she should go over and tell Maribel about it. Something very vague, but it was a picture of her cousin Santos in the middle of a bullfight arena, surrounded by a jeering, mocking mob. Maybe it didn't mean anything but the anger-filled picture took a while to fade. Maybe I should go warn his wife about my premonition. No, I don't really know her that well, and we hardly ever talk. About anything. It might seem too abrupt, and besides, who wants to hear about possible bad news, especially now that she has her baby and can't do anything about anything concerning her husband in prison.
I hardly ever even see her, anyway. Still, maybe I should tell my Mom and let my Mom bring it up

next time she goes over to Maribel's for morning cafecito?

Maybe, maybe not. Since I'm not sure, just not today. How come sometimes, we women have trouble making up our minds?

XXXVII

The letter to Inmate # 52 1-11 had numerous creases and folds—having been read and re- read numerous times—and remained in the envelope (with Maribel's return address) on a corner of a desk. This is where Santos studied the crude map that he had made, detail by detail over the past several weeks. Mari's previous letter had informed Santos that José Rumaldo had survived the Winter Flu season, but it seemed as though he might have a severe case of asthma. It was this possibility that drove Santos to the decision, reckless or not that he should make at least one attempt at breaking out, or be tormented by his conscience for the rest of his life.

What no map or written document could show was that *La Mala Suerte* would be paying a long-due visit to Champagne for his next fall further into disgrace.

Santitos had talked Louie into trying to escape from this hellhole. Yes, the endless, monotonous, tedious, nerve-pinching, dreary days can make a man do foolish things, and Louie could actually fall for the reckless plan that Santos proposed he be a part of. Santos had fallen into mental laziness and had failed to consult his second mind when he came up with his present idea for escape. Now that his roommate, Louie Mascarenas, was also working in the kitchen with him and old man Morgan, Champagne had conspired to explore an underground passageway that, according to Santos, led beyond the outside wall of *La Pinta*.

"I've done my research on this, Louie, and I'm telling you, we can go through this passageway to their mystery room, which is beyond the big wall, then climb up and break out."

"What research? How do you know about this?"

"Believe it or not, one day, while I was in the library, I checked out this book on public architecture and, stuck right there in the middle of the book as a huge book marker, was an old map of the north side of this place. How lucky for us that we work in the north side kitchen and have traveling privileges, *qué no*?"

If it seemed too good to be true, it was. *La Mala Suerte* smiled. That was two weeks ago.

After the thirteenth day of pressure, Louie had agreed to go along with the Champagne Liberation Plan.

At 8:58 a.m., after informing the Shift Supervisor that they needed to go downstairs to get a couple sacks of potatoes, Champagne and Louie walked downstairs to the food storage room. They made a left turn down an old, unlit hallway that had been revealed on the old map in the old public buildings architecture book. With their hands on the wall on their right, they walked and walked and walked. *La Mala Suerte* made an invisible exit. The echoes of their footsteps halted at exactly 9:05 a.m. Santos lit a match on the rusted metal door ahead of them, the light reflected on sickly-yellow droplets.

"This is the room, *jodido*! I told you the map was right."

Louie dampened Champagne's enthusiasm.

"It smells like shit down here."

"Who cares what it smells like; beyond this door is our freedom. *La Libertad*."

The glistening drops went back to black as the match burned down.

"Sánchez, are you sure this leads out of the prison grounds? I don't remember there being a tiny *bosque* around the outer fence, and, and it is way too wet down here . . . eeeeh . . . *¡qué hedionda!*"

Leader and chief break-out expert Santos held his nose as he declared, "We'll just have to put up with the stink until we get this damn door opened, and we're out of here!"

A match suddenly lit behind them!!

"I wouldn't open that door if I were you."

After Champagne and Louie's hearts began beating again, and they resumed breathing, they asked, in unison, "Why not?'"

Old Rick Morgan shuffled closer to the shuddering pair.

"The only thing on the other side of that metal door is a whole lot of aged sewage. Don't you know what this is?"

"The Mystery Room? An old storage room?"

"Try an abandoned cesspool."

Louie slammed his fist against the humid door. "Champagne, you stupid son-of-a-bitch."

"Shhhh, *señores*, I don't need to remind you. This area is off-limits, and we shouldn't even be down here."

The voice of age and experience whispered authoritatively.

Louie drew back his threatening finger from Champagne's face and turned his attention to the old soldier.

"So, Morgan, what are you doing down here?"

"Okay, gentlemen, I guess, since you just had to come snooping around down here . . . " He paused and looked over his shoulder. "I'm going to have to let you both in on a little secret. Of course, if this little secret of mine gets out, both of you will wake up the next morning with a shank up your ass and a bed sheet rope tight around your throats."

Champagne's face gradually broke into a sly grin.

"Before Rosco Jonson died last month, he told me that you had a private still that had provided the entire cell block with booze for the past twenty-seven years. So, the rumor all these years was true? Down here is where you brew your famous *mula*?"

"You guessed right, Sánchez. Now I haven't exactly figured out how to make any champagne, but I think my customers are pretty happy with my raisin wine and my apple cider."

"So how do you get these potatoes and raisins and apricots to turn into booze?"

"A little yeast, some sugar, a lotta time and some practice. Now should I happen, in the future, to accidentally be missing a bottle or two of my famous home brew . . . "

"Don't worry, Morgan, we're not going to rip you off. Just give us a 20% discount from now on and we'll forget all about this secret location." Louie grinned.

"Your secret is safe with us, Mr. Morgan," added Santos, as he respectfully patted the brewmeister on his bent back.

"Glad to hear it, Champagne. Now I'll let you in on another little secret."

Old man Morgan drew them both in and began whispering. "I normally wouldn't be down here on a Friday; cuz the guards do their weekly check on this day. It's just that they got assigned some special security detail for some meeting with the warden. That's what my contacts in the warden's office told me last night."

Louie turned his accusing, black eyes to Santos and spit out his realization.

"I doubt we'll be spending much time here in the future anyway. Sánchez, you stupid bastard, did you know that the average septic tank has 8-inch thick concrete walls? Oh, we'll just climb up and break out, right. After about three years of chipping away at cement."

Louie pushed past Santos, shaking his disillusioned head.

In an attempt to lighten the mood, and change the subject, Champagne blurted out, "*Ese* Louie, we better get back with these potatoes or somebody's going to start missing us in the kitchen."

Pause, then survival consciousness kicked in.

232

"*Vámonos.*"

"*Bueno*, Morgan, *al rato.*"

"See ya guys. Remember, this is our little secret. Oh, and you get your discount on all future purchases of spirits," Morgan, the entrepreneur, reiterated.

"*Seguro que sí.* Nobody knows but us sewer rats."

§ § §

Four stories above the stinky folly taking place in the damp basement, a couple of extra security guards stood like cornstalks outside Warden Eichwald's office. Actually, having extra security outside his office was not all that unusual. Eichwald had so many friends, enemies, contacts, associates, partners, plotters, and co-conspirators in high, low—in fact, mainly low places—that high-security meetings were held an average of three times a week.

Three cockroaches scurried out under the door as Anthony Salvatore Giovanni began to speak in a combination stale garlic/burnt-coffee cigar-breath voice.

"Well, back to business. Gentlemen, as we all know, the governor's race isn't that far off and if we're going to ensure Warden Eichwald's re-appointment, we'll have to make sure that Governor Wooten is re-elected. That means a well-financed campaign which is where Gato Negro Productions comes into the picture."

"What's that? What about our negroes? Civil rights for the encarcerated? Eichwald, aren't we complying with the federal regulations?" Corrections Board Member Walker Cannon asked.

Governor Wooten's trusty aide, Rusty Barks, leaned over and spoke in a loud voice, "Turn up your hearing aid, Cannon."

"What's that? Oh, yeah, my hearing."

Once the dust re-settled on the warden's desk, Henry *I'll-take-care-of-it* Puente spoke up, ignoring Walker Cannon's question. "In other words, we need some reliable cash flow for an effective campaign."

"*Exactamente. En punto.*"

Boy, did Vásquez hate it when sleaze ball Puente did that, throwing in Spanish phrases when talking about legally-questionable strategies?

"I'm open to ideas."

Barks finished his loudly whispered summary in Wooten's sunburned ear, and Eichwald gestured with one of his 23-carat gold pens.

"I suppose one of my cell blocks could accidentally burn down but the turn-around time for the large insurance reimbursement to my nephew's construction company wouldn't come in for months."

"Thanks for offering," Giovanni noted, "but, you're right. We don't have that kind of time."

Puente, ever the advocate for newer approaches, adjusted the black tie over his huge stomach and spoke. "I've got a quick fix solution until we come up with a more elaborate money maker. I'll simply raise the rents at the J & J Apartments. It's been months since the last rent hike."

The *víbora* looked at the *puma* for approval. He nodded his head. Giovanni's combination bad-breath reached the farthest corner of the office with his grand question.

"All in favor of a rent increase?"

"Aye," muttered Vásquez.

"Aye," stated Puente.

"Aye," gloated Eichwald.

Clueless Corrections Board Member Walker Cannon confirmed with an "Aye."

Bzzzzz. Bzzzz. Bzzzz, whispered Rusty.

After a hesitation, Governor Wooten hoarsely muttered, "Aye."

Four stories above the encounter of the prison moonshiner and his unexpected septic tank guests, the latest nasty business meeting of the Gato Negro Productions broke up. Rusty Barks helped Governor Wooten out of his chair and handed him his gold-plated cane as the *víbora*, the *puma*, the fountain of ideas, the newest appointee to the Corrections Board, and a head crook at the prison milled around, creating a low hum.

A fruit fly headed toward the nervous man in a threadbare pin-striped suit but sensed an evil presence, as foul as an abandoned cesspool. It changed its flight pattern and splattered itself on a window that looked out onto the volatile inmate exercise yard. Business, as usual, in the prison where thieves were sent to be rehabilitated, and guarded.

XXXVIII

Father Galli, the respected and dignified Catholic priest who occasionally visited the Misión de San José, blew out the candles. Maribel's voice sounded frail in the dusty adobe dark.

"*Padrecito*, could I talk with you about my husband?"

He had noticed that she had not left after the morning Mass.

"*Seguro qué sí.*"

He was a full-blooded Italian, but like many of the descendants of immigrant miners and farmers who had relocated from Colorado (where they settled after leaving Sicily and Italy), he was now fully bi- lingual in English and Spanish.

After tearfully explaining the situation with Santos, Maribel checked to see if José was still sleeping. He was.

"*Mi hija*, naturally, the mother's instinct is to protect her children, but before you divorce your husband to get away from all this bad business with the gangs and drugs and so on, why don't you give it some time. Pray about it. The Church respects your need to be in a temporary state of separation. I wouldn't advise to stay and subject yourself and your child to danger. Still, my advice would be for you to pray to Our Lord for strength and guidance during this time of crisis for your family."

236

Fr. Galli hoped she would change her mind . . . for now, anyway.

Josecito began to stir. It would be time for his morning feeding very soon. Father Galli concluded by giving her *la bendición* and his final *consejos*.

"Pray for patience for yourself, for wisdom to make good decisions, and for your friendship with this *comadre* of yours to be a blessed and protected relationship."

"Delfina."

"Sí. With your friend Delfina. Finally, feel free to come back to me for counsel whenever you need *y te prometo que* you and your *familia* will be in my prayers. Put your faith in the Holy Spirit, *mi hija*. And pray that sometime in the future you might be able to reunite with your husband with these *conflictos* resolved and behind you both."

She noticed a light in his eyes when he closed the old cottonwood door. Halfway home, Josecito began to sob and Maribel stopped in her tracks, dumbstruck by how similar José Rumaldo's cry was to his father's voice when he hurt deeply. Maribel resolved to remain physically separated but, she knew now, their souls were deeply inseparable.

§ § §

The Holy Spirit woke Fr. Galli up at the usual time: three a.m. In the icy jaw of January cold or the still-warm blanket of June, this faithful servant of God was stirred by the constant promptings. By 3:30 every morning, he

237

had already silently recommitted himself by reading the Divine Office, a prayer he united with, in both English and Latin. Fr. Galli next reviewed the life, trials, and lessons for whichever saint was honored on this day, and then he moved on to his personal prayers, some of them in adoration, some for thanks but mostly petitions for favors.

That young lady, Maribel Sánchez, her son, José, and her convicted husband, Santos, were lifted up in *oración*, even as they slept and dreamed. As did at least 92% of the rest of the population.

§ § §

Magdalena Moya was also deep in communion with her Heavenly Father, asking for mercy on her earthly father and, oh, so many other parents and their young.

§ § §

Although he would never be able to explain it in ten thousand years, Mad Dog Montoya awoke abruptly knowing that, although he could fight and kill whenever he felt the urge, he would never be able to actually harm Champagne Sánchez again, but he did not know why.

§ § §

At three in the morning, a large, physically scattered, but spiritually united congregation of prayer warriors was awake and at work, with self-adopted tasks and supplications.

Many were men like Fr. Galli, who followed in the line of priestly service of the order of Melchizedek. These men did their part, from early morning until past the dawn—which marked the stirring of commerce, strife, chaos, and some love—to try to keep the world from falling apart. Men and women praying in the pre-dawn. The biggest secret on the planet. Men and women. In service. In balance.

§ § §

The key in the door jangled, and the cheap plywood door swept open. Hmm, he's thinner than I expected, Walter Shines mused silently. Then prison librarian Shines wearily gestured to the far wall.

"You say you're interested in anything, huh, Champagne? You've only been here a matter of months. Once you've been here for years you either go one way or the other, it seems. After you've read all the books in here, you're more interested in the world, or you end up not giving a damn about anything in this hollow world but maybe your next cigarette."

"And you?"

"Oh, I'm in the first category. See, I get out on parole in three months, I've got hope."

Big grin. "Anyways, on that far wall are your law books. Outdated and hard as hell to understand. Of course, if you have a lot of time on your hands . . ."

"Over there?"

"That's our New Mexico section. Anything you want on the history, geography, culture."

Shines jerked a glossy, over-sized paperback off the shelf and slammed it onto the green metal table.

"This here's our latest addition to the collection, courtesy of the local Chamber of Commerce. *Who's Who in New Mexico*. You won't find too many convicts in there, though! Ha, Ha!"

Walter's laugh reminded Champagne of the grinding gears of the *Fruta de Oro* 18-wheeler.

"Over here we've got our fiction section."

Carefully taking a thick volume from the top shelf, Walter narrowed his eyes and broadcast his grin.

"How about a great long novel? *Les Misérables* by Victor Hugo."

"What's it about?"

"In this one, some guy steals a loaf of bread, ends up in prison, and then he . . . "

"Never mind. What's this?"

"Ahh. *Don Quixote* by Miguel Cervantes."

"And what's that one about?"

"Let's see, Don Quixote is this old guy who reads all about knights and chivalry and then he gets the crazy idea that he can make something out of the rest of his life by . . . "

"Do you have something more modern?"

"Champagne, these are the classics. Most of them are about shit that happened a long time ago, but the lessons still apply to today."

Santos' eye caught a deep blue hardback cover.

"And this one?"

"There you go. *Life is a Dream.*"

"What happens in this one?"

"Well, see, this king takes this prisoner out of his cell and then switches . . . "

"Uh, Walter, never mind."

Santos put the book back and then sat on the cold metal chair.

"Maybe I'll just sit here and think for a while."

"Well, you go ahead and do whatever you want," Walter Shines muttered as he transferred the newspapers from his librarian's desk to the gray metal periodicals rack.

Putting things in place, in order, was one of the great joys in Walter Shines' life. Now that he was due to be released after eleven years in the joint, he felt a great fear that life on the outs might not be as orderly, or ever could be. For now, however, he relished placing today's copies of the *Albuquerque Journal* and the *Albuquerque Tribune* on the top slot, the *Santa Fe New Mexican* and the *Las Vegas Optic* right below, the *Socorro Sun,* the *El Paso Times* and *the New York Times* underneath, and so on. A place for everything and everything in its place; now this was life at its best for Walter K. Shines.

§ § §

"The hell with this!" Adelita whispered angrily to herself.

A couple of nearby scholars in the darkened Zimmerman Library scowled at her. Researching out-of-state parking lot companies was boring and not exactly going to shake up society. She thought to herself, No, I think there's an institution a little closer to home that could use a real shake up. I think I can do a quick write on this and turn it into Professor Romero for my next contribution to the *Lobo*. But I can also do more than that, for my real goals as a journalist. I need a break from the burning issue of parking lot politics anyway. She made a beeline to the card catalog.

Adelita was sitting on the floor up on the ninth stack—where the ghosts of past scholars whispered from time to time—a dozen hefty volumes at her feet. Her eyes widened as she read the list of contractors who had bid on, received, and completed construction projects at the State Pen for the past four years. Hmm. Eichwald and Sons, Gato Negro Productions, Eichwald and Sons, Gato Negro Productions, Gato Negro Ventures, Gato Negro Associates, Gato Negro Affiliates, Gato Negro Unlimited, Gato Negro LTD., Gato Negro Productions. Hmm.

§ § §

Champagne looked down and there it was, in black and white, on page forty three. In the section of Most Successful New Companies in the Land of Enchantment was a captioned photo of the Board of Directors of Gato Negro Productions. What caught his eye was the strange

242

coincidence of the two men in the center of the picture with their arms around each other and toothy grins on their faces. The *víbora* and the *puma* next to each other. Special Agent José Vásquez and the People's Lawyer, Anthony Salvatore Giovanni. Coincidence?

Adelita's Notebook #3,111

¡Qué escándalo! Wow, my research up in the stacks of Zimmerman Library has confirmed what my intuition has been leading me to. Provable corruption in the State Corrections Department.

Favoritism within state government. Should I really be surprised? Land of Enchantment? More like Land of Entrapment and Land of Embezzlement. But is this an opportunity. The chance to make my name, stake a claim in investigative journalism. After this Watergate Affair, the heroism of Bob Woodward and Carl Bernstein is well-known. Is it time to show the world that las mujeres can be just as brave, skilled, and driven by integrity as los hombres? Or do I know what I'm getting into here? Could El Profe actually be right in his (always) over-cautious consejos? Maybe I should first establish myself, either in a job, a news organization or in name or reputation before I go after a big kill. I know what he means about having a base of readers and having a place to go to each morning, as in a job. I don't have that yet. I'm only able to get an article published in the Trib as a guest columnist. And there's no contract between them and me, in other words, no protection. They could just choose not to run my big exposé if I pursue this prison contract business. If I already could count on the safety of a contract, then I'd have more leverage.

The fact remains, the City Desk editor still calls all the shots (of course he could always make his name ever bigger by discovering new talent—me!) If I was already established I'd even have readers in other cities and states through syndication that could follow my exposé, week after week. But I'm getting ahead of myself.

Like Professor Romero always says, "What could be the repercussions, for years, of putting this story in print?" Could there be possible retaliation against me? My mom? Santos, in prison? Pursuing this and publishing it could get complicated in ways I can't even imagine.

XXXIX

Inmate #52 1-11 felt splendid about this day. Today he would be free. No, Inmate #52 1-11 was not due to go before the Parole Board for several months, but today, after making a couple of final deliveries, Champagne Sánchez would wipe out the remainder of his debt to La Familia and be a free man, once again.

Libertad, he thought to himself as he carried a specially prepared dish of tamales from the kitchen to the serving line and put them onto Mad Dog's plate when he came forward.

Champagne grinned as Montoya nodded in acknowledgment, "I'm sure these vegetarian tamales have green *calabacitas* inside, right?"

Champagne spoke through a smile, "Sure do. By the way, by my count, that makes us even, doesn't it?"

"That's right, brother. You are now a free agent again."

Montoya unwrapped the cornhusks, removed the stuffing, snuck the $20.00 bills into his prison grays and winked over at Champagne.

Freedom. Santos almost sang it out loud. Spotting Jesse Villa in the lunch line, Champagne went back to *la cocina* and retrieved a tray of specially-prepared chile rellenos.

Face to face, Sánchez grunted to Villa, "Today's rellenos are high in cholesterol. Must be all that white flour and *manteca*. After today, you'll be on a diet, eh, Villa?"

"Yeah, you're right. After today's meal, I'll have to look for somebody else to help me keep on my diet, *ese*."

Santos wiped down the dinged-up chrome counter and cast a glance at Villa as he cut into the stuffed green chiles and pulled out little plastic bags filled with white powder.

Villa gave him an inconspicuous thumbs up and ate his sides of *frijoles y arroz*.

"No more obligations, no more debts." Santos darn near chanted the mantra out loud while pushing his cart.

Stopping in front of Ramón Valdez's cell, Champagne pulled a special hardback Bible out of the bunch and whispered, "Valdez. Today is the Day of Reckoning, as they say."

Valdez grinned for the first time this year.

"Open that up and you will find a Revelation, *ese*."

The bag in the hollowed-out section brought an almost painful smile to Ramón's face.

"*Órale*, Sánchez, I'd call this delicious."

"Actually, if you check your records, I'd call us even."

Valdez counted up the marks in the margin of a hand-penned *Paño* taped to the wooden desk and nodded.

"*Pos, qué milagro.* You did it, Champagne. *Al fin*, you're finally square *con La Familia. Vaya con Dios, carnal.*"

Valdez did not know it and would not have believed

it, but Santos actually went on his way, his path already guarded and made smooth and sweet as honeysuckle by those pre-dawn prayers from Maribel, Fr. Galli, Magdalena Moya, and other people he didn't even know.

Adelita's Notebook #3,121

¡Qué Milagro! Es un placer leer las palabras tan poéticas as those of this new Poeta I have discovered. This Lorna Dee Cervantes, from the Bay Area, writes of her surroundings, her life, and her struggles. She is uniting with those of other mujeres, Hispanic, Black, Anglo, but especially Latina to try to live lives free of oppression. It's her gentle, at times, y fuerte, a veces, hermana bi-lingual ways of expression. She, and others like Jenny Montoya are brave.

What inspires me is how Lorna has had the coraje to not let el sistema stop her from getting her work out there. She has self-published some small chapbooks of her poetry that I have discovered, and they show that our self-determination is what will cut though the macho attitudes that we Chicanas have to face in our homes, nuestra cultura, and en la sociedad. But we can still be women at the same time as being soldaderas, whether in the battlefield for equal pay for equal work or in the home of la familia where we insist upon respeto when asking for it just doesn't work.

And, of course, even though I am named after una de mis ancianas, there is the historical precedent de la Revolución Mexicana, of the Adelitas that stood by their men in the battle. Sometimes they resisted with rifle or pistola, on occasions sustaining sus hombres and themselves with spoon and pan, y siempre fighting, with love in their corazones for La Familia.

As Che said, "At the risk of seeming ridiculous, let me say that the true revolutionary is guided by great feelings of love." In fact, that is what we Latinas bring to la batalla, whether in the kitchen, the streets or yes, the newspaper office. And, not to be forgotten, to the coffee shop where we weave our poesías out of the many-colored strands de la vida, personal and political. Qué milagro that I am also discovering the voices of my comadres de poesía like Lorna Dee from San Francisco, like Ángela de Hoyos from Texas, and like Jenny Montoya from my own Alburquerque (from Old Town, no less!) who are helping to create a new path for us as writers. Qué milagro that I have been blessed with the time to write, as both a reporter and a poet. After all, sometimes the obvious has to be poeticized and, on occasions the mystical has to be clarified, but always, we have been called to witness and feminize and express the truth . . . to sing the many songs of our hearts.

Poema por Augusta, *en Los Cielos*

Amor fue tu misión
tu misión fue tu liberación
la verdad tu lección
honor en tu corazón
mujer de fuerza,
mujer de gracia,
mujer de las estrellas
en la distancia
(Poem for Augusta, in the Heavens)

(Love was your mission
your mission was liberation
the truth your lesson
honor in your heart
woman of strength woman of grace
woman of the distant stars)

by Adelita Zoila Augusta Chávez

Adelita looked over the beginning of a poem for her great, great, great Grandmother on her mom's side, the proud Augusta Fiero, an *Adelita* who had fought, *mano a mano*, with Emiliano Zapata, in Mexico during La Revolución. Although most of the 'Adelitas' spent their time reloading *pistolas* and *fusiles* for their men and cooking their meals, Augusta supposedly picked up a gun and proved herself as fierce as any of the *soldados* that she fought with. If only Adelita knew more about her brave ancestor, but so many stories had been lost when her great, great Grandmother crossed *la frontera* into Aztlán, now called the Southwest.

§ § §

The meeting was almost over. Governor Wooten's snoring reached a crescendo. His trusted and so far unindicted-for-assorted-crimes (knock on wood) aide, Rusty Barks, nervously tapped both feet.

"So, any more New Business before we adjourn?" Tony asked.

"I've got one thing. We need to decide what to do with the cash that came in from the Tykie Mendoza bust. Any ideas?"

After a more-than-pregnant pause, Henry Puente answered his own question.

"Well, I've got an idea. I propose that we hold off on any more real estate deals till the market gets better. So, why don't we diversify?"

"What'd joo have in mind?" Tony shot back.

"Fireworks." This caught everybody's attention. Even José Vásquez opened up one sleepy eye.

"The R. & T. Fireworks Company is up for sale. I say we buy it and keep it running year- round. No reason why people shouldn't have Roman candles for New Year's Eve and for birthdays."

"Why not? If we can afford it." Giovanni sputtered with greed as he slivered closer into the group.

"We can't afford not to." Puente tapped his pen on his notebook of calculations and exhaled a small cloud of burnt expensive Cuban tobacco.

"All in favor?" Giovanni polled while attempting to hide the blatant greed in his eyes by putting on a pair of dark sunglasses.

Proposed. Passed. One abstention. The snoring Governor.

§ § §

The meeting at the warden's office that afternoon was not so smooth. The governor's Secretary of Corrections was trying to deliver bad news.

"I'm concerned about the reactions of the inmates," Warden Eichwald cautioned as the twitch in his right eye fluttered faster.

"Screw the prisoners," Mr. Gino Franco retorted while scratching his fat ass.

"Tell them we had budget problems and had to cut the overtime for guards. They're doing time in a prison not a country club, and they've got to get used to it. As Secretary of Corrections, I'm ordering recreation time in the yard and visiting hours to be reduced at all correctional facilities in the state. Including the youth facilities.

"You're the boss. I'm just warning you; we'll probably have a few protests over this." Now his left eye twitched too.

Franco's arms wiggled in space as he retorted.

"Screw those Liberals! The hell with the American Civil Liberties Union!"

"No, I'm talking about protests inside."

"All the better, I hope they do protest. That'll justify our clamping down on the bastards."

Eichwald walked over to the coffee table and picked up the *Albuquerque Journal.*

"So that's it, huh? This is part of the governor's 'get tough on crime' strategy, huh?"

Franco settled back in the overstuffed chair. Eichwald humbly placed a long envelope with the Gato Negro Productions' black cat logo on it in Franco's hands. His eyes grew wide.

"No," he blurted out, and he put a hand on his chest as if his heart had skipped a beat.

"I don't believe it. After all this time?"

"Believe it, Gino. What you are holding in your hands is an official invitation to finally join in with Gato Negro activities and holdings."

Mr. Gino Franco, the so-far-unindicted Secretary of the Corrections Department, felt really superb about this day. Talk about criminal behavior.

XL

It didn't even make good nonsense. Santos had not had a visitor in months, was not even expecting one, and then they call him down from his cell for a special visit from . . . No! It couldn't be! Special Agent Vásquez?

But, sure enough, standing in front of him on the other side of the chipped-enamel table was Special Agent José Vásquez. What the hell could he possibly want?

"Santos, Special Agent José Vásquez."

"I know who you are, and you know who I am. What the hell do you want? If you don't mind my asking."

Santos sat and Vásquez did, too.

"I'm going to just speak honestly here if you don't mind," Vásquez spoke very matter- of-factly, realizing that it was impossible to pretend that he was here for no other reason than to ask Santos for a favor and only Santos might be in a position to help.

Vásquez tried to act like he felt neutral about the favor he was leading to, but his hunched back and jerky movements showed that he felt a genuine fear of a possible shanking by Santos, after all these years.

"Got a cigarette?" Vásquez almost jumped at the mere request by Santos.

"Huh? Oh, yeah. Here." Champagne burned a hole in his eyes as he slapped open the lighter and sparked it.

Vásquez's hand shook ever so slightly. Santos' second mind registered the slight tremor and informed his first mind that Vásquez, in spite of the tough exterior, was here to beg for something. These long, numerous months in the *pinta* had sharpened his intuition, along with his reflexes.

"As much as it goes against the very grain of my nature, I'm here to ask you a favor."

I knew it, I could just smell it, Santos thought.

"I wonder why I even agreed to meet with you after they told me who the 'special' visitor was."

Champagne blew smoke in Vásquez direction.

"If it weren't for you, I wouldn't be here in this corner of hell."

"You put yourself here."

"I think I'll just go back to my cell. I don't have to listen to your shit."

Santos raised his voice. "Guard? Guard! Take me back."

"Hey, wait. Stop. I'll make it worth your time. What do you got to lose?"

Unfortunately, that appeal almost made sense or at least *good* nonsense. Santos gestured for the guard to never mind.

"I'm not here to argue. I admit it. I really need your help with something. It's my sister's only child. Joaquin Lucero. Ya know him?"

Champagne stared him down, searching for any hints that there was a possible *movida* behind Vásquez' visit and request, any possible 'set-up' engineered by the

254

Warden or *La Familia*, and nodded his head behind three large rings of smoke. No, Santos' second mind concurred with his first, that this miserable wolf, with the shaky voice was dealing straight with him.

"He's still a kid, he doesn't belong here."

"I don't think I belong here, either. So?"

Santos looked right through the broken man before him. Behind those cold, gun-metal bars, a certain truth was always revealed.

"Joaquín was hanging around these little gangster wanna-be's, stealing cars. I should have been keeping a closer watch on him. No father around."

Santos nodded. I wouldn't know anything about that, now would I?

"At any rate, word on the streets is that you've got clout with *La Familia*, as well as some of the other prison gangs."

Sánchez shrugged. "Could be."

"Only you can guarantee his safety. You know, prevent him from having an accident in here. Sánchez, I'm asking you to give him *esquina*. He doesn't know anybody up here."

"And what do I get in return?"

"I could talk to my old friend, Warden Eichwald, about giving you some privileges. Mobility. *¿Tú sabes?*"

"*Ya lo tengo.* I've already got mobility, *sabes?*"
"Maybe give you extra visiting hours?"

Pause. "The person, the one person I would like to have a visit from, hasn't been here in almost a year. I gotta get out of this hopeless place where souls are forgotten. You want *protección* for your nephew, you gotta offer me something I want . . . and don't have."

He took a long slow drag on his cigarette and exhaled a huge cloud of Marlboro smoke.

"What would that be? What can I offer you?"

Santos' research time in the library was worth it now.

"I know you know people in high places around town. You move up my parole hearing, and nobody touches little Joaquín. Deal?"

Vásquez didn't answer right away.

"Deal?" Champagne pressed.

"Alright, it's a deal."

Vásquez betrayed his anxiety with the slight tremble in his hand as he wrote his phone number on the back and gave his card to Sánchez.

"Anytime you need to get ahold of me, call this number. They'll get a message to me."

Champagne grinned to himself as he took one last drag from the suddenly tasty cigarette. Vásquez got up to leave, stopped in his tracks, and turned to face Champagne.

"By the way, Santos, you know for years I've held a terrible, hateful grudge against you. I always blamed you for Mónica 's depression."

"So tell me something I don't know."

"Anyway. Recently, Mónica got over all that, got married, and now . . . now I'm going to be a grandfather."

256

"Well, congratulations, Grandpa. And your point is?"

"My point is . . . I want to say . . . I want to say . . . I'm sorry."

"Yeah, well, I'm sorry for every minute of every day I have to be in this cruel cage. Where hearts are constantly breaking. Bad faith rules this place.

Must be nice to see your own flesh and blood whenever you want. Wish I could say the same. Have a good day, Agent Vásquez."

The sound of Vásquez' echoing footsteps had not completely faded when Champagne Sánchez's mood rapidly soared, and his soulful eyes grew wide. He discovered a key piece in the puzzle he had been working on for months. On the side of the business card that didn't have Special Agent Vásquez's hand-scrawled contact phone number was the inscription: José Vásquez, Co- Director, Gato Productions.

XLI

Adelita's Notebook#3,193

Cancer. There. I've done it. I made up my mind and did it. I actually wrote that awful word here in my journal. The very word seems to carry power, a dread, and it's-too-late meaning that reduces me to a helplessness I've never known before. When you hear the word cancer spoke about you or someone you know and love, it's all the more terrifying and irreversible. That word. Isn't it supposed to be somebody else's word? Why mi familia?

The doctor says the word cancer and then it ceases to be abstract. It becomes the awful indelible word, the word that incesantly appears in front of you wherever you go and wherever you are and whatever you do. The word wakes you up several times throughout torturous nights, wipes out any dreams you might have slipped into, and then suddenly CANCER!

You can't die, Mamá!

But she can. Some words feel worse than Death. Worse than Betrayal. Unwanted, unwelcome, rejected. But, Cancer? I can't get used to it. And yet, the doctors start talking, start explaining: "This test shows" and "Inconclusive" and "Our options are." It's just that when it is your own mother. Don't you understand? It's my mom you're talking about; she's not just another patient.

But after a while, it is possible to calm down. The doctors tell us that cancer can be cut out, that cancer can die. The physicians and technicians, after all, they are here to help. And then you're not so alone. There are other people, and you see how brave they have to be when we can't.

There's that guarded, that cautious, that very tentative little hope. "We are hopeful that we have caught your mother's breast cancer early." Early. Another hopeful word. Early, no really, early is my connecting word to hope. If Mom's breast cancer has been caught—that life- saving, that God Blessed, that merciful E-A-R-L-Y—then this time next year, I could be writing about the things I did with Mom because, by the grace of La Merced, the cancer (now with a small c) was caught early. I hope that I will be able to write about us, Mom and me.

Por ejemplo: After a successful surgery, Mom and I enjoyed going up north to touch, dig, and gather the Tierra Sagrada in a handkerchief from El Santuario de Chimayo, and we brought *it back home. It will have been a part of Mom's healing, as it has been for so many hundreds of other faithful ones.*

I pray that a year from now I am able to write, por ejemplo, about the memory of visiting relatives down south. The melodies of their aged Spanish wishes, spoken by Sofia and Mom's other aunties, the music of their conversations about times long past and about blessings. Here, now, in the present moment, where los ancianos, the wise ones, have learned to live. I hope that a year from now I will be able to write, as I am now, to describe having enjoyed so many minutes, so many days and weeks spent in a different way of being, not thinking about the past or future, but feeling life in the real, full, present time.

I'm finally getting it that now is all that exists. Yes, cancer is here, has not gone away, but it's not the only thing or word here. No, our presence is what's bigger and stronger. Our time, here, being fully conscious is what is real. Now that's a word, a word with new meaning. I like the simplicity, the sound, the look of that balancing word. Hope. H-O-P-E. One vowel says its name; the other is silent.

XLII

Maldito's mournful feline cries woke Maribel promptly at three a.m. José Rumaldo dreamed on. Mari immediately began saying a silent rosary for Santos, knowing that something painful was going on with him. Something always was, when his old cat cried out.

§ § §

In one house in the pre-dawn stillness, Carmelita Rojas, the neighborhood town crier, otherwise known as *La Mitotera,* ironed a handkerchief. She was going to give it to Doña MariLuz, in hopes that Father Galli would bless it before she gave it to Alicia Crespín, who had a son who was leaving for fame and fortune in L.A. *Ay,* the land of illusions, rock bands, and six-lane freeways.

§ § §

In another quiet corner of the *barrio, comadre* Delfina prayed for *la pareja* as well as for the souls of her deceased husband, her hard-working journalist daughter, extended *familia,* numerous friends, the souls in Purgatory, and so on. She prayed herself to sleep.

§ § §

Doña MariLuz, *la Curandera*, woke herself up and set about dutifully arranging certain *yerbas* out on the woven mats to catch the full moon light. She set aside the *oshá* for old man Gallegos for endurance and healing his lungs. She put some *yerba buena* in a plastic baggie for a calming tea *remedio* for Maribel, who needed to stay *tranquila* for her baby. Doña MariLuz set aside some *malva* for her sister, Magdalena, to use as a home-made shampoo.

§ § §

In a colorful dream of *bailes en la carpa* of his youth, old deaf Mr. Gallegos heard *conjuntos*, lively mixes of *acordeón, guitarras, bajo sexto,* and *voces del cielo* in perfect harmony. They overflowed with *música del corazón y del alma*.

§ § §

Comforted by Maribel's compassionate purring lullaby, black Maldito cat-dreamed herself back into a corner of sweet milk-universe sleep.

§ § §

Then, somewhere around 3:30 a.m., everything just stopped for a moment and there was a total eclipse of sound. Then hearts started pulsing their songs, crickets began their rhythmic dialogue, dreams went into Act Three, and the day prepared itself for another round.

XLIII

Santos' second mind was already on the job, psyching himself into not getting his expectations too high, but allowing preliminary plans for the possibility of an early release.

"Santos Sánchez!"

The screeching voice sounded like it had to have come from a demented cartoon character on this fine early morning, but Champagne kept a straight face, a serious face, and a serious attitude.

"Yes, sir. I'm Santos Sánchez."

Mr. Cartoon Face gestured for Santos to enter the second story makeshift office with the *Temporary Parole Hearing Room* Magic-Markered cardboard sign taped on the outer wall.

"Come in, Mr. Sánchez, and have a seat."

Cartoon's chalk-white hand, palm up, cued the introductions.

"This is Mrs. Higgins, Mr. Taylor, Mr. Hutchinson, and I'm Bill Schwartz."

The only difference between them all was that Mrs. Higgins wasn't wearing a tie and Mr. Taylor's Coke-bottle glasses made his eyes look like green oranges.

Cartoon's screech started up anew.

"Mr. Sánchez, normally your hearing would have

been scheduled in with all the others for our regularly-scheduled Quarterly Meeting, but since some members of the Board had to be here on other business anyway, Warden Eichwald asked that we make an exception and review your case today."

Santos nodded in his best I-know-you've–got-the-power look and spoke like he had just graduated from kiss-ass college.

"I greatly appreciate this. I feel that I have made the best of my time here and I've learned my lesson. When I get out, I'll be a changed man."

"*If* you get out."

Mrs. Higgins was the perfect picture of the mean principal and the white pin-curls that encircled her head said *Warning* in no uncertain terms.

"What evidence do we have of your rehabilitation, young man?"

Champagne bit his tongue, but his cool mind prevailed and he started again.

"With all due respect, Madam and Sirs of this Parole Board, I was part of a small select group of inmates who chose to speak to some teenage visitors from the Youth Diagnostic Center who visited here last week, plus, I . . . "

"Why should we consider early release, Mr. Sánchez? How do we know that you have truly turned your life around permanent?"

"Excuse me, Mrs. Higgins," Ned Hutchinson interjected.

He then handed her a note that read: *Warden*

Eichwald did request that we give this case special consideration. A special reminder that Cell Block B, Mr. Sánchez's Cell Block, is being investigated for alleged overcrowded conditions that could be alleviated by a reduction in the population. Being a legal thorn in our side, it is believed that the lawyers for the State Corrections Department would appreciate all due consideration.

Santos did not see the contents of the note but he noticed that Mrs. Higgins read it with a frown. He needed to help his own cause.

"Please. You all on this Board know I've made mistakes. I'll admit it. I did stupid stuff before coming here, and even some while I've been here, but I think you should know of the good things I've done while I've been here."

Santos' sincere pleas took the tension down three notches.

"Could you give us some more examples?" Mrs. Higgins inquired as she tidily folded the note.

"Yeah, sure. First of all, I would like for you to know about all my good work with the St. Dismas Christian Ministry."

"What?" Mrs. Higgins' blood pressure jolted up three notches. Santos proudly repeated, "The St. Dismas Ministry. I've been involved with them."

Oops. The sympathy of the members of the Board dropped thirty notches and they lowered their heads, except for Cartoon, who shook his head in some pain. Wrong. Wrong. Wrong. Mr. Taylor spoke up first.

"Did he say what I thought I just heard him say?"

"Just another mistake." Ned sighed.

"What? What's wrong?" Santos really didn't know.

Today's daily newspaper was passed from one Board member to the next.

§ § §

About fifteen minutes later, alone in his cell, Santos got a copy of the newspaper and read the headline that secured their decision and his further descent into hopelessness.

Champagne silently read the headline: "St. Dismas Ministry Investigated over Alleged Ties to Street Drug Gang. Pastor Roger Reportedly Missing."

XLIV

The scent of crisis filled the air. This mixed with the pungent aroma of a variety of *yerbas* that MariLuz Moya had used to minister to Delfina. Death was carving into Delfina Chávez, cell by cell, and MariLuz spoke sternly and compassionately.

"*Señora* Chávez. You are in a wrestling match with *La Muerte. Las yerbas* have limited power with your sickness. We are going to have to take you to the doctor, *pero de pronto.*"

§ § §

"This is unfair. They're taking away our rights!"

Tykie ripped the mimeographed memo off the dayroom bulletin board and grabbed the attention of half the inmates around. Ever since being transferred to Cell Block B, Tykie Mendoza had earned a reputation as a hot head with a short fuse. It was so bad that even Champagne, over in the corner watching The Price is Right, on an eight-inch black-and-white portable, kept his distance.

Mendoza was reacting to the notice that time allowed in the yard and visitors hours were being cut and now Montoya was whispering in his ear.

"Tykie's right. We can't let them do this to us."

"I think we gotta send a message back to the warden,

qué no?"

Tykie flicked the plastic lighter open and lit the memo on fire. Now he had everyone's attention.

"*Órale,* people. let's show them what we think of this bullshit."

It happened so quickly that Santos and his little group didn't even have time to get across the room. In about three minutes flat, Mendoza, Montoya, and half-a-dozen other inmates had lit a couch on fire, thrown playing cards into the outer hallway, ripped the wire off the intercom on the wall, and created a contagious interruption. Mack Heinrick, a guard with a reputation as a bully, fired a single shot that stilled the mini-riot. Tykie Mendoza lay bleeding.

Montoya broke the shocked silence. "Champagne. *Oye,* Santos. It's your *carnal, ese.*"

Santos leaped over the smoldering couch and lifted Tykie's head up against his own chest.

Valdez, from the outer circle around them, yelled, "Guards, get a doctor! This man's losing a lot of blood!"

The tremble in Heinrick's voice made audible his inner fear.

"It was turning into a riot. I had to do something or else."

"Shhh. I think he's trying to talk."

Montoya put his face close to Tykie's as he breathed hard. Tykie coughed.

"Santos? That you?"

"*Aquí estoy,* Tyke."

Santos moved in closer, cautious but confident.

"Man, I can't breathe. Feel like I'm choking."

"Shh. Don't try to talk, *carnal*. There's a doctor on the way, homeboy."

Santos rubbed his shoulder.

"*Sabes qué*, bro? I've caught bullets before, but never anything like this, man. I don't know if I'm gonna make it this time, know what I mean? I can't feel my legs and my arms, my arms, my arms . . . "

The atmosphere of compassion was so contagious that even Mad Dog softened, trying his best to sound encouraging.

"*Cálmate*, bro. Don't talk like that. *Debes tener fé.*"

"Montoya's right, Tykie. Show some faith, *vato.*"

Tykie's voice sounded like a child's. "*Familia.* I never got to start my own *familia. Oye*, Santos, you got a boy, *qué no*?"

"Yeah, man. I got a boy, but I haven't even seen him yet."

A gurney echoed through the far corridor.

Tykie began to sob.

"But you got somebody to pray for you, *verdad*?"

"Yeah, but you got somebody to pray for you, too, *ese*. You got us to pray for you, Tykie. Did you hear what I just said?"

Santos held Tykie in his arms but his breathless body grew heavy. A wet, real tear of surrender crawled across the black tattooed tear on Tykie's left eye onto his throat where Santos noticed, for the first time, the tattooed words, next to a pair of dice, in the Old English style.

270

"Mi Vida Loca."

Tykie's eyes fluttered shut. His heart stopped. The doctor arrived. Too late.

§ § §

The doctor entered the waiting room and took off his glasses so his vision would be blurred. On purpose. He spoke the words like a business report that he had been forced to deliver too many times before.

MariLuz held Adelita's hand.

"The bad news is that the cancer was a little bigger than we had expected. The good news is that we may have caught it in the very *early* stages. We'll want to operate right away. Did you have any questions?"

They didn't.

Adelitas Notebook #3,317

The tragedy of when almost all words lose their meaning . . . There are some situations in our lives when words are so inadequate, cannot describe, mean nothing. But we're stuck with them. Our thoughts are connected to words, and our thoughts just can't, just don't, just won't stop. After a while my thoughts shift away from me and Mom. Away from this situation and this place in time. My thoughts wander, like ants, cautiously, to wonder about that woman with the coal-black hair over there, alone in this waiting room. Does she have a daughter? A mother? A sister who is going through surgery right now? Underneath her dark maroon sweater, what terrors, doubts, disappointments or what aspirations, hopes, plans does she carry in her heart for herself and her sister? her cousin? her aunt? or possibly herself?

Strange how, after the shock of finding ourselves in challenging, sometimes overwhelming circumstances, we can start to feel empathy for others in similar situations, as well as feel tremendous respect and gratitude for these doctors, nurses, technicians, and orderlies.

Before, they seemed so invisible, so ordinary, so all-the-same. Now, the work of their minds, eyes, and hands can be the living means and expressions of that word: Hope. I can't look at doctors with neutrality anymore. They are all special to me because they are all special to my somebody special. I can't look at any of the other people in the waiting room without caring. Call it contagious compassion.

XLV

Maribel wiped the tear from her eye. She put the black and white picture of Santos, leaning against the white plaster of their *chante*, smiling during better times, back on her altar and lit a new beeswax candle. What am I going to do now, she wondered, as she put the geranium back in its place on the altar.

"Go back to the beginning?" she asked herself out loud as she walked over to José Rumaldo's small bed.

Halfway there, she stopped at the picture of Delfina on the darkened hallway. She made the sign of the cross on the image of her best friend and said a silent prayer, in her heart.

"If that's all I can do, then . . . "

Mari remembered that Fr. Galli had told her once that sometimes all we can do, in certain situations, is to surrender to God's will and pray.

Mari picked up a couple of José's little stuffed mice and glanced at his other sleeping toys. The thought of Santos not being here to watch his son growing up ripped her heart sideways. She almost stumbled over José's wooden blocks and plastic dinosaurs.

"What is all this for?" she sobbed. "There is something more important."

§ § §

Santos leaned back against the concrete and put his plastic Bic pen and worked-over paper down.

"What am I gonna do now?" he asked the unhearing and unspeaking universe.

Santos had just written a kind of poem/remembrance to read at Tykie's upcoming Memorial service.

"Go back to the beginning?" offered Santos' cellmate, Louie Mascarenas.

Louie had been telling Santos, for days, to write about his and Tykie's days coming up together.

Champagne didn't feel that would be good enough. He sighed, "If that's all I do, then . . . "

In Champagne's mind, there was an argumentative voice that insisted that no part of a person's life can be summed up by words, no matter how eloquent. The limits of words, *ese* . . . So why try? For him, at this time, words were inadequate, couldn't describe, and almost meant nothing. He also thought that he couldn't look at even the meanest, most suffering and suffering-causing inmate with neutrality anymore.

§ § §

Louie thought back to the bloody scene in the dayroom of B Block a couple days ago and sorrowed out loud, "What was this all for?"

To get their minds on something else, Louie switched on the radio, catching the desperate preacher's voice, mid-scream: "There is something more important!"

§ § §

For the first time, Adelita trusted a personal decision with Professor Romero. She had come to him and shared the news of her mother's illness.

"What am I gonna do now?" she sobbed as she handed him the Withdraw From Class Without a Grade card.

He shook his head. No. He had previously asked her to postpone any decision to quit school until after tomorrow. The day of her mother's surgery.

"Go back to the beginning?"

No, he shook his head. Romero had already showed her that she had turned in 80% of her semester's required assignments. She had already been published six times in the *Daily Lobo*. Plus, there was that trio of Guest Author pieces printed in the *Albuquerque Journal*. He had noticed. Extra Credit for that. Her participation in the Intern Program was splendid. No, no dropping out. He offered her the option of doing one last, self-designed piece. As long as it was accompanied by some journal entries, documenting her thoughts at several stages of her research. He pushed the optional assignment description towards her.

Adelita was surprised at the thick stack of paper and asked, "If this is all I need to do, then what are all these extra pages for?"

Romero lifted the top two pages off the stack and pointed to the title on the packet underneath.

"There is something more important."

She read the title of the Xeroxed article: "How to Keep Your Peace While Finishing Your Piece" by Professor Romero. The subtitle read: "Spiritual Tools for Recovering Workaholics."

§ § §

"What am I gonna do now?" Dr. McAllister muttered to himself.

It had been a long, continuous day of operations. This was his last surgery of the day. His mission: follow-up on the previous surgery to locate and remove any remaining cancerous tissue from Delfina Chávez' breast. His dilemma was the shock at finding so little infected tissue after he made the incision.

"Do I go back to the beginning," he asked himself. After re-examining the primary spot, he concluded, without a doubt, that the lump that had shown up on the x-rays appeared to have shrunk significantly. Hmmmm.

He cut the small area of tissue and thought to himself, "If that's all I do, then what was all this for?"

But he knew that, however small the cancer, it would have spread had it not been removed immediately. It just always amazed him that such a large opening had to be created to get at the small poison inside. Although still feeling fatigued, he told the assisting nurse that he would close the wound himself.

While he worked on stitching up the suture, his fatigue and his world-weariness rapidly disappeared. He realized there was something more important. The use of modern medicine was his talent and ability and duty, and people like Delfina Chávez and her daughter counted on it.

Dr. McAllister then mused, smiled, and thought of the peace and joy on the faces he would encounter as he told the elder and younger Chávez women of the successful surgery. Dr. McAllister consoled himself with these thoughts and reflections that helped him transcend his aching feet and burning hands. All of this was for all of that.

§ § §

Champagne suddenly awoke to the desperate coyote's cry, wailing out in the thirsty midnight desert, outside the cold bars of his sleeping cell. The wild animal's lament was replaced by the memory of his father's gravely voice, humbly singing the old *alabado* :

"Alma, pues en mi passion, me has acompañando fiel y digo con mi corazón, de tus culpas el perdón, te pido,por siempre, por siempre."

("Dearest soul, during my passion you have stayed faithful to me, and I say, with all my heart, that I ask pardon for your sins, for ever and ever . . . ")

XLVI

"What was I thinking?"

Santos silently asked himself, repeatedly. "All my life what have I been thinking? Or not thinking, that I should have. Even worse, not doing, that I should have. I am so alone," he reflected wordlessly.

It wasn't the aloneness that comes when they transfer your cellmate and now you don't even have a guy like Louie Mascarenas to talk to, even though you never did share what was really in your heart or mind. You couldn't and didn't do something like that in a place like this.

No. This was the kind of loneliness that haunts you when you wonder what you did with your life besides sleep, eat, drink, shit, talk, cry, laugh, think; but you really did nothing good to change this *pinche* world. However small our little worlds really are. Did I do nothing I can have some pride in having accomplished? Did I just live for myself and do a lousy job of even that?

The engulfing sadness was swallowing him *en un grande onda de tristeza*. He lay on his hard, stinking bed and shut out the decaying cries of grief that reverberated through the corridors of this 24-hour house of bitter pain.

Champagne had gotten to that plateau of solitude that most men and women get to, if they live long enough. That ungentle, harsh, and bitter void that can't be filled

278

with literature, movies, music, money, sex, time, power, or dreams. Santos was in that scary space where the mind and the heart can't be consoled by accomplishments or family, by travel or rest, by companionship or solitude. Santos had reached the end, that too-real place beyond which it is impossible to go, to hide from, or to remain in.

Santos cooled himself in a pool of truth. Now he knew that there is no such thing as a curse to blame your troubles on. Now he knew about the love of a father for a son. Now he knew of the gift of grace.

Like the way the planet halts during a total eclipse, no, even bigger, like the universe holding its breath for one sacred moment.

Santos Sánchez spoke to God with his entire being and gave up all he had or was. This was one-on-one. For the first time in his existence, he stopped grasping, wanting, holding, or being. He surrendered. Totally.

A few moments later, the universe began breathing again, the earth continued turning, and Santos began being. Just being. But. In a new way. Santos was now in the center of serenity.

The Bible that MariLuz Moya had once sent with Maribel when she used to come and visit, fell off the shelf and landed, face open, next to him. He read a few lines and then rolled into the most peaceful dream sleep of his entire life.

"Love bears all things, believes all things, hopes all things, endures all things."

1 Corinthians 13

XLVII

Santos leaned out of the cedar-smelling canoe on the river of dreams and saw his father's face reflected where his own should be. The shock transplanted Santos back to that wolf-bite cold night in the front seat of his dad's car, frozen in a still parking lot. Then the sounds of beer- soaked laughs and wild *gritos* muffled behind the red-lettered Cisco's Barbershop window echoed in between the breaths of the incoming wind. That familiar paralyzing feeling of being left alone frosted Santos' shoulders and face. Then something unfamiliar happened that changed everything. This time, Santos looked into the face of the haunted *Pachuco* outside. He wore a black trench coat and pointed a shaking small gun straight at the boy in the icy claws of the Chevy. Santos ducked and then heard his father's voice yell like a bullet aimed at the stranger out there.

"*Cabrón, déjalo solo.* What the hell are you doing around here, anyway?"

The scared 19- year-old with the gun leaped and crossed old Bridge Boulevard in five sudden jumps and melted into the hungry mouth of a January freeze. It was quiet as death. Then Santos heard his own heartbeat start up again, steady as a *Ranchera* band in his ears.

And his father's son looked into the watery brown

eyes of Eddie López. The father who chased away the danger. The father who, at the last minute, remembered him and left the beer, the poker friends, the *pachanga* of a desolate Saturday night. The tears from his father's pained face said more than any *dichos* or promise, or *canción* or prayer ever could.

La Soledad recognized herself across a century from the Basque country to *el Valle Sur*. A picture was completed and made mature in the moment of dream-world understanding. Forgiveness strengthens the one that gives it and blesses the one that receives it.

Awake. Champagne Sánchez had outgrown his old life. The world was no longer a rabid dog that could take a bite out of him, in any possible way. He now walked differently. The universe once again breathed, spun, wrecked, and got up again. The planet whirled, lit up, darkened and then glowed again.

Champagne walked with an inner strength felt by the others as he strolled past them down the corridor to the dayroom.

On his way in, Barney Stewart made the mistake of asking, "Hey, Champagne, did you make parole?"

Santos didn't even blink or get out of step but calmly marched in as Billy Thompson whacked Stewart on the head.

"Shhh. It didn't go well for him."

But it didn't matter.

Champagne sat by himself near the Price is Right crowd and pulled his Bible out and read to himself as the crowd pokered, TV-watched, smoked, joked, and dominoed.

The relative peace and order was broken by a young man's voice.

"Just leave me alone, eh?"

It was Joaquin Lucero, Vásquez' lost nephew, and Champagne had been watching over him out of the corner of his eye. Lucero's face was twisted in pain as Montoya reached out and grabbed him by the neck.

"You owe me money, punk." Mad Dog was pissed.

The crowd in B Block Dayroom moved outward to let Champagne by as he floated, not walked, over to the disturbance.

"Let him go," Santos gently ordered.

"This punk burned me. We bet, fair and square, on the Bronco game. Now he doesn't want to pay."

Champagne removed Montoya's arm and pulled it backwards as he commanded, "I don't care what it was. He's not to be touched. *Me entiendes?*"

Montoya started to stand, caught himself, and sat back down.

"My arm, Champagne."

Santos continued to burn a hole in Mad Dog's eyes as he let go of Montoya's arm.

"What's he owe you, Montoya?"

"Twenty bucks. But, hey man, who does he think he is?"

Champagne peeled a couple of $20 bills from the small roll he pulled from his pocket. He shot a glance at the two guards who quit staring, who forgot about rules against contraband and who looked away.

"Spread the word, Montoya. Nobody touches the Lucero kid."

Montoya rubbed his arm where the soreness throbbed.

"*Órale.* Nobody touches him."

On his way back to his meditation spot, Jessie Villa whispered to Champagne, "Hey, Sánchez. This the Lucero kid that Vásquez talked to you about? Why you going out on a limb for him?"

Champagne stopped in his tracks.

"Why not?"

"You didn't get paroled. Hell with his nephew, right?"

"*No le hace.* A deal's a deal. I always keep my word. That's the way it is."

Sánchez went back to his Bible, the Price is Right crowd returned after a brief message from the sponsor, and Montoya put in an order for more cigarettes from the canteen with the guards who accepted $20 for not busting him with contraband that was the other $20 bill that they confiscated and agreed to deposit in his Canteen account.

Another day among the many. In a changing universe.

XLVIII

Mercy was in the air. Adelita had just gotten her mother into bed and there was a knock at the front door.

"*¿Hay alguien?*"

"Come in, the doors open. Is that you Mrs. Sánchez?"

Maribel rushed in, past the living room and then into Delfina's bedroom. She put the marigolds on the nightstand and bent over to carefully embrace Delfina.

"*Dios te bendiga, comadre.*"

"*Igualmente, comadre.*"

"And God bless you, Adelita."

Mari gave her a greeting *abrazo*.

Delfina spoke with an angel's contentment in her voice, "I thank you, *comadre*, for all your prayers. They got all the cancer out!"

"Thank God the operation was a success. You look really great, Delfina."

"God has been good to me. I feel great. It feels so good to be back here, even if it is an old creaky house."

Maribel sat in the chair Adelita brought for her.

"Oh, did you hear? They're going to build some new J & J Apartments in that lot across from Dorinda's house. If you want to get on the waiting list, I could call."

"Maribel, thanks. Really, I'd rather stay here. Wouldn't we, huh, *M'ijita?*"

284

"Sí, Mamá. We're just fine here."

Delfina got that smile in her eyes.

"*Díme*, how is José Rumaldo doing?"

"Oh, *comadre*, he's been crawling a lot. And, his first birthday is on March third, *fíjate!*"

"Where does the time go?"

Adelita nodded, "Excuse me, Mamá. Maribel. I need to do some more typing. I'll be in my room."

"Okay, *M'ijita*." Delfina continued, "One thing I was reminded of, going through this operation *y todo*. How short life is, *qué no*? How precious little time we have here."

"*¿Verdad, no?*" Maribel echoed.

"*Verdad. Sí. ¿Sabes qué*, Mari? I think you should think about giving Santos another chance. Not that he deserves it. It's true, he did some pretty stupid things, *pero*, we're all human, right? We all make mistakes."

"*Tienes razón*, Delfina. I've been praying on it. As soon as the time seems right, *comadre*."

Delfina laughed that old, familiar laugh.

"*Ay, qué vida*. Remember the Grand Opening of the Chante Sánchez Restaurant?"

"How could I ever forget? Remember? That was the first painting I ever sold!"

Adelita interrupted their laughter. Her tone was somewhat serious, meaning business mixed with asking permission.

"Mamá? Mrs. Sánchez? I'm doing some investigating that has to do with the prison. I'd like to talk to Santos about some things going on there. What do you think about me getting my name put on his Visitors List?"

Mari felt another layer of resentment crumbling away.

Mari looked at Delfie, who nodded yes.

"Yes," Mari answered, "if you want I will make sure your name gets put on the list. If you go see him, tell him he's still in my prayers. And that I miss him. And Josecito misses him."

Adelita's Notebook #3,401

I'm a little scared. What the hell have I gotten myself into? I could have just gone on observing the situation, pretty much de lejos, getting as close as I wanted to, when I wanted to, and how I wanted to. But now, once I go and see mi primo, El Champagne, as some call him, what will change? It's been quite a while since he's seen me—actually since that horrible scene at the city jail, my first real glimpse at the justice system. I have so many questions, concerns, and doubts.
Will Santos have expectations of me? Will he be disappointed if I get some of his story out and nobody cares or does anything about the way he's been burned (the way Profe Romero seems to think)? Or will he already be so cynical that he won't give a damn? I have heard that inmates rapidly, some permanently, become contemptuous and scornful.

Maybe he'll trust me but maybe I'll change? Could it be that the more I see, the more I'll understand what I'm up against? I don't want to give up on la causa, or on Santos, or on my own determination and strength of will. Our vecina, Magdalena, tells me that she keeps me in her prayers, (just like I know that my mom does, in spite of her weak condition) y, Santa Maria, do I ever need them now.

I even wonder if I'm not partly getting into this just to spend some time away from having to watch Mom suffer (although she is getting a little better every day). Why does life contain so much suffering? Still, even at its most challenging, there always seems to be a reason to get up tomorrow and do something con el día que Dios me dió.

Adelita put her pen down and placed her journal on her nightstand, next to the pre- surgery picture of *Mamá*. She glanced at the faded black and white snapshot of her mother and her father that she kept taped to the wall, close to her bed. Delfie told her before her surgery that the time had come for her to know that her father, Modesto Chavez, had died of a heroin overdose when she was just three years old. Adelita had been too young, all these years, to understand, but Delfina wanted her to know that her dad was actually a good man, just careless. It was the very first time he had ever experimented with drugs. The 'fallout' of War.

287

§ § §

While pulling his surgical gown off at the end of the long, long day, Dr. McAllister flashed back to pulling off the gown that he wore as an altar boy, all those years ago.

Remembering those early mornings at San Felipe Church, McAllister recalled that the priests there always spoke of hearing confessions. He then wondered how his practice would be different if he thought in terms of hearing his patients. He also knew that hearing his patients and their family members would mean taking into account what they didn't say as much as what they did. He could model his 'listening to patients' after what Diane-Martinez Hursh did with her acupuncture recipients.

Dr. McAllister was now haunted by the face of Adelita, the daughter of Delfina, the woman whose cancer had shrunk without explanation. Why was Adelita's father not there with her in the waiting room when he came out to share the good news? Did she even have a dad?

§ § §

Champagne looked at the handkerchief on the scratched-up, ink-splattered table in front of him. His left hand held the off-white cloth flat and his right hand fingers gripped around a ballpoint pen. *La Merced* patted his shoulder and praised Santos.

Self-respecting *Pinto*, you knew how to make time serve you instead of just serving time.

You got one of your homeboys to teach you how to create this art form born in jails or prison cells called *Paño arte* on handkerchiefs and pieces of torn pillowcases or sheets. Look at the hourglasses, cell bars, sexy women, pairs of dice, men *con bigotes* looking like Emiliano Zapata, Tragedy-and-Comedy masks, prison guard towers, stylized peacocks and the merciful face of Our Lady of Guadalupe, all creatively combined in blue or black ballpoint pen ink collages on the white mini-canvasses. They hang on the walls for decoration or are folded into letters to wives, children, girlfriends, or fellow gang-bangers on the outs as a way to communicate hope, grief, sorrow, faith, understanding or just basic self-expression. You realize that, for the first time in your life, you are drawing, Santos. You're putting down on handkerchiefs images that were born in your head and ended up on the cotton square in front of you. You realize that you're making Art in the middle of Hell. Not a bad way to make your time serve you, #52 1-11.

Santos made several image-filled hankies and included banners with the words 'Maribel, por Vida' or 'Mi Hijo, José' encircling perfect hearts and roses on his *Paños*.

§ § §

Maribel tore open the envelope from prisoner #52 1-11 and unfolded the white handkerchief with the ink images and the word 'Respeto' in the Old English script-style and found the five twenty dollar bills (and the Official Canteen Account Withdrawal Form) with a short note written in Santos' crude cursive scrawl.

"My dear Maribel. I earned this in the Prison Shop and it's for you and for toys for mi hijo, José Rumaldo. Hope it helps."

XLIX

The sickness-of-the-soul that had haunted Santos for so many years lifted. Consequently, a lot of things about him changed. He only spoke when he had something to say; he would still laugh, once in a while, but not too much at anything cruel or vulgar. Champagne no longer walked as much as he seemed to float or roll from place to place. Nothing seemed to bother him anymore and some old defenses were gone.

So, when informed that he had a visitor, Santos simply responded, "I'll be ready in a couple minutes."

Sitting in the Visitor's Room, a few couples quietly murmuring all around them, Santos faced the professionally-dressed Chicana across the table, his cousin, a notebook in her hand.

"Mr. Sánchez, I know we've never been close and you probably are wondering why I'm here."

"Call me Santos, *prima*. Yes, we hardly know each other. Our paths haven't crossed that much. You've really changed since I last saw you, but you are Delfina's girl, right?"

"Right. I'm her only child."

"I heard a little about you. You're the one in college, huh?"

Adelita blushed. "That's right. I'm studying journalism. In fact, that's why I'd like to talk to you. You see, I'm in this intern program and I'd like to interview you."

"Adelita, I don't think that would be such a good idea. We had somebody in here from *The People's Voice* the other day. We trusted her, told her a lot, and what came out of that was a three-day lockdown, transfers like crazy, harassment. I'm afraid not."

"*Pero escúcheme*, Sr. Sánchez, er, Santos. I believe there's a lot of injustice in the court and the judicial systems, especially against Latinos as well as Black and Native Americans and poor whites, but the only way people can change the *sistema* is if they're informed."

Pause. Santos smoothed out a wrinkle on his prison-issue shirt.

"Adelita." Pause, "How are my wife and kid doing? You must see Mari sometimes, *verdad*?"

He knew by her partial-smile what she was going to say.

"She's doing better these days. Your son is growing and seems happy. In fact, Mrs. Sánchez, uh, Maribel, told me to make sure and tell you that she misses you and that you are in her thoughts and prayers."

Something inside warmed his blood and sang to his soul.

"Do me a favor, Adelita. Don't forget to tell her that I still love her very much and care for her even though I haven't seen her in too, too long."

"*Te prometo.* I'll go over today and give her that message."

"'*Lo agradezco mucho. Bueno,* so what do you want to know about things in here, *en la Pinta?*"

She excitedly opened her notebook and got out her trusty Bic fine-line pens.

"Well, for starters, did you guys get the new TV sets for your day rooms that were donated by Gato Blanco Electronics last month?"

"You kidding? Word around here is that those tax-deductible TVs were sold off by Warden Eichwald, like all the other donations that somehow get lost in transit on their way here. In fact, before I tell you all about this printing press that was supposed to be relocated here to be used in the Print Shop, let me ask you something."

She put her pen down, something Adelita rarely did.

Santos Sánchez leaned forward and lowered his voice.

"I think we should look at the bigger picture here. Would you be able and willing to do a little research for me?"

"Yes, I would, Mr. Sanch- . . . Santos."

Santos glanced to either side, then clarified, "See, the materials in our little library here are somewhat limited to donations and there's this project that I'm working on. Your technical assistance would be greatly appreciated."

"Anything to help, I mean it."

And she did.

"First of all, you need to understand that any and all

mail I receive is read and searched, so I'm going to set up a code that you will use to tell me about certain connections I am investigating. You'll want to start writing, now, in your notebook."

And she did.

"José Vásquez, the F.B.I. Agent, will hereafter be referred to as the *Puma*. Tony Giovanni, the People's Lawyer, you've heard of him, right?"

She rolled her eyes and nodded.

"Giovanni will be called, in all of our communications, the *Víbora*. Henry Puente, the local real estate baron will be referred to as the *Rey*. Our esteemed Warden Eichwald will be the *Buitre*. Governor Wooten is the Peacock. Ned Hutchinson, of the Parole Board . . . "

By the time the two-hour visit concluded, Santos Sánchez had given Adelita plenty to keep her busy during her time in Zimmerman Library on campus. Adelita flew out, justice on her mind. As she walked out past the gates topped with razor-barbed wire, she reflected on how tranquil Santos had seemed. Hmmm. That cousin of mine sure seemed at peace with himself, even though he's in the midst of all that human misery. I wonder what it takes to become a person so comfortable in their own skin.

Santos floated back to his cell, almost nothing in either of his two minds.

L

"Da Da?" Little José Rumaldo shook as he leaned against the altar and pointed to the photo of Santos.

Maribel bit her knuckles to hold back a sob, and then she said, "Yes, José. That is Da-Da. That's your father, Josecito."

The knock on the door distracted them both, "¿Comadre, estás lista?" Delfina yelled from outside.

"Just about ready, Delfina. Come in, amiga."

Maribel picked José up and put him in his used stroller. They were on their way to the Albuquerque Zoo.

The best friends half-listened to Mary Howard, the local Channel 9 news reporter as she wrapped up the morning broadcast.

"Finally, speaking of the local economy, prominent businessman Ned Hutchinson announced, last night, that he and his associates will be publishing local, as well as regional writers of Southwest fiction, satire, and folklore. The company will be called Gato Negro Books, Inc."

Adelita's Notebook #3,497

Gato Negro Books? Are they serious? This new publishing venture by Ned Hutchinson is . . . oh, this is beyond crazy. Maybe it's just a tax write-off scheme or something like that. Still, it is tempting to think about putting together some of my poems. If I took a look at the articles I've had published in the Journal, plus the ones that I didn't submit. I wonder if that would constitute a small book of essays. Or would they be considered too topical, without lasting value? May I should get some advice from that Editor I met, Marcela Landres. Hmmm.On the other hand, once you get published, once those words are out there, it's impossible to rein them back in, as Professor Romero has warned. If it's in print now, in a sense, it's in print forever. And what would I want to be known for, if I had to be known for anything? Exposing corruption? Bringing some beauty into the world, or offering another way of looking at things, through the publication of some of my poems? Yet so much will be out of my hands and depend on the publisher and the editors. Ultimately, what gets out there and in what form?

The one thing that is mine, that I do have—and it can be consoling—is at least some control over my writing process. My morning free writes. Here in the 7:38 a.m. New Mexico sun, after and during coffee, and before that loud, noisy, distracting world intrudes and drowns out the quiet beauty. These are precious gentle, soul-nourishing moments. Playing with words can be

an in-spiriting activity. Time can sometimes be
kind.

LI

Months had passed. José was trying to walk and talk more, and was succeeding. Maribel had started visiting Santos. The bitter sadness at having to say "*Adios*," to his wife and kid grew deeper each time. The man ached with sorrow.

Today, after his morning prayers, Champagne addressed a letter to Special Agent Vásquez.

Later on, Champagne watched an Orson Welles black and white masterpiece called *The Third Man* on TV for the ninth time.

"Harry Lime never grew up. The world just grew up around him." Champagne declared in perfect unison with Italian actress Alida Valli.

Later on, Champagne picked up the latest copy of *The People's Voice* and read a short article on a nurse, Cathy Chávez, from the North Valley who had used her bilingual skills to communicate between the oncology doctors, the children with leukemia, and their parents on treatment plans. (There was also a sidebar piece on Cathy's husband, Ruben, who worked in the Gang Intervention Program, struggling to produce a truce between warring street gangs.) It wasn't just politics in *The Voice* these days. They were also taking notice of some local, silent heroes. Santos got inspired to write some *recuerdos* in the hardback journal that Maribel had given him during her last visit. After reflecting on his reflections, Santos began a new entry.

"I am going to have to be the father to José Rumaldo that I never had. This will be the main part of my life's work."

§ § §

Sixty miles south, Josecito played with the red and blue finger-paints that Delfina had given him. Maribel began a series of Sacred Hearts that she would add to the half-dozen Guadalupanas that she would leave for sale on consignment at the Old Town Basket Shop. Little did she know that one of her Virgen de *Guadalupe* Retablos would end up in the hands of the mother of a popular Chicano actor, Edward James Olmos, who bought one while visiting in Old Town.

Adelita's Notebook #3,499

The Peoples Voice? Hmmm, well, why not? Why not write for them, for at least a season? Fact is, from what I have heard, their circulation keeps growing, phenomenally fast with every issue (especially now that they have proven that the Governor's re-election committee accepted so much money from rich Texans). They've gone from once a month to every other week, and rumors are that they'll be coming out weekly. Restaurants, bars, and art galleries are tripping over each other to take out ads in the hip new newspaper. Although they are only offering me a probationary contract, I have the confidence that I can hack it. They contacted me; I didn't have to seek them out. There was some mention of my integrity and independence fully in evidence in pieces that they had seen and admired from the Journal.

The Journal . . . hmmm. If I do accept this probationary position I'll have some leverage with which to approach the Journal, perhaps with a request to move from guest writer to, at least, part-time permanent. With graduation not too far off, maybe temporary full-time. Hmmm. I don't think I have anything to lose. Hmmm. I could develop a solid reputation by doing a season of work for The People's Voice, right? And now that Santos has given me the leads to these outrageous connections between Giovanni, Henry Puente, Warden Eichwald, the governor, etc . . . Since The Voice is always willing to take risks, I may need them as much as they seem to think they need me. The timing may be just perfect, perhaps an answer to prayers. Who knows, maybe with the growth of The Voice, that could end up being my dream job.

I'm leaning towards taking their offer. It would be consistent with living by one of my main mottos, that one from Kris Kristofferson: "I'd rather be sorry for something I did than for something I didn't do."

Yeah, I think I'll make the leap.

A couple miles East, MariLuz Moya sang De Colores, and the man sitting in front of her, for the first time in years, heard every gentle, healing note. After months of taking MariLuz's remedies, Old Man Gallegos was getting his hearing back. Word by word. Song by song.

§ § §

Just around the corner, Fr. Galli, after his evening prayers, gently strummed *Mi Redentor* on his Pimentel guitar and hoarsely hummed himself closer to the Saints.

§ § §

Irene, Adelita's distant cousin, put the finishing touches on her lesson plans for the upcoming week. It was time, once again, to do a check on what was going on in her fourth graders' lives, as so much from home eventually surfaced at school and it helped to have some insight into the live-in boyfriends, the users back on their drugs of choice, the latest family to have the head of household suddenly unemployed, and yes, their positive achievements, too, like the parent going back to school, the re-unification of couples, the successful graffiti clean up program, the fireman father who coached the baseball team and so on.

Only the student holding the Talking Stick could speak as the others in the circle had to respectfully listen until their time to speak truth, or pass, came. It was a very effective form of communication that she learned from her dad, Papa Ru, who had learned it from some Native Americans that he worked with in his capacity as a Gang Intervention Leader counseling Cholos. As Irene finished, her sister Celina, who was taking classes to become a teacher, came over to visit, bringing Annalisa, with a drawing of Grandma's zinnias, and Niko who had a drawing of an ice-cream cone, with a slice of bacon on top, to show off. Uncle John tore himself away from the Lobo basketball game on TV to look at the masterpieces. One day it would come to pass that future students like a future Santos or Tykie would be lucky enough to get a teacher like Irene or Celina or, who knows? Maybe even Annalisa or Niko would go into teaching . . .

A group of cousins gathered at Bill and Emily's house to put together a care package of things to send to cousin Santos: Marlene and Richard were donating some packages of *carne seca* (dried pieces of elk and deer meat dusted with Chimayo red chile powder), Margaret and Tony were sending him a new Bible to replace the one Santos had worn out, Susi and Jon put some cassettes of songs by Chicano bands like Thee Differentials and the Vintage Band for Santos to enjoy, and Joey was parting with his collection of Elvis Presley (from the early days at Sun Records) as well as a five-pack of brand new handkerchiefs for Santos' *Paño* artwork.

Sam put a cassette of his drum playing into the box of drawings by Noelle that would soon be sent up to Santos in Santa Fe. That same box held some photographs by Victoria and a book on Chicano murals for Santos that Deanna got for him during her last visit to the Chicago Art Institute. There were also some sketches made by Silas that his mom, Angel, made sure were part of the surprise. Jonathon sent a picture from one of his rock-climbing trips in Europe and Megan shared one of her small paintings of a jaguar. The package was complete when stuffed with some prayer books from Delilah and Raquel and one of Joey's Special Olympics ribbons.

§ § §

A couple miles north, Adelita Zoila Augusta Chávez opened the envelope and read the news, in black and white, that a probationary position as an investigative reporter for *The People's Voice* was hers. Her ninety-day probationary period was due to begin with her first day of work on Monday.

LII

With a barely-contained fury, Agent José Vásquez, envelope in hand, walked briskly behind Guard Robbins down the hallways, around several corners into Cell Block B to the front of the cell where Champagne Sánchez wrote dutifully in his journal, with a barely-contained passion for the truth, today's reflections and insights.

"What the hell is the meaning of this?" demanded Vásquez, crumbling the envelope with one paw.

Champagne didn't even look up. Or stop writing. He spoke authoritatively.

"Meaning should be clear. Inmate #52 1-11 has finally completed his personal investigation and made some key connections between certain pillars of the community and certain prominent local investors."

"I think you're bluffing, Champagne."

"Willing to bet your current freedom from prison on it? Better think again. You could someday find yourself in here."

Champagne calmly put the finishing touches on a *Letter to my Boy* as he removed the bookmark from his journal and finally looked up. The bookmark was a modest business card with the nicely typeset inscription: José Vásquez, Co-Director. Gato Negro Productions.

"Gato Negro." José whispered in a voice of panic.

"Yes, as well as Gato Blanco, Gato Colorado, Gato Azul. My how things have grown. If I don't hear back from you, or a representative from Gato Negro, and all the other fronts, a story is going to break, in *The People's Voice*. Every Thursday after this, a new revelation will come out. You won't be able to get a volunteer job after that, trust me. Unless it's here, in the joint. Wouldn't that be something, having you as a fellow *pinto*. Ha ha! Also, I don't think that Henry Puente, Ned Hutchinson, and the other guys you know very well will appreciate those articles coming out, either."

"Alright, alright. I get the point. You've got me. Put a stop on those stories, okay?"

"On the other hand, Tony Giovanni could probably care less what the public finds out about his financial ties, but Warden Eichwald and the governor? Different story."

"Alright, alright! Dammit. I'll start working on this as soon as I leave here. Just keep in mind, I can't control how the Board will vote on this list of requests."

"Aw, come on, José. As co-director, I think you can be most persuasive when you need to."

"Santos, why are you doing this to me?"

"Do you really need to ask? Am I just doing this to *you*? Think about what I am trying to do for me."

Pause.

"Okay, José. Think about it like this. Like you, I would like to be able to see, talk to, and hug my wife and son whenever I want. Every day. No waiting for visitor hours. Just *a familia*. Now, if you don't mind, I've got some writing to get back to."

The New Business items at that Friday's Emergency Board of Directors Meeting of Gato Negro Productions and its various subsidiaries were voted on in record time. Someone had brought them all together for the first time. True consensus. The votes were unanimous. Actions would be taken immediately. Talk about operating efficiently.

Adelita's Notebook #4,007

Out of the blue and into my soul. After class on Thursday, Antonio, whom I hadn't spoken with in weeks, asked if I wanted to join him for un cafecito y plática at the Common Grounds. At first, he mainly expressed admiration y mucho respeto for the several articles that I've done recently for The People's Voice on the growing escándalo involving the Republican Secretary of State. The Voice, by the way, is now the hottest weekly in town. Every copy flies off the newsstands on Thursday afternoons. In fact, Antonio asked me for any tips I might have about how he could get hired on, and then he laughed and said, "Not really. I wouldn't in any way want to compete with you. You took the initiative to get that job, and you're the best at it. La Raza, in fact toda la comunidad, needs you there."

He got nicer and nicer as we talked. Then, out of nowhere, he told me that it's been a while since he broke up with his girlfriend. "We just weren't compatible, we found out. Not politically, socially, or spiritually." Then, he said, "I won't put you on the spot now, but if you would just think about it maybe we could go see one of your foreign films at the Student Union Theater and go out for dinner afterward. Just think about it. I'll talk to you after class next week, okay?"

What's that they say about good things coming to those who wait? So now I'm thinking about it, but I really don't need to. Hmmm. Maybe I should start imagining where I'd like to go out to eat afterwards. No, not the Dog House, as good as those red chile, cheese, and onion-filled hot dogs taste; how about a meal at the Barelas Coffee House-nothing like those carnitas or tamale plates and not to forget their menudo con posole. Actually it's time to stop writing and go get something to eat.

LIII

He finished packing by placing the faded pictures on top of the prison-issue cardboard box they had given him. He took a look around for the last time at the graffiti-filled, cracked concrete wall and the steel wall of bars that had kept him in here for too long.

He wondered what it would be like to spend his first night sleeping without the sound and smell of metal doors and the decaying echoes of suffering men.

He wondered about all that had changed on the outs. And he was amazed by how much he had changed within. He thanked his first mind and his second mind for their life-saving friendship.

He wondered if that poor, misguided *vagabundo*, Eddie López, ever made peace with himself before he died. Santos remembered him in prayers, morning, mid-day and night. He had a deep curiosity about the condition of the soul of his old friend Tykie Mendoza. He felt reassured that the souls of his father- and mother-in-law were at rest.

He looked outside through the too-small window and spotted the greasy-black limousine as it arrived for the sole purpose of transporting prisoner # 52 1-11 straight from the Santa Fe Prison to the special press conference at the KiMo Theater in Albuquerque. He squinted his eyes in disbelief as thought he saw an apparition of long-gone Maldito, leaping in the shadows.

He laughed to himself at how fast life changed and at how being patient brought magnificent rewards. Like they say, he thought, Good things come to those who wait. Most of all, he knew that sometime today, after the emergency press conference and all that hoopla, he would spend the night with his wife and son.

Now Santos truly walked like a man who had gratefully outgrown his disbelief.

On his way out of Cell Block B, around the corners, all through the hallways, Santos Champagne Sánchez thought about how ironic it was that he was going to be released. After he surrendered—to the Divine—he had been set free, and always would be. His old life lay on the cold concrete floor, an invisible, matterless, skin of days forever gone.

La Mala Suerte and *La Soledad* watched him disappear through the gun-metal doors on his way to 'the outs,' inhaling freedom with every clean breath. They shrugged at each other, done with their attempts to try to make a *'Champagne Sánchez Curse'* a reality. Resigned to the fact that they had failed, they turned and walked back down the smelly and clanging corridors of *La Pinta*. Plenty of other *vagabundos* to keep them busy.

LIV

Champagne grinned a little grin and dropped the old cigar butt to the pavement and stomped it out. Champagne smiled at the limousine driver in the front, who had enjoyed conversing with him all the way.

"Thanks for the lift. You don't need to wait. I'll be driving home with my wife and kid. Just leave the cardboard box, uh, here. Here, in the box office of the KiMo theater. I'll pick it up on my way out."

He glided over to Adelita, who had just stepped out of the back seat of the limo.

"Really glad you're here, cousin. How did you like the ride?"

She grinned and nodded.

"You know, that research of yours really helped. So, here we are. Ready for the big doings here in the KiMo? Soon as I can, I'm taking you, your mom, Mari, and José out for *tacos de pastor* at El Festival, over on north Fourth Street."

Santos was so pumped he didn't give Adelita time to answer any of his questions or comments; he was a free man, speaking freely.

Adelita looked down.

"Oh, you don't owe me anything. Just glad I could help. Well, I think we better get in there, they're supposed to start the press conference any minute now. They can't do that without you. And I need a minute or so to wipe off my clothes."

He smiled from ear to ear.

"Yeah, time to take care of business."

On their way through the Pueblo Deco doors, past the *maiz*-colored tiled walls into the cozy lobby, Santos took one backward glance at the corner of Fifth Street and Central. From under the Von Hassler murals showing scenes of some Pueblos, he thought about a previous life of his, lived on these same streets of *machos, Malinches, pobres, payasos, xolos y ángeles*, but, back in the day, lived with a constant glance over his shoulders.

In the lobby, Adelita waved goodbye.

"Well, I'm on the job, now. See you later, *primo*. I'll be up front with the other reporters. Time for me to represent '*The People's Voice*'"

Adelita swept in with the crowd and disappeared into the restroom for a quick mud "clean up." Before Santos had a chance to take in his surroundings, prominent businessman and soon-to-be publisher Ned Hutchinson reverently took him by the arm and headed them down an aisle toward the long table and chairs set up on the bare stage.

"I understand you've been doing some writing these last few months, Mr. Sánchez. After this business here, maybe we could sit and talk about a publishing contract. Maybe you could write about some experiences from, er, uh from your incarceration experiences, huh? I understand that memoirs are going to be a real hot item this fall."

"I don't know about that. Maybe. Mostly, I've been writing for myself. We'll see."

Ned directed Champagne onto the stage to the empty seat in the middle of the row of well-padded chairs. Champagne poured himself a glass of ice-water as he surveyed the crowd in front of him. Oblivious to the nervous buzz, about eight rows down to his left, sat Maribel and Delfina, tranquil expressions on their faces. Mari smiled and lifted José Rumaldo from her lap. She helped him wave his little arm. José laughed at the whole world around him. Seated next to them was the flamenco dancer and special education teacher known simply to her students and their parents as Miss 'B.'

"Testing one, two, three," Ned muttered into screeching microphones.

Mr. Wasson from the KiMo sound crew adjusted the sound board. Anchorwoman Mary Howard gestured to cameraman Frank Zuñiga, who aimed his camera, and his assistant, Laurence Manzanares, switched on the bright stage lights. Frank focused on Valentina, sitting in the second row, putting away her nail polish and smiling for the TV camera that then turned toward Ms. Howard. Her voice was business mixed with charm.

"This is Mary Howard, reporting live for KQUE, from the KiMo Theater Press Conference hosted by Gato Negro Productions. Scheduled to begin at any minute now, it is expected that local attorney and Gato Negro board president Giovanni will announce . . . "

Mary Howard continued her commentary briefly, and then Frank aimed his camera at the slightly-disheveled man standing and speaking into the mike.

"Good morning, ladies and gentlemen, fellow shareholders, and members of the press," mumbled The People's Lawyer. "I want to thank you all for attending and for showing up with such a short notice. I, myself, was driven over here directly from . . . well, never mind. Let's start."

Champagne began to take inventory of the well-groomed and expensive-suited group to his left and to his right. There were a few that he couldn't identify and some he began to recognize from their photos in the *Who's Who in New Mexico* book, courtesy of the Chamber of Commerce. On his left was the *Rey* of the local real estate racket, Henry Puente. Next to him was, well, what do you know, Perry Lewis, Warden Eichwald's Special Assistant and Advisor. Next to him was Gino Franco, Secretary of Corrections, and he didn't seem to look all that happy on this momentous occasion.

State policemen, as well as special agents who usually accompanied the governor, didn't normally attend press conferences but a small army were on hand, standing next to the stage and up and down both main aisles, watching every move that Santos made and whispering into their miniature headsets.

It probably didn't help that every once in a while someone would holler, "*Viva Santos Sánchez!*" and "*Órale pues*, Champagne!"

Yeah, the 'hometown crowd' was arriving, chewing gum, laughing and shaking hands with each other, offering *"Buenos días le de Dios"* and other respectful salutations in the ever louder buzz of a growing crowd.

To Champagne's right was a significant representation of all those major movers and shakers, as identified and honored by the Chamber. Each and every mover checked his or her watch repeatedly, fidgeting as though sitting on saguaro cactus limbs. Their eyes darted in all directions like paranoid schizophrenics in a psych ward.

Why, here was Bill Schwartz, Ned's partner on the Parole Board and the Director of the Stocks and Bonds Division of Gato Negro Productions. To his right sat Rusty Barks, Governor Wooten's trusty aide and the Chairman of the Governor Wooten Re-Election Committee. Next to him, a man looked down at his folded hands. Special Agent Vásquez seemed to be doing an awful lot of self-reflection. Most of those people Champagne only knew through Adelita's research and his subsequent letters to them. They were pretty spiffed up for the occasion. And really, really nervous.

Anthony Salvatore Giovanni, The People's Lawyer, wiped the sweat off his brow and continued speaking into the microphone. "At this time, it is my extreme pleasure to introduce to you the newest nominee to our Board of Directors, a dynamic and truly visionary young man, Mr. Santos Sánchez!"

All 630 seats in the old KiMo were filled with people from all corners of the community and from so many stations in life. Everyone in the audience leapt up, from Magdalena Moya to Professor Romero, from the lead singer of the West Ella Band to all those cousins who had sent Santos packages of deer jerky, cigarettes, handkerchiefs, and candy, only days and weeks ago. Santos then stood and acknowledged the thunderous applause, grinned, and gestured for the crowd to sit down.

While they quieted down and sat, Giovanni went on. "Mr. Sánchez comes to us in his capacity as a nominee to be the new Chief Executive Officer of the NuMex Utilities Corporation." Enthusiastic applause, especially, for some strange reason, from all those gathered movers and shakers.

Giovanni went on, "I would like to note that Mr. Sánchez will also be asked to serve as Committee Chair for the governor's new Ex-Offender Employment Program."

More applause with movers and shakers throwing in a whistle or two.

Giovanni added, "Also, Mr. Sánchez will be appointed to the position of Treasurer for the Governor's Re-Election Campaign, if he will accept this offer."

Applause, hoots and howls from the movers and shakers and the other curious and happy *plebe* including Irene's fourth-graders up in the balcony, everyone leaping to their feet. It was too much. Too much to take in or understand after so much time spent hearing human beings curse and threaten each other with every breath.

After Santos raised his arms and managed to get

them quiet and sitting again, he spoke softly with a tranquil authority. Everyone, including old man Gallegos savored every sincere word that Santos offered. Mrs. Jaramillo, quiet in a corner and recalling his vacuum cleaner sales talk so long ago, marveled at his improved presentation skills.

"Thank you, Mr. Giovanni, Gato Negro Board members, members of the press. *Estimado público*."

He caught Maribel wiping a tear from one eye.

"*Familia y amigos,* and to a very special *amiga, mi prima, Adelita. Mi amor Mari y mi hijo, José Rumaldo.* There was a time when people called me 'Champagne,' but now I appreciate just being called Santos. These days I have a greater understanding of the lives and the ways of los Santos."

He took a deep breath and felt the moment in its fullness.

"I'm honored by your faith in my ability. I appreciate your offers of jobs and positions and all. But . . . "

It got so quiet you could have heard a cat walking on a lawn.

"After careful contemplation and thought, I have decided to ask the Gato Negro Board to excuse me from these offers for positions of power and to ask for a little favor."

A shocked murmur spread around the gathered crowd; family, friends and friends of friends looked at each other in pure surprise. Most of the movers and shakers on the stage had faces of pure terror at the possible revelations that might be coming from the gentle, but self-assured voice of Santos Sánchez in the next several minutes.

Adelita put her pencil down and looked up, wondering, is he going to expose the whole large conspiracy, right now, in front of all these *Burqueños* with live TV coverage?

The murmurs of shock spread like electricity through the KiMo Theater, growing in intensity. Santos spotted Josecito sticking his hand into his mouth. Probably getting another tooth. Santos glanced at the box seat section on the right-hand side of the balcony in time to see *La Mala Suerte* being chase off by a rejuvenated *La Merced*. In the wings of the stage, to Santos' left, was MariLuz, encircled by the protective smoke from a sage smudge stick. She hummed a prayer to St. Michael, the defender against evil. A calm descended on the gathered crowd as the ancient healing smoke drifted over everyone's head. Even the *Maestros* of the *Mexica* dance group, Ehecatl, Paz (Mapitzmitl) and his wife and spiritual sister, Rita (Yeikoatl) Zamora had shown up to bless *la comunidad* with their *danza* and other aspects of *Floricanto*, gathered behind the theater scrim, onstage, but hidden.

"All I've ever wanted was just an even chance to provide for *mi familia*. If the Gato Negros, here, would give me a loan, I would simply like to start my own combined tamale, fireworks, and landscaping business."

Most members of the audience and the press corps looked at each other trying to understand his simple request. But for Maribel, Adelita, and Delfina, it struck them as both somewhat funny, yet, given the changes they had seen him go through, it made sense, in a *pura vida loca* sort of way.

With the crowd hanging on his every word, Santos pondered what he had just said and, the power growing inside his being, he continued, with renewed assuredness.

"Seriously, the way I look at it," he continued, his finger pointing upward, somewhat philosophically, "I would get a chance, with my small business, to sell my *tamales* in a different neighborhood every day while I got some landscaping done and I could end off the day selling fireworks, year-round, to the kids *a dondequiera*."

"Of course, as with all business dealings, there would be a few conditions that would have to be met before I sign a 'memoranda of understanding' with Gato Negro Productions."

In a smile that communicated undeniable knowledge of the leverage he now possessed, Santos spoke slowly, clearly and with pure intention.

Pointing at his temple, narrowing his eyes, he declared, "Yes, I learned about the law, about getting agreements in writing, about memoranda and all kinds of things while I had time to think." He looked over at the suits. "And so a few more little requests, ¿está bien?"

The movers and shakers squirmed but nodded.

"*La plebe* of *Burque* are going to need a *Clínica de la Gente*. However, in addition to the doctors and nurses that will be available to people in their community, this *clínica* must have *consejeras y curanderas* that can provide our traditional healing methods and *las yerbas* to young and old."

The applause was deafening. The movers and shakers shook their heads in agreement. What else could they do? MariLuz acted like she knew he'd do this all along. *La Merced* was dancing in the aisles.

"I'm sure we could get our *Mexica* dance group, Ehecatl, to dance for the grand opening, *que no?*"

Paz (Mapitzmitl) & Rita (Yeikoatl), walked out, onto the stage, to thundering applause. The dancers joined them, drummers too, and they began a traditional danza to bless the gathering of souls. The crowd went wild.

When the dancers were done, it got quiet, Santos looked into the eyes of Ned, Bill Schwarz and Gino and spoke to their souls.

"Agreed?"

They exchanged glances and nodded.

"Okay, we'll get that in writing. Now, the next thing. Prison."

He paused and let that dread word shock the audience, although the threat was not lost on the movers and shakers who shook slightly, in their seat.

"The time of inmates in *La Pinta* wasting their days doing nothing or hurting each other out of pure boredom is over. We need meaningful jobs in our jails and prisons, like learning how to work on everything from cars to computers. Real skills have to take the place of making license plates for ten cents an hour."

The people applauded, the press corps wrote, and

the movers and shakers trembled but agreed.

"Ladies and Gentlemen, and I'm sure the Gato Negro directors will agree with me on this, (the heads on the movers and shakers nodding furiously), some funding for community newspapers, like *The People's Voice*, and funding so that our young poets and journalists from Barelas, San José, Martineztown and Duranes can have a place for their writings to be shared with us all."

Santos noticed Adelita's tears of joy as he took in a deep breath.

"Ladies and Gentlemen, boys and girls, friends, supporters—*especialmente* Mari, Adelita, Delfina—we have a lot to do, so I'm going to stop now. The details for the Gato Negro future projects will be worked out in the days ahead. But for now, let me say, *gracias, gracias a todos*, thank you for being part of this glorious day. Thank you for being part of my new life. And now, it's time for me to go home with my wife and son. ¡*Gracias a Dios!*"

The People's Lawyer stepped back up to the microphone. "I speak for the Board in saying that we look forward to meeting and planning with you, Mr. Sánchez. We will be forming a Community Projects Committee with you as the Chairperson." Heads bobbed and smiles appeared. "Tomorrow you can come up to our main office for the funding for your landscaping and tamale business, Santos."

Santos raised his hand and leaned his head toward

the crooks, narrowing his eyes. "Funding, yes, in cash, no checks."

"In cash." Giovanni nodded until his hair flopped in his face.

From his place up on the stage, Santos caught Adelita's eyes, and winked at her. She then realized that, yes, this *was* the most important assignment of her current journalism career. Adelita put no words on paper, and for now, that was alright. The words, images and emotions of this moment were all locked in her memory. She would remember it all and write it all up later, but in this sacred moment a precious memory came to her. Adelita remembered the look and feel of her first journal- a big Red Chief notebook.

Santos walked off the stage, brushing past Margie Baca, the bi-lingual teacher, and her son, Patrick, over to Mari, Delfie and *el niño*, José Rumaldo, to the sweet music of hometown applause from Magdalena, MariLuz, old Man Gallegos, Miss B. and the other joyous souls. Andrea Luján, still seated in the theater balcony, said a quiet prayer of thanksgiving.

Unseen by any of the 630, representatives of the press, family members, or movers and shakers was a quiet meeting in the wings that was a source of soulful peace. There, in the blessed dark, was a short encounter and blessing from *La Merced* to Eddie López, who now drifted forward with fatherly pride and with the movement of a soul, finally, at peace.

§ § §

Close to the doors in the lobby of the KiMo Theater, Santos embraced Maribel like the way skin holds onto blood. Santos tenderly picked up José Rumaldo and looked into those big brown eyes as if for the first time. As he gazed into those eyes of wonder Santos looked beyond 'Burque, beyond East L.A., beyond Nuevo México, beyond Aztlán, beyond the old Basque country and beyond the cradle of his ancianos de España. Santos gazed past sin and forgiveness, past mistakes and lessons, past marching songs of war and peaceful songs of Healing. Santos saw beyond the 20th Century, the Middle Ages, past suffering and grief, even beyond redemption and grace. As he looked into his son's eyes, Santos Sánchez saw, at last, Innocence. Santos put his arm around the soft shoulders of Maribel and they turned to walk out, followed by *la Inocencia*.

Santos Sánchez López was now the man that he was always meant to be.

§ § §

Underneath the balcony metal railing of sand hill cranes the community celebrated. In the middle of the milling crowd, in the lobby, a hand on her shoulder caused Adelita to spin around. It was Professor Romero. He spoke to about a dozen college freshman admirers, who clung on his every word.

"Students, I want to introduce you to a real pro. It wouldn't surprise me if she ends up earning herself a Pulitzer Prize someday, based on the awesome job of investigative reporting, as evidenced in the series of articles that we have been following in *The People's Voice* and other publications. We can't wait to see what you expose next. But students, the other most important thing to remember is that journalism that chases after the truth, no matter where it leads, can actually change people's lives. I don't want to keep you away from your job any longer, but I just wanted to say, students, this is a model reporter, and a hero of mine, Adelita Augusta Zoila Chávez."

Cheers, triumphant laughter and smiles continued their contagious rounds.

Santos, Maribel, and José swam out through the admiring, loving crowd, exiting under the Von Hassler mural that showed a Pueblo woman gazing over the purple mesas, through the art Deco doors onto Central Avenue and all those low riders, *genízaros*, street saints, *manofashicos* and *babosos* riding in limousines. The reunited family waved to Delfina, who proudly walked over to her daughter's side.

Adelita's Notebook #4,153

Sometimes life is just right. Not often, but it happens. For just a few brief but cinnamon- sweet moments, everything can feel fine, comfortable, secure, tranquil. Full of grace and love. Mamá came up to me after the press conference at the KiMo Theater and hugged me and told me, in that voice of pure love, "M'ijita, I am so proud of you." That's when I knew that all of the long, uncertain hours, the sleepless nights, the coffeed afternoons of struggle, the questions- without-answers and the answers-that-came, the wisdom given, the words carefully written and rewritten and re-rewritten were all worth it. My mother's approval, admiration, and respect were all that mattered, all that really counted in my heart of hearts.

I know that time goes too fast, como una mariposa en una tormenta—a butterfly in a storm—but it is all worth the struggle for that simple, short glimpse de paraíso. No one will ever be able to take away these precious minutes, hours and days spent con mi mamá, talking, laughing, and yes, many silent, no-need-to-speak moments. This what Heaven must be like—just being. Amor en silencio. Quiet communion. Una unión de almas para siempre. Vivo en amor.

LV

Santos' arm was around Maribel like a cottonwood branch protecting a lilac bush. He inhaled a couple deep breaths of North Valley spring air that sneaked in through the open kitchen window and exhaled, *contento*. "Ahh, *pintos refritos y qué suave.*"

From where he sat, he could see the candle burning near the picture of him on her altar in their bedroom. Mari sat on his lap. José Rumaldo played on the floor by their feet.

"There's been a candle burning for you on my altar and a prayer burning for you in my heart every minute you've been gone. I never stopped loving you," Mari whispered.

"I never stopped loving or thinking about you, either. Honey *querida.*"

"Ah, *mi* Santos. *Mi muy querido* Santos."

After they said all that they needed to say, and Josecito had long been put in his crib, they went into their bedroom, danced the secret dance of *amantes*, and then slept the dream of life- long lovers in the nest of their intertwining arms.

§ § §

Before the kiss of mid-summer dawn, MariLuz Moya began her morning walk along the *acequia*, praying and talking to her sacred herbs and plants.

§ § §

La Señora Mendoza placed some marigolds at Tykie's grave and finished day nine of her latest Novena of prayer for his soul.

After putting the sacred wafers of Holy Eucharist safely in the golden tabernacle, Father Galli changed into his faded-blue, torn, and worn overalls, and then sat down and plucked a lively melody, *El Mosquito*, on his custom Jerry Starr *requinto*.

§ § §

Old man Gallegos dreamed of Isaias Sánchez, leading the singing of *La Entrega de Los Novios* at a wedding and Gallegos harmonized along, in his sleep.

§ § §

Frank Zuñiga pounded out another screenplay in the pre-dawn stillness.

§ § §

Adelita slept right past her usual extremely-early wake-up time, redreaming the perfect ending she had composed the night before.

§ § §

Delfina, in remission, now treated every moment like it was the appearance of the first wild strawberry of spring. Strong in peace, she dreamed about her Adelita, as a six year-old, writing in her red Big Chief tablet.

§ § §

Rudy and MariAnne put Piccolina, their intelligent and always-in-trouble dog, into the back of the old Dodge pick-up truck where she settled into a curl as they headed north towards their favorite camping spot. They would soak in the healing hot springs after a hike in the Jemez Mountains. On this trip they found a couple of stray cats that they brought home and named Chapulín and Josette.

MariAnne continued her prayers for healing and, at the wheel of the old Dodge, they headed South to Corrales. Rudy thought about maybe writing a book about some of the things they had enjoyed, suffered through and learned. Maribel dreamed, for the first time in months, about a new knitting design because she knew José was actually dreaming, after these rough, challenging months. Maribel also dreamed, in bright, singing colors about Santos showing José Rumaldo how to draw peacocks in ballpoint pen ink, and how to plant the corn and the marigold seeds in the ground.

§ § §

José Rumaldo dreamed vanilla, chocolate, and swirled ice cream cones. José dreamed, back and forth, between smashed bananas and dripping cones and his mama's voice and the big Da Da lifting him up in the air.

§ § §

Maldito Segundo, named after his first playful cat, pounced on Santos' foot and did battle with it until his buddy awoke.

Santos got up, opened a can of tuna with egg, and forked some onto Segundo's plate near the sink, something he had done hundreds of times for his first *gato vagabundo*. He paused. The world had changed. It was no longer a mad mongrel with a bad case of rabies, ready to pounce. It was now like the clay that Santos had played with in the first grade. It could be anything he made out of it.

Santos looked out at the bright-green Sandia Hot chile plants in the backyard and said, from his soul, "Thank you, God, for another day of life."

Just got back from seeing Salt of the Earth at the Student Union Basement Theater with Antonio. He took me to the Frontier Restaurant, across the street from campus, and we warmed up to our spirited conversation, fueled by grilled cheese sandwiches and their fiery hot Hatch green chile stew. We expressed our mutual admiration for Rosaura Revueltas and her stoical, saintly portrayal of Esperanza, the wife of Mine Workers Union Leader Ramón Quintero (Juan Chacón, in real life).

Antonio and I both kept talking over each other, recalling the heroism of the men in fighting for their rights and dignity, and the super-heroism of the miners' wives, who endured so much in support of their men during the long struggle, eventually taking their places on the picket lines. And then we talked about how that classic film vividly told a story that needed to be told.

In a small, modest, but necessary way, that's what we are doing, and what we need to keep doing: Telling the story, the way Antonio is doing in his articles in the Daily Lobo about the struggle of the students to keep open the Women's Studies, African-American Studies, Native-American Studies, and Chicano Studies Centers. The Campus Planning Committee has proposed

329

bulldozing the buildings for more space for a pinche (as Santos would say) parking garage.

Antonio couldn't stop telling me about how important it is for me to keep researching, to keep writing, and to keep publishing in The People's Voice about la política en Nuevo México, an ongoing, never-ending project.

I think about how I want to keep telling that story, but not just that one. I want also to tell the stories about Santos and Maribel, about my mom, Delfina, about MariLuz and Fr. Galli, Tykie and Magdalena, about them all.

It makes sense. It is up to me to tell the story of Santos, after all, I knew what it was like to have grown up without a father, like Santos did. Maybe it will be a book. I can imagine, some day, bringing that crazy manuscript to Floricanto Press . . . in honor of my Mexica herencia, that belief in the strength de la cultura . . . . Maybe even a book of poems I've been working on in bits and pieces, in addition to la política.

My mind is frosted with the sparkling crumbs of last night's dreams. I am going to shake off the visions and focus on a song of my soul.

"Adelita's Notebook" (Leche)

*My Mom told me that leche (milk) was one of my
first words . . .*

*I called the snow that I saw outside our living
room window 'leche' one Wintery morning. So
many years ago . . . and then I learned Chaquegüe
. . . atole . . . atolli . . . Mexica . . . Spanish . . . Aztec
words for Porridge . . . gruel . . . corn meal English
words for the same blue corn breakfast treat that
gave me strength for those mornings . . . so long
ago   in the morning of my life to get what I
needed, to say how I felt, to express who I am .
. . I learned more words. And it amazes me that
words don't wear out like tires, clothes or pencils
y ahora, I use the same words in a changed and
changing world*

*'palabras de poder, dame tus consejos, estás
conmigo, aquí y muy lejos' when calling on
my Guardian Angel I use words that I learned
in schools . . . to criticize schools I still use las
palabras de resistencia . . . to resist the lies
told in false history books, and to transcend . . .
transformar . . . cambiar . . . celebrar our legacy,
historia, cultura y memoria . . . I still use words to
empower myself y mis hermanas, mis compadres
y comadres, mi familia and my friends to reclaim
our place, physically and spiritually en Nuevo*

México, Aztlán, América . . . living both 'out there' and in here . . . in my words . . . knowing, at last that, if watered with the miraculous rain of love, the seed of solitude blossoms into the flower of freedom and redemption . . .

45279642R00207

Made in the USA
San Bernardino, CA
04 February 2017